Stellar 3

SCIENCE-FICTION STORIES

EDITED BY

Judy-Lynn del Rey

A Del Rey Book

BALLANTINE BOOKS • NEW YORK

A Del Rey Book
Published by Ballantine Books

Library of Congress Catalog Card Number: 77-4376

ISBN 0-345-25152-0

Manufactured in the United States of America.

First Edition: October 1977

Cover art by Darrell Sweet

TO
ALL MY FRIENDS ON THE
RANDOM HOUSE/BALLANTINE SALES FORCE
WITH
GRATITUDE, ADMIRATION AND
AFFECTION

Contents

No Hiding Place

Jack L. Chalker

1

It was a sleepy little river town, sitting on the silt bed beside the mighty Mississippi. The town of Newtownards, Louisiana, was a waystop for the steamers and barges that plowed the mighty river; it had been a refueling and rest stop on the waterway to New Orleans or up toward Vicksburg since 1850. It was a very small place, and the town hadn't changed much in the century-plus since the first river steamer piled on wood for the long journey north.

The people were a quiet sort, with little ambition and with that sense of peace and tranquillity that only an isolated community atmosphere can give. This isolation gave security of sorts as well, for the town had not been settled by the almost legendary Bayou folk of the surrounding lush, tropical swamplands, but by hardy capitalists who picked their location on the river for profit.

The Bayou people had become more legend than real by the twentieth century. No one alive could remember seeing any of the quiet, backward swamp folk for a long, long time, and even those who claimed experience with the mysterious backwater people were only half believed. Certainly the Bayou's secretive inhabitants were no longer any threat to the community welfare and, at best, were merely the poor people out in the sticks.

1

A town like Newtownards was a difficult place to keep a secret. The art of gossip had fallen into disuse simply because there was nothing the locals could whisper to each other that wasn't already common knowledge. Crime, too, was a rarity, and the town kept only two local policemen, two old war veterans whose major duty was checking the more deserted areas for hoboes and other itinerants who might be drifting through and looking for a free place to sleep. For anything more serious, a state police barracks ten miles to the south kept watch on several small towns in the swamp, which was a favorite hiding place for escaped fugitives. But since Newtownards had little to offer men on the run, being the most public of places, the only troopers who had visited the place officially came for ceremonial functions.

The town, as did all small communities, had its history, and it was especially colorful. Rackland's Maurauders had ridden through, back when the country was split and Grant was mapping his strategy, and had set up an observation post in the town's one mansion—deserted Hankin House, empty since the founder of the town and builder of his castle had fled, insane. Colonel Rackland's valiant party used the hilltop to look for any signs of Farragut's ships heading up the river toward Vicksburg, and for any signs of Yankee soldiers lurking in the swamps to the west. There, too, they had met the fate that had haunted Hankin House since 1850, when, after only three months in his new home, Josiah Hankin had suddenly gone mad and attempted to kill everyone nearby, while babbling of a horror in the house.

The old juju woman had come after that. She had originally warned Hankin not to build on the knoll, for, she said, a demon lived within the hill and would take all who disturbed its rest. She had not seen the thing, of course. But her grandmother's people, in 1808, had declared the hill a sacred place of worship, where weird, bacchanalian rites had been carried out by ex-slaves who lived in the Bayou. Now, the juju woman had warned,

Josiah had paid the price, and so would all others who disturbed the demon who lived in the hill.

Yes, Hankin House was the town's true pride. In an open society, people, being human, still must talk of something, and the locals had talked about the old house for better than a century. The townspeople didn't really *believe* in *Obi* and voodoo demons living in hills, but they remembered, too, that Josiah had been the first, not the last, to meet a strange end.

Colonel Rackland and two of his men had died by fire in that house, without a single part of the house itself being even singed. The lone survivor of his command had come down the hill a white-haired, raving maniac. Fearful townspeople had investigated, but found nothing but three bodies and a still, ever so still, empty house.

The house was vacant, then, when Farragut finally *did* move his force up the Mississippi. It had remained a still, silent, yet expectant spectator while the town wept at the news that at a place called Appomattox the world had ended. The house had slept while pioneers traveled the mighty river in large steamboats, moving beneath the hill on which the house stood.

Then in March of 1872, on that very same day that U.S. Grant was taking the oath of office for his second and tragic presidential term, Philip Cannon bought the house. Cannon had profited from the war, and even more from its aftermath. But his shady past seemed to be so very close behind him that he was always running, running from his past, his shadow, and himself.

He was running west when the ship he was on docked for fuel in Newtownards, and he had seen the mansion sitting majestically above the town. "Fit for a king," Phil Cannon thought, and despite the anxiety of the townspeople, he located the last Hankin relative, paid her off, and the house was his.

Cannon spent lavishly, building up, refurbishing, until the twenty-two-year-old house looked as if it had been built the day before, a shining monument to Josiah's taste for Gothic architecture and to Phil Cannon's desire to feel like a king.

And Cannon loved it. He became, by virtue of the smell of money, a very big man in Newtownards, and no one asked about his past. People with noble pasts seldom go to live and work in a tiny town in the midst of a swamp.

Then, one day, almost exactly two years after Cannon had moved in, the big man failed to put in an expected appearance with his usual pomp, strutting as he always did with his little saloon-girl on his arm.

It was not just the townspeople's dislike of the unexpected, nor their concern for the legends, that made them immediately investigate. Many had shady dealings with Cannon and they grew panicky at an unscheduled disappearance. So, a group of businessmen walked up the road to Hankin House and knocked. When they received no answer, they tried the door and found it unlocked.

The crystal chandelier Phil Cannon had imported from Spain tinkled as the hot wind blew off the river and through the open door into the main dining room.

They found *her* head, eventually, taken off her slender shoulders as if by a giant razor. They never did find Phil Cannon's.

As was the case when Josiah went mad, the servants were nowhere to be found. There was speculation that the juju people had a firm hold on those servants and that they might have done away with Cannon and his mistress as revenge for some of Cannon's shady dealings with the swamp folk. But no one ever found the servants, and the cleavage was too clean to have been the work of any sword or knife.

And so it was that Hankin House was closed again, and more generations passed as the silent old house looked on. The original panic and talk of a juju hex had caused some townspeople to cry out that the building be razed to the ground. But since Cannon's will left the old place to his local business syndicate, such talk was quickly suppressed. Besides, by the time talk became action everybody was convinced that the servants and the Bayou people had done the deed.

Hadn't they?

In 1898 the battleship *Maine* sank in Havana harbor, and America for the first time since the War of 1812 went to war a sovereign nation. One of the eager volunteers had been Robert Hornig, a youthful captain with the Fifth Cavalry Brigade. He had fought in Cuba, was wounded, and then returned. He chose as his point of disembarkation both from the war and the military the port of New Orleans, for he was a man with no family save the army. Now that he no longer had even the army, he was a man without a direction—only a discharge and a limp.

When he stopped off on the river trail westward at Newtownards he was immediately struck by the charm and simplicity of the town. He was also fascinated by the old deserted house atop the hill, and this fascination grew when inquiries to the locals brought forth bloodcurdling stories.

The house cost him a bit more than he actually had, as all important acquisitions do, but it was worth every penny to Captain Hornig. A lonely man, he loved the old place as a man would love his bride.

After a while, he was no longer alone. An orderly named Murray, who had also faced the test of battle in Cuba, passed through, as much a drifter as the captain had been. Here was the man, thought Hornig, who would at least temper the loneliness and who might also aid in financing the renovation of the house. Although the captain was a crusty sort, the young orderly liked both the man and the town, and assented.

They found Hornig at the bottom of the grand stairway, his body sprawled out on a rug in the entrance hall. Murray's body was in the dining room; he had been shot through the heart with a pistol, a pistol never found. The coroner's verdict of a murder-suicide did not fit all the facts, of course. But what alternatives were there? At least, this time, both victims still retained their heads.

Again the house was shut up and remained so until 1929, when Roger Meredith moved into the house with his wife and daughter. A heavy stock-market investor, he had selected Newtownards and the house carefully as a quiet and peaceful place in which to bring up his child and to escape the hustle and bustle of Wall Street, where his services were no longer required. He was quite a comfortable millionaire and originally a Louisiana boy as well, and so the townspeople offered little protest at his arrival.

When little Carol Meredith was observed—bloody and hysterical, crawling up Main Street not seven weeks after the family had moved in, her face full of buckshot—they said it was another murder-suicide, the last act of a man driven mad by the collapse of the stock market. As usual, the coroner's jury did not bother with details. How could a small man like Meredith ever throw his wife out of the west window? How did he, himself, inflict the merciless blow to the head the doctor stated had killed him? And what of the little girl, lying in the arms of storekeeper Tom Moore, life oozing out of her, who turned her face to his and, with a queer, maniacal smile, whispered as she died: "Daddy shot it!"

World War II came, and passed, and the house remained empty. No longer did fancy riverboats ply the Mississippi at the foot of the hill, but the town remained. Freight traffic had increased, and those ships still needed fuel.

Wars, hot and cold, passed, and generations came and went. The old house sat silently, as always, its mysterious demon undisturbed. Until one day . . .

August was a bad month for Newtownards. It was horribly hot and as humid as the air and the laws of physics would allow. Most people at midday would close their stores and stretch out for a nap while the intolerable heat of the day dissipated. But in the schoolyard, under the shade of a tall, old tree, there was activity.

"I am not yella!" the red-haired, stocky boy of about

fourteen yelled to the tall, angular leader of the group of boys, "but nobody's stupid enough to commit suicide, Buzz Murdock!"

The tall, blond-haired teenager towered over the object of derision. "Ya must be, ya half-Yankee!" Buzz Murdock replied haughtily, and not without a deliberate sneer. He was playing to his audience now, the group of young teenage boys who formed the Swamp Rats, a *very* exclusive little club.

Ricky Adherne, the redhead, bristled, his face becoming so red and contorted with anger and rage that his freckles almost faded to invisibility. The "half-Yankee" tag had always stung him. Could he help it if his no-account pa had been from New York?

"Lissen," said Murdock, "we don't allow no chickens in the Rats." The other boys made clucking sounds, like those of a chicken, in support of their leader. "If'n ya caint prove t'us that ya ain't no stupid chicken, ya bettah git along home riaot now!" continued the leader.

"Lissen yuhself!" Adherne snapped back. "I don't mind no test o' bravery, but jumpin' inna rivah with a sacka liam is a shoah way ta diah quick!"

Murdock put on his best sneer. "Hah! Weall wouldn't be so afeared. We's Swamp Rats and ya ain't ouah type. Git along home, kid, afore we beat on ya!"

Adherne saw his opening, and he dived in. "Hah! Big ol' Swamp Rats! If ya *really* wanted a test o' bravery—why, you'n me, Murdock, we'd go upta ol' Hankin House at midniat and sit 'til morn!"

Murdock was in a bind and he knew it. He'd have to go through with this or he would lose face before his followers—*that,* he was smart enough to figure out. But, damn it all, why'd this little punk have to pick Hankin House?

It was 11:22 P.M. when town policemen Charles "Scully" Wills and Johnny Schmidt got into their patrol car—actually a loaned state police car with a radio connection to the Hawkinston barracks in case of emergencies—to make the rounds for the first time that night.

As they drove toward their last checkpoint, Hankin House, Schmidt thought he spied a bluish gleam moving about in one of the old structure's upper windows. But when he blinked and looked again the light was gone. He mentioned his suspicions to his partner, but the older cop had seen nothing; and, when the light failed to reappear, Schmidt told himself he was just tired and seeing things in the night.

The two men made an extra check of the seals on the doors and windows of the old house, though, just to be on the safe side. Nothing human could get by those seals without breaking at least one of them, this they knew.

When all the seals proved to be intact, they left the old, dark place for town and coffee. They'd make their rounds again in about three hours. Both men settled back to another dull, routine night.

It would not be dull or routine.

There was a sound like a hoot-owl, and Ricky Adherne advanced on the little party of boys waiting in the gully near the roadside. Hankin House looked down, grim and foreboding, in the distance.

Murdock was scared, but he dared not show it. Adherne, too, was scared, the sight of the old house by moonlight being even more frightening to him than was his previous all-consuming fear that his mother would check his room and discover he wasn't there. Throughout the evening he had mentally cursed himself for suggesting this stupid expedition, and he'd convinced himself that the Swamp Rats weren't worth the risk. But he still had to go, he knew. His personal honor was at stake. Newtownards was an open town, and he had to live in it, and with himself as well.

The chirping of a cricket chorus and the incessant hum of june bugs flying to and fro in the hot night air were the only sounds as the small party of boys, Murdock and Adherne in the lead, walked up the road to the old manor house. Suddenly they saw headlights turn onto the road and barely jumped into the tall grass by the roadside in time to miss the gaze of Scully and Schmidt as they rode up to the old house. Minutes passed like hours, but no boy made a move. Finally, after an eternity, the car returned and sped back down the hill.

"Man! That was *real* close!" Adherne exclaimed in an excited whisper.

"Shaddup, punk!" called Murdock, who felt like running himself but who, also, had to live in Newtownards.

The old house sat dark and silent as the group reached the tall front steps.

"Now how d'we git in, smaht guy?" Murdock demanded, believing he had discovered a way out of this mess. But Adherne, now pressed on by Murdock's sarcasm and the will to get an unpleasant thing over and done with, was already up on the porch.

"If'n we kin jest git this here crossboahd off'n the doah, we kin git in thisaway," he whispered, not quite understanding why he spoke so low.

Together the frightened boys pried off the wooden crossbar whose nails had been rusted and weakened by weather for better than thirty years. After much tugging the board gave, and one Swamp Rat fell backward, board in hand, with a yelp.

A blue flickering light shone in an upstairs window. Suddenly it froze.

"It's open," one boy whispered huskily.

Murdock swallowed hard and drew up all the courage he could muster. He suddenly pushed ahead of the red-haired boy, who stood statuelike, peering into the black gloom. "Me first, punk," he snapped, but the tall leader wondered why his voice sounded so strange in his ears.

First Murdock, then Adherne, entered the blackness.

The blue light in the upstairs window, unseen by any of the waiting boys encamped below, moved away from the window. And the climax to a strange quest, spanning not one century but more than a score, was close at hand.

2

As the small scoutship lifted from the landing grid and rose into the sky above the peculiar red-green surface of the planet men called Conolt IV, a signal flashed in a larger, more formidable, and very alien vessel hiding in the darkness of space. As the tiny Terran scout pulled free of the planet's thick atmosphere, the alien ship's commander gave a crisp order and set out after his prey.

The scoutship pilot, a giant Irishman named Feeny, spotted the dark raider just after leaving radio range of Conolt IV's spaceport. He punched a button on the ship's instrument panel, where myriad dials and switches lay before him.

"Doctor, I'm afraid we've been had," he said, his voice calm and smooth. Intelligence men did not break under pressure and survive.

In the aft compartment, Alei Mofad, a cherubic, balding man in his late sixties who was known as *the* scientific genius of his age, jerked up with a start.

"How far, Feeny?" he asked in a level voice.

"About twelve thousand, Doctor, and closing fast. Too damned fast."

Mofad turned and examined the small cabinet which, aside from the bunk and his own person, was the only other thing in the compartment.

"Feeny, how much time have we got?"

"Ten, twelve minutes at the most. Sorry, Doc. Somebody made one *hell* of a slip here."

"Yes, yes, I know, but no use crying over bad security now. I shall require at least fifteen. Can you give that much to me?"

"I can try," the pilot replied dryly, and he began to do more than try. As Mofad worked feverishly to connect his equipment to the ship's power supply, Feeny began trying every maneuver in the book.

The alien spacecraft swung around out of the planetary shadow and shot a tractor beam, its purple glow slicing through the icy darkness of space. Feeny saw the beam only a fraction of a second before it was upon him, and his split-second reflexes urged the tiny scoutship upward, evading the powerful magnetic beam by inches.

The enemy craft swung around again, and for the second time shot out a purple ray from its bow tubes. Again Feeny dodged by inches, banking left and downward as he continued to fight the hopeless duel, playing as if the two ships were master fencers, with one swordsman now disarmed but yet agile enough and determined enough to avoid his deadly opponent's thrusts.

Feeny knew he could not keep up the game indefinitely, but he was determined to give his illustrious charge as much time as was required. He dodged, banked, dropped up and down, all the time playing for Mofad's precious, essential seconds, while at the same time sending out a distress signal to the cruiser that should have been waiting nearby to pick them up, but was actually a hulk of twisted metal, the loser of an earlier duel with the enemy craft. Twelve minutes passed . . . thirteen . . . fifteen . . . and then the goal was passed.

Eighteen minutes after the game had begun, it ended, when Feeny's lightning reflexes were no longer quite quick enough, and he began to tire. A tractor beam lashed out, enveloping the scoutship in a purple glow, pulling the tiny craft slowly toward the greater ship in the grip of the magnetic field.

"Doctor, they've got us," Feeny called into the ship's intercom. "Are you ready?"

"Yes, Feeny, I'm leaving now," came the physicist's reply, a tinge of sadness in his voice as he thought of the fate to which the faithful pilot had to be abandoned. "Do you want me to do anything, Doc?" Feeny called back.

"You've done enough, but yet you must destroy this machine. You know the detonator." Then, more softly, "Good-bye, Feeny."

Alei Mofad reached up on top of the plasticine cabinet and removed a small box. He stepped into the cabinet then, and vanished.

The two ships collided with a *thunk* which reverberated down the corridor of the smaller ship. Feeny rose from his pilot's chair and began the walk back to the aft compartment, struggling under the excessive gravity taken on when the two ships had linked and begun to roll. But he was too slow. The midsection airlock blew open before him, separating him from the precious cargo in the aft compartment. He stopped and stood straight, erect. After all, one died with dignity.

A creature entered the ship, a weird giant thing that could never have been spawned on earth. Humanoid was the closest to Terran that you could get, descriptively, for it stood erect, towering a full seven feet, on two thick, stiff legs. But it wore a chitinous exoskeleton that, as natural body armor, was as strong as sheet metal, yet half-transparent, so that the viewer could get a glimpse of veins, muscle tissue, and even the creature's brain. The two very long arms differed from one another. The right one, which ended in a five-digit hand whose fingers were extremely long and triple-jointed, bore a pistol, aimed at Feeny's head. The left arm, however, ended in a massive set of razor-sharp pincers—the Sirian ceremonial claw, used as a two-fingered hand or used in many Sirian rituals, including the mating ceremony of the species.

Colonel Rifixl Treeg, Hereditary Colonel of Empire Intelligence, fixed one of his stalk-like eyes on Feeny, the other on the door to the aft compartment. There could be no outward expression intelligible to a Terran in that face that resembled the head of a lobster, nor any sound, for the Sirians communicated—it was believed—telepathically. The alien colonel motioned with his pistol for Feeny to move back into the pilot's cabin.

Feeny complied, staring in fascination at his first Sirian. Only a few Terrans, such as those in the original discovery expeditions like Mofad, had *ever* seen them.

The Sirians ruled a great stellar empire of allied and vastly different races. They did not fight wars; they directed them.

Feeny decided on a desperate gamble. If he could surprise the Sirian, at least long enough to run to the far wall and throw the generator-feed switches, it was possible that he might be able to blow up the ship.

Treeg watched the Terran captive almost halfheartedly; this was not the prize he was after. As he stepped backward, another member of the Sirian crew entered, partially blocking the colonel's view of Feeny. Feeny saw his chance and dived for the switches. The Sirian who had just entered swung around and fired his pistol at the advancing Feeny. The Terran lurched back with a cry and was instantly consumed by the white-hot pistol fire. Only a burning heap on the control-room floor betrayed the fact that anyone named Feeny had ever existed.

Treeg was annoyed at the killing; he preferred his prisoners alive for interrogation, as his orders specified. There had been talk of late that the old colonel was getting too old for his duties, and this slip would not help his position with the High Command. Still, he was more than annoyed at what he found in the aft compartment—or, rather, what he did not find.

There was a bunk and a plasticine cabinet of dubious purpose. Nothing else. Alei Mofad was not on the ship. Treeg went over to the cabinet and examined it with both eyes. Apparently the only moving part was a small relay on the side which flipped up and down, up and down. Atop the cabinet were two small boxes, each without any writing—just thin little boxes with two buttons, one red and one green: purpose, also unknown.

The law of the survival of the fittest breeds certain characteristics common to all races who struggle to the top, and Treeg exercised one of those characteristics— he beat his fist in frustration against the compartment wall. He then turned and stormed out.

In every age there is a special one, a genius who can see beyond the horizon—Copernicus, Edison, Einstein, and the like being prime examples.

And Alei Mofad.

An explorer and trader in his youth, as he approached middle age, a wealthy and industrious man still full of life, he had built a great laboratory on the quiet Federation world of Conolt IV, and he had applied experience to experiment. His findings became the cornerstone in the later fight between his own people, the Trans-Terran Federation, and the other giant stellar empire he had aided in discovering, the Sirian League. The Terran-Sirian War of the Empires was a bitter, no-quarter clash between two equally ruthless and ambitious centers of power, born out of jealousy and greed and fed on misunderstanding and hate—too much alike in the way they thought to ever get along.

And in the midst of the conflict, Alei Mofad broke the fabric of time itself.

His original machine was still in his laboratory on Conolt IV, along with his notes and specifications. His newer, larger, model which Terran Command insisted be brought to Terra itself for its first public demonstration had been loaded secretly on a small scout. Then the doctor and one intelligence man had attempted to sneak off planet without arousing any curiosity, to link up with a cruiser off the sixth planet in the system. But Sirian allies could pass for Terrans, and their spies on Conolt had blocked the attempt. So Terran Control Center was left with just one clue, one hope of obtaining the crucial formulae that would make the Mofad computations on Conolt IV make sense. Mofad had that in his brain—but he had stated that, if he could escape, he would somehow place the location at the Terran test site, Code Louesse 155. They would use the original machine to retrieve it—and, hopefully, Mofad. But, the formulae were hidden in time itself. They knew where, but not *when*.

For the machines were still imperfect. The day would come when whole armies would be transported across space and time to the enemy's heartland in the remote past, then brought up to the present, an indetectable army of occupation.

Rifixl Treeg, too, had a time machine and the controls to make use of it. But he knew neither where nor when.

"The physics is quite beyond me," said the Empire's top physicist. "Mofad is someone centuries ahead of us all. However, the Terran pilot's failure to destroy the cabinet after Mofad escaped in it gives us more information than you might suspect, my dear Colonel."

"Terran intelligence knows what's happened, too, by now, and they have a head start," Treeg replied. "What can we do? You've already told me you can't duplicate the thing without Mofad's basic formula, and we can't get the formula without Mofad. It seems that he's beaten us."

"Pessimism simply will not do in an intelligence officer, Colonel Treeg. I merely told you that we could not duplicate the thing; I never said we could not *run* it."

"Ah!" exclaimed the colonel, and then he suddenly drooped again. "But we still don't know where or when. Terran intelligence at least knows *where,* although, as you tell me, the thing's too unpredictable for them to know *when.*"

"Where is not a problem," replied the physicist. "Obviously the *where* requires a setting. Since Mofad wasn't there to unset it, the machine will transport you to the right place, never fear. Your own intelligence reports show the original test site to be in the northern and western hemisphere of Terra herself. Since I credit the doctor with foresight, that's where anyone using the machine will go. At this point we are even with Terran intelligence. But now we go ahead of them."

Treeg suddenly stood extremely erect, the equivalent of a start in a race that could not physically sit down.

"You see," the scientist continued, "Mofad also had the time *period* set. The machine will follow through there, as well, but not exactly."

Treeg slumped. "Why not exactly, if—"

"Because," the scientist went on in the manner of a professor lecturing a schoolboy, "the machine is imperfect. It will transmit within, roughly, two centuries, I'd say. The disguised control panel here," he said, pointing to a spot on the machine, "is elementary. We can regulate the time sequence much better than could old Mofad, who had to go blind into a two-century span. We could make short jumps in time, with our agent searching the immediate vicinity for traces of Mofad. Since an agent, friend or foe, could appear only minutes after Mofad—even if that agent left days later by our standards—he would have to hide the thing fast. Was there any sort of transcribing equipment missing from the scoutship?"

"Yes," replied Treeg, "a minirecorder. You mean—"

"Precisely. That recorder is somewhere very near the point of emergence, and it contains what we must have. Terran intelligence does not have our present dials, so it will have hundreds of centuries to search. We may yet beat them. Who will you send?"

Treeg was still smarting from the lashing given him by the High Command for allowing Mofad to escape. There had been thoughts all around of retirement.

"Me," he said.

The two Sirians stood by the machine. The physicist began: "The device is based on a geographic point of reference. Mofad in his haste left the two portable units behind, an inexcusable blunder, but one very fortunate from our viewpoint." He handed Treeg a small box that was surprisingly heavy for its three-by-five-inch size and that only contained the red and green buttons which had interested Treeg when he had discovered them.

"This is the portable triggering device. When you want to go, we set the machine, and you step inside. Then you press the green button all the way down, and the machine transforms you into some sort of energy form we don't yet understand and resolidifies you on a preset point determined by the cabinet setting. When you wish to return, you need only return to your exact point of emergence into the other time and place and press the red button down all the way. This will reverse the process. I don't pretend to understand it—this is what we need in the way of Mofad's formulae, that mathematics which will tell us the how of the thing. Let's say that the machine somehow rips the fabric of time and place, which are linked, and that the tear is mended when you reactivate the device, thereby restoring you to your point of origin.

"I advise you to mark your point of emergence on Terra carefully, though. You must return to it exactly or you will remain where and when you are. Are you ready?"

Treeg nodded, and with an effort squeezed his rigid body into the upright cabinet. The scientist examined the control panel. "I have preset it—I think—for the earliest possible time. I will count down. When I say *Now!* you are to press the green button. All right. Five . . . four . . . three . . . two . . . one. . . . *Now!*"

Treeg pressed the button.

The first thought he had was that there had been no sensation whatever. It bothered him; this tampering with time should not be so quiet nor so sudden. But—one moment he was squeezed uncomfortably in that cabinet on Sirius; the next moment he was atop a lonely hillside surrounded by lush, green swamp. Below the hill a large river, glittering in the sunset, flowed its way past the spot. The time was 1808, forty-one years before a man named Josiah Hankin would found a town on the flats below, a town he would name after the Belfast street on which he had been born—Newtownards.

Treeg was overcome by the wildness of the place and by the idea that he was the first of his race to travel in time. The air, he noted, was sweet and moist, and it was almost as hot here as his own native world. He stood there on the hilltop, a grotesque statue silhouetted in the setting sun, and thought. He had all the time in the world. . . .

He heard a rustling in the undergrowth.

Four men crept through the dense marsh grass, looking not at the hill and its weird occupant but out at the river. Two were old-time pirates who had fought with Laffite years before and had then changed occupations to become Bayou smugglers, finding the new line of work just as profitable but less risky.

The other two were renegade slaves, who joined the Bayou settlement as a sanctuary where they could relax, free from the fear of the law in a society where it was not race, but brains and muscle, that made a man a man. All four of them loved the art of smuggling, taking pride in it in the same way as a jeweler would pride himself in his skillful work.

Treeg had no ears with which to hear the men, and so, oblivious to the danger below, he began walking down the slope toward the base of the hill. He had decided that Mofad would surely have made traces in the virgin land if this was indeed the correct time, but he had a duty to perform, and all the time he would ever need. So he decided to check all the same. In the military caste society of his birth the first rule taught every youngling was "Never underestimate your enemy."

"Damn and double that stinkin' Joe Walsh," growled Ned Harrell as his eyes strained to catch a glimpse of a flatboat on the great expanse of the river. "If that pig's double-crossed me I'll— Hey! Did you hear that?" A crash and crackle of underbrush sounded nearby.

Carl, a giant black with a fugitive's reflexes, had already jumped around. Then he screamed. They were looking at a giant demon out of hell come down from his high hill, a demon with the face of a monster and the look of the swamp.

Harrell instinctively grabbed his rifle and shot at the thing in one motion. The bullet struck the Sirian's midsection, a strong point in his body armor, and bounced harmlessly off; but the force of the blast knocked Treeg back, and he grabbed a long vine to keep from crashing to the ground. The initial surprise of the attack wore off almost immediately, and Treeg saw the situation for what it was—he was faced with a bunch of primitives, and scared ones at that. Treeg, a born killer trained in his art, charged. Three of the men drew back, but Carl stood his ground. Stopping a few feet away, the Sirian surveyed the Terran who was as big as he.

The big black man charged, and Treeg stepped aside, letting his adversary sail past. The Sirian had spotted Harrell furiously reloading his rifle and wanted to eliminate the threat. Drawing his pistol, Treeg fired. Harrell went up in smoke and flame. The two others ran off, the short black man known as Eliot shouting: *"Juju! Juju! Oh, God, we done raised a juju!"* as he stormed through the brush.

Carl had recovered from his missed lunge and, rising to his feet, charged at the back of the monster. He knew he was facing a demon, but he also knew that demons could be wrestled into submission—and Carl was the best wrestler of them all.

The Sirian went down, caught completely off guard. He had forgotten his initial and greatest threat while shooting at the others. Carl pounced on top of him and for a few seconds the two wrestled, the big black man not being able to do much damage to the hard-shelled creature, while Treeg found himself pinned in a viselike grip, not being able to free either claw or hand. They were stilled in a test of brute strength, a frozen tableau as Carl sat atop the giant creature and strained to keep those arms pinned.

Treeg was virtually helpless if downed, and he had to be able to roll over in order to bring up his claw. He heaved with all his might, at the same time marveling at the strength of this soft Terran ape, as he thought of all Earthmen.

Foam poured from the mouth of the frenzied Carl as he struggled against the giant creature's strength in that death grip. Finally, after a few seconds that seemed to both to pass like hours, Treeg felt a slight slackening as the man tired, and he kicked over to one side. Carl went sprawling over, and Treeg rolled to his right, at the stunned man, claw raised.

Rifixl Treeg had a terrible time bringing himself to his feet again. Rigid, unbending legs propped out, he used his long arms to lift his body semiupright, then grabbed an overhanging vine and pulled himself erect. He then looked down at the cut and bleeding body of Carl, a Terran. He had been more impressed with the courage and skill of this one creature than with any he had encountered before. The primitive should have run away with the rest of his group, yet he had chosen to stay and fight. He had been closer to winning than he knew, for Treeg had been tiring as well, and a mighty blow into the pulpy Sirian face would have penetrated into his brain, bringing instant death.

Treeg resolved not to underestimate these Terrans again. He had often wondered why such seeming weaklings were any threat to the Empire. Then a saying one of his early tutors had drummed into him suddenly came back as he stood there: *Ignorance is not a synonym for stupidity, nor savagery for fear.*

Treeg cast one eye in each direction, looking for a sign of the return of the natives in force. He did not want to be caught off guard again. But he found no signs of any life save the crawling insects and flying birds; so, keeping a watchful eye, the Sirian decapitated the Negro, using the ceremonial claw, in the age-old gesture of respect for the dead of war. He then made his way around the hill, searching for the signs of a more civilized man's presence. He found none and, regretfully, walked back up the hill, back to where a stone marked his point of departure.

From back in the swampy glades, a group of cautious Bayou men and women, attracted by the sounds of a struggle, watched in awe and fear as a great demon stood atop the hill, visible as a fearsome specter in the last fleeting rays of the sun.

And suddenly vanished.

Treeg tumbled out of the time cabinet and onto the floor, unconscious. It was only a split second since he had vanished from the laboratory, but it was plain to the Sirian physicist that the colonel had been through an ordeal. The red blood almost completely covering the claw proved it, and Treeg was carried to the hospital, where Carl's blood was washed off and he was left alone to sleep off his exhaustion.

3

Less than two days later, Treeg was ready and able to try again. He had learned a lot about his enemy in his first try. This time, unhampered by the apprehension of transition, the passage to Terra was even easier to take. Yet this time, too, it held a surprise.

Treeg stood in a primitive dwelling made of wood. The size of the room was very large, and it was lavishly furnished. A great, long table divided the room almost into two parts, with chairs stretching endlessly down each side. At the head of the table was a great, padded chair where the master of the house would sit. A long mirror hung on one wall and, overhead, suspended directly above the center of the table, was a massive iron chandelier.

Treeg's first thought was that there had been some sort of mistake. The jump was not more than forty years, he thought, and those primitives of the swamp were surely incapable of making such a dwelling as this. But, of course, forty years brings inevitable change, external as well. The dwelling and the small town below were products of outsiders, who had used the time to carve a slice of civilization from the swamp.

In that time that shrewd old trader Josiah Hankin had built a town and a mansion. He had also been warned not to build on the hill. An old juju woman had prattled about a demon, one her grandmother saw, who lived in the hill and could disappear at will. But Josiah was a hardheaded man, and he laughed.

It was almost midnight. The servants had retired, the

slaves had been locked in their house. Josiah sat in his study studiously examining the previous month's account books. But as far as Treeg was concerned, the dark house was empty.

The Sirian took a small tube off his wide utility belt, the only clothing he wore. The tube snapped to life, its brilliant blue-white glow illuminating even the darkest corners of the large room. Treeg narrowed the beam after an initial visual scan of the place, and he began his search. Although not conscious of sound himself or capable of fully grasping what it was, he still moved softly and carefully, knowing that the Terrans possessed a certain sense that he did not.

Then, in the most comic of ways, Rifixl Treeg tripped on the edge of the lush Persian carpet at the doorway and hit the floor with a crash, the blue torch flying against a wall.

Josiah jumped at the sound. He had never been quite comfortable in the wilds and was always a little jittery after dark. Cautiously, the old man tiptoed out onto the landing above the grand stairway and looked down into the dark entrance hall. He heard the sound of movement as Treeg dizzily and with great effort hoisted himself back to his feet. Feeling certain that a burglar was in the house, Hankin went back and got out his old flintlock pistol.

In the meantime Treeg, oblivious of discovery, had started his methodical search of the dining-room area, looking for spaces likely to hide a small recorder. He felt certain that the recorder was hidden in an obvious place—a place somewhere in the house, and one where a Terran searcher would be likely to look, since, were it hidden too well, Mofad's own kind would miss the object of their search.

Josiah crept softly down the stairs, loaded gun in hand. The sounds of movement in the dining room continued. Raising his pistol, the old man stepped across the threshold of the room, now lit by a strange blue glow.

Treeg, very near the door, chose that moment to turn

around. As he did so, his right arm swung around and hit Hankin hard, sending the old man reeling back into the hallway. The gun fired on contact, but the ball missed its mark and lodged instead in the far wall.

The Sirian walked toward the old man, who was just getting to his feet. The fellow looked up and into the pulpy, grotesque face, screamed, and ran for the front door. Treeg, being slower, did not give chase as the old man sped out the door and down toward the slaves' house, screaming hideously.

Treeg quickly resumed his search. He was certain that he was still too early in time, and so, with only a few more seconds to survey the downstairs layout—and with pursuit probably imminent—he stepped back to the point just behind the great chair that sat at the head of the long table and pressed the button.

Josiah Hankin, driven mad by the horror that had touched him and pursued him, saw monsters in place of bewildered slaves. He grabbed a heavy stick off the ground and started after one of the men, a field hand. The others finally subdued him.

Hankin would live out his life in a New Orleans sanitarium, always babbling a description of the truth that men of 1850 could only accept as the ravings of a maniac.

Private Fetters jumped nervously as Colonel Rackland entered the house. Rackland grinned. A tall, gaunt man with a now-famous blond goatee, he delighted in scaring his men. It kept them on their toes.

"Well, Private," he drawled, "have you seen any signs of those wicked old Yankees yet?"

Fetters relaxed. "No, suh, but ah'm keepin' a shahp lookout, suh."

Rackland smiled again, and went over to the old padded chair that they had uncovered and put back where it rightfully belonged—at the head of the dining room table. The table was ideal for maps and conferences, and the east windows of the room gave an excellent view of the broad expanse of the Mississippi.

Two more men came in—the rest of the observation-post team, one of several Rackland had set up along the riverbank. Rackland walked over to the windows to confer with the new arrivals, and Fetters asked if he could be relieved. This granted, he walked over to the big chair. That saved his life.

Rifixl Treeg appeared between Fetters and the men at the windows, so close to the private that poor Fetters was knocked down. Treeg wanted no surprises and acted by reflex this time, drawing his pistol and firing point-blank at the men at the window.

The wide beam caught all three at once, and each man screamed once, then died from the intense heat. Fetters was only singed slightly, and he saw the creature in the room. One look was enough. Fetters managed to leap up and jump out one of the windows, then ran off, screaming and yelling for help as he raced down the hill toward the town below.

Treeg cursed himself for allowing one to get away, reflecting sourly that that seemed to be all he was doing of late. He made as quick a search as he could, but decided that if this place was being used by these men—seemingly soldiers—Mofad's presence would be marked in some way. Still, he made the rounds of the usual hiding places and then looked over the other downstairs rooms as well. His duty done, Treeg walked back over to the focal point just behind the great chair and pressed the red stud.

She took one look at the creature and fainted, something which puzzled Treeg, who was ever ready to kill but was unused to potential victims dropping unconscious without pain as a precipitant. He decided to kill her while she was out in order to save problems later. Then, despite the fact that head-taking was usually a ceremony of honor, he sliced off the woman's head simply because it seemed the easiest way of killing her.

For once, Treeg allowed himself every luxury of time. He had no reason to believe that anyone else was about, but he kept one eye on the main hall anyway. Lucky for him he did.

Phil Cannon bounced down the stairs, gun in hand. He had watched as the weird creature severed Mary's head cleanly with that claw, but the vision had not driven him mad. Cannon had lived too long and done too much to be scared of any monster that simply was more foul than he. He had accepted Treeg as a reality, probably some sort of unknown animal from the swamps, and he had reached for his .44.

He felt no emotion at Mary's passing. People were things to Phil Cannon; they could be replaced. What mattered was killing the thing in the dining room before it killed him.

Treeg saw movement out of the corner of his eye, drew his pistol, turned, and pulled the trigger. The shot was wide and on a thin beam as well, and it missed Cannon, who darted to cover behind the wall partition, completely. Cocking his pistol, Cannon dropped low to the floor, then darted out, firing a volley at Treeg. One shot struck, and though it did Treeg no harm, it had the force to make him drop his searpistol.

Treeg realized that he had no cover and no weapon, and decided immediately that he had to rush the man. He bounded across the dining room and reached out, but Cannon was too fast.

"Com'on, you brute," Phil Cannon whispered, "com'on out where I can get a clear shot with this thing."

Treeg decided to oblige, chancing that the Terran would aim for his midsection. It was a risk, but there was nothing else to do. He charged, and guessed correctly. Cannon fired into the Sirian's chest, to no effect; but Treeg, ready for the blow of the bullet, was able to keep up his charge. Hand and claw reached out for Cannon, picked him up and threw him into the dining room, where the con man landed with a *snap*.

Treeg made certain that the man was dead by severing his head, but as he started to move the body, part of which was on the focal point, he saw people running for the house, attracted by the shots. Treeg decided that this time period was without doubt still much too early for Mofad anyway, and he pressed the stud.

When he arrived back in the Sirian laboratory, he discovered that Phil Cannon's severed head had come along as well.

Cannon's servants, running in the front door in response to the shots, stopped short at the gruesome sight in the dining room. Crossing himself, the butler said: "We'd all bettah git out of heah fast. They's gonna think *we* done it."

So it was that the town investigating committee found two bodies, one head, and were able to place the blame on the servants.

Murray was in the dining room when Treeg appeared. Stunned for a moment by the creature's sudden appearance, he recovered before Treeg could effectively act and ran to a wall, on which a prized pistol sat, ever loaded, the captain's symbol of his life.

Treeg advanced on him, and Murray fired once, the bullet glancing off Treeg and putting yet another hole in the old house's wall.

The Sirian reached out and grabbed for the young ex-orderly, but missed and fell to the floor. Murray, in dodging, was thrown off balance and fell, too, but he retained a grip on his pistol.

Treeg saw the pistol and lashed out his hand, catching the man's arm in an iron grip. They struggled, rolling along the floor, each trying for possession of the pistol. The gun suddenly reversed under Treeg's mighty pressure, and fired. Murray jerked, then was still. Treeg had killed him by forcing the muzzle of his own gun to his side.

Rising, he went immediately to the dining-room doorway, not taking any chances on another Phil Cannon coming down the stairs.

The captain was standing at the head of the stairs. At the sound of the struggle he had painfully gotten up from his bed, where he had been for several days, fighting an old leg wound that had flared anew. At the sight of Treeg he drew back. His bad leg gave out from under him, and he fell headfirst down the grand stairway. When he hit bottom, he lay still, his neck broken in the fall.

Treeg looked down at the body, which was undeniably dead, a bit stunned at this death. It was, at least, the easiest of the lot, and Treeg was glad of that after his tussle with Murray.

This time the search was not interrupted, and Treeg explored the upstairs as well.

The little girl was playing with her doll in a corner of the dining room. She didn't see Treeg, who stood for a second pondering what to do. Younglings meant adults nearby.

Treeg was correct. Meredith walked down the stairs, spotted Treeg, and grabbed his shotgun, which was in the hall in preparation for a day of hunting. He stormed into the room and fired point-blank at Treeg before the slower-moving Sirian could react. The buckshot spread across the room, parts of the shot striking Treeg in the face; others, deflected, hit the little girl in the face as she watched in horror. Treeg blundered about in pain and in rage and lashed out in all directions. Roger Meredith froze as he caught sight of his daughter, bleeding and in shock, inching along the wall. He was thinking only of her when one of Treeg's blows smashed into his head, killing him instantly.

Mrs. Meredith came running in, and all but bumped into Treeg. He grabbed her and threw her hard away from him, doing so with such power that the unfortunate woman was thrown out of the east window to her death.

Treeg didn't see the child, could think only of getting back. The pain bit at him, driving him almost into a frenzy. This allowed little Carol Meredith to back out the dining-room door, out of the house, and to make it to town, where she would bleed to death in a merchant's arms.

Treeg stabbed at the button on the time-distorter

unit, but nothing happened. Suddenly, drawing in great gasps of air, racked by nearly intolerable pain, he realized that he was not precisely over the focal point. With effort he stumbled to the place behind the big padded chair and pressed the stud again. Again nothing happened. He panicked. He pressed, and pressed, and pressed. Finally he pushed the red button instead of the green.

It took two weeks in a Sirian hospital to heal the wounds sufficiently for Treeg to continue. Command had all but ordered him to get another man, but Treeg knew that if he chose another in his place, he would be finished—a final failure. The finding of Mofad was no longer a mission with Rifixl Treeg, it was an obsession. To a born warrior retirement would be a living hell—he would commit suicide first.

This time he was very cautious. As soon as he emerged in the darkened house he drew his pistol, prepared to fire on sight. But the dining room was empty, the furniture piled in one corner. Everything was covered with white sheets, and a thick carpet of dust and cobwebs was everywhere. Treeg glanced around in relief. The house was unlived in at this time.

First he checked the traditional spots, and then the rest of the lower floor. For the first time he was completely uninterrupted, but he never let down his guard. Slight pains in his face reminded him to keep vigilant. His pale blue torch flickered as Treeg mounted the grand stairway with effort.

He found a body at the top of the stairs—a fresh one. Treeg, to whom all Terran apes looked alike, knew this one on sight, every feature from the tiny mustache to the potbelly burned indelibly into his brain.

Alei Mofad, in the initial stages of rigor mortis, lay on the landing, dead neither by murder or suicide, but from a weak heart deprived of its medicine.

Treeg felt a queer thrill run through him. This was it! Even on this mad planet, Terra, he felt, he was still in command of himself.

Mofad had been upstairs, obviously. But had he been

going up, or coming down? Coming down, Treeg decided from the angle of the body. Treeg stepped over the body of the scientist, dead in a remote area, remote in time and space—dead many centuries before he would be born. He walked down the second-story corridor.

The master bedroom, in the same dusty condition as the dining room, nonetheless had the look of being used. A big old stuffed chair, the same one that had been in the dining room through many reupholsterings, stood in the middle of the room, a stool resting in front of it. Clearly Mofad had spent his time here, awaiting Terran security, fearful that he would be overlooked and stranded. As Treeg searched the darkened room, his eyes caught the glare of headlights outside.

The police car pulled up and two men stepped out. They checked the front and back doors, and then went back to their car, got in . . . and drove off. Treeg waited a few seconds to make certain of their departure, then resumed his search. It would be midnight shortly, and the moon shone brightly in the window.

Suddenly Treeg glanced out the window again, nervously checking to see if the car would return. After a moment he made out a small group of figures creeping up on the house. Youngling Terrans, he decided. He watched as they moved closer, then up and out of sight underneath him.

Treeg crept out of the bedroom and back over to the stairwell. He watched the front door. After a while, it started to move. This time Rifixl Treeg would not be caught off guard! He switched off his light and melted into the shadows, still watching.

Two young Terrans entered cautiously, even fearfully, each one seeming to urge the other on. They stood for a moment in the hallway, then went into the dining room, where moonlight flooded the interior. They pulled two chairs off the heap, very carefully, and sat down, backs to the wall. In silence, their eyes wide, apprehensive, they gazed at the open door.

Treeg decided that, with the others outside who

might run for help, he could wait them out. He relaxed a bit, and leaned against a wall to wait, one eye fixed on the front doorway and the other on the entranceway to the dining room. He wasn't about to run and give the prize away. It was too close!

Hours passed, and Treeg fumed with impatience to get on with his search. But it was evident that for some reason—perhaps religious—those boys, scared as they obviously were, were going to stay the night.

Johnny Schmidt and Scully Wills drove back up to Hankin House. They had gotten bored as usual and decided to give the route a fast, clean check before turning in.

As their headlights reflected against the dark shingle of the house, Schmidt caught sight of a small figure running around the side of the place—a figure he knew.

"Hold up there, Tommy Samuels!" he cried, and the boy, who was more scared of the night than of the police, stopped, turned, and obediently came back to the front. Slowly the other Swamp Rats appeared as well. The game was up, and Tommy was known to be a blabbermouth anyway.

"Now, just what the *hell* are you kids doing up here at this time of night?" the irate officer demanded, and in confused snatches the entire story was told.

"Well," said Schmidt disgustedly to his partner, "we'll have to go in and get them. Let's get it over with." With that the two men mounted the steps and threw open the door.

At that instant a bored and impatient Treeg, curious as to the meaning of the flashes of light outside, chose to risk a peek from his hiding place. So his face was fully outlined in Schmidt's casually aimed flashlight beam.

"*Oh, my God!*" yelled the police officer, who dropped and drew his pistol. Treeg jerked back, but not without sound.

"Did you see what I saw?" Scully whispered huskily.

"I hope not," replied Schmidt, and then a thought struck him. *"The kids!"*

"Buzz Murdock! Ricky Adhernc! You two get outa there fast, on the run, when I give the word," Scully shouted. "Then run like hell for town and tell 'em to bring help. We got *something* cornered upstairs."

The two boys ran out, joined their frightened compatriots, and ran down the hill as fast as their legs could carry them. None of them would give a warning! They hadn't seen anything.

"Scully, get out to the car and call the state troopers. Tell 'em we don't know what it is but to get some heavy stuff up here and *fast!*" Scully crept back out the door and ran for the car. There was noise on the second floor, as Treeg retreated to the master bedroom. He knew from the way they reacted that these men were armed professionals, and he wanted a good place both for a stand and for a view of the road.

He set the pistol charge to high intensity and aimed for the patrol car below at which the unfortunate Scully was standing, giving his call for aid to the state-trooper barracks. The beam lashed out from the upper window, exploding the car with a blinding glare and shock wave that was seen and heard in town. People awoke, looked out, and saw a burning heap in front of Hankin House.

Schmidt was knocked flat by the blast, but quickly picked himself up and stationed himself behind an overturned hall table near the stairs. Whatever was up there he was determined to *keep* up there until reinforcements arrived.

Treeg knew that with only one man downstairs he could get away, but he would return a failure, return to death. Better to make a stand here, he decided, and at least *find* the recorder, if only to destroy it. If the Sirian Empire didn't have it, then at least it would not be used against them.

A small group of villagers ran up the hill. Treeg saw them coming and aimed a shot that exploded the earth just in front of them. Men started screaming. Those unharmed ran back toward town.

Lights went on all over town, including those in the house of National Guard Major Robert Kelsoe, who had two advantages. He had a full view of the old mansion from his bedroom window, and he lived next door to the Guard armory.

Treeg fired a third shot, on wide beam, that cooked swamp grass and vegetation in a five-foot path down the hillside. He did not know where the other Terran man was lurking, but felt that he wouldn't charge without help. And the hilltop shots would discourage anyone coming to help. He continued his search.

Schmidt heard the thing moving furniture around upstairs. He tried to imagine what it was and what it was doing up there, failing on both counts. But he was Newtownards born and bred, and he knew the legends. He knew that he had just seen the demon of Hankin House and that no matter what it was, it was solid.

Major Kelsoe wasted no time in opening the armory. He didn't know what was going on, but he had seen the beams from the house and knew that some sort of power was loose up there. Three of his Guard unit were awaiting him at the armory, and they discussed what they had seen and heard as they broke out submachine guns.

It was eight and a half minutes since Scully had called the state police. Two cars roared into town, having done eighty along the narrow road. They matched Scully's incredible radio report, cut off in midsentence, with what the Guardsmen had seen. The state police corporal looked over at a far rack. *"Hey!"* he exclaimed, "Are those bazookas?"

A few minutes later a cautious group of men, three of them armed with bazookas, crept up the side of the hill to Hankin House.

When they reached the summit and were standing in front of the house, across from the crater left where the patrol car had exploded, Corporal James Watson found his voice and yelled: *"Wills! Schmidt!"*

Schmidt heard the yell and called back, "This is Schmidt in here! Wills was caught in the blast. This thing is unbelievable! It's upstairs moving stuff around at a fearful rate. Come in slowly, and watch it!"

As if on a commando raid, the men zigzagged across the road and up onto the porch, seconds apart.

"Thank God," Schmidt sighed when he saw them. He spotted the bazookas and said, "Get those things ready. The thing's sort of like a big crawfish, I think, and that body armor will be awfully thick on a baby his size. The thing's got to come down this way—maybe we can give it a bellyful."

Treeg was thoroughly frustrated. Not being able to hear anything at all, and not having seen the band of men creep up and into the house, he fancied himself still with only the problem of the lone sentinel below.

Mofad must have hidden the recorder downstairs after all, he thought disgustedly. He'd have to get rid of that pest down there and then have another look.

Quickly Treeg stepped out onto the landing, over Mofad's still body, and started down the stairs slowly, pistol in hand.

The bazooka shell, designed to penetrate the toughest tank armor, sliced through his body like a hot knife through butter. The great, alien body toppled headfirst down the stairs and landed with a crash at the feet of the men below, almost exactly where Captain Hornig had lain after his fall.

Colonel Rifixl Treeg, Hereditary Colonel of Empire Intelligence, was dead.

The newsmen had left; the police and Guard had finished their examinations of the building, and the alien body, or what was left of it, had been carted off to Washington, where baffled biologists would almost be driven mad in their unsuccessful attempt to identify the thing. The physicists regretted that the bazooka shell had passed through the curious beltlike container the creature had worn, destroying forever the new science in the ray-pistol power pack and the portable time link.

The excitement was all over, and Hankin House was again boarded up. There was talk of finally tearing the old place down, but in the end the house gave the economy of the tiny town a much-needed boost. The only tourist attraction in the state that drew more year-round visitors was the Latin Quarter of New Orleans.

4

A man, Terran, materialized in the hallway, almost on the spot where Rifixl Treeg's body had fallen. He removed a sheet of paperlike material, upon which was written the location of the agreed-upon rendezvous Mofad had established before he had ever left Conolt IV. The slip stated: "LOUESSE 155—EMERGENCY LOCATION IN CASE OF ENEMY ACTION. POINT OF REFERENCE 221."

The agent mounted the stairway, turned at the landing where Mofad's body had lain—he who now was at rest as a John Doe in the potter's field—and went directly into the master bedroom.

The place was a shambles. Treeg had moved everything around, torn down cabinets, mantels, and other such hiding places.

"Now, where the devil would I hide a minirecorder in here if I wanted a place another Terran would probably find but a Sirian probably would not?" That was the problem.

Where?

After some exasperating searches the agent crossed his arms, stumped, and surveyed the room. Dammit, Point of Reference 221 in this house was the master bedroom!

The agent suddenly felt tired—he had had a day that spanned twelve centuries. He decided to sit down and think the problem out. Grabbing the overturned master's chair that had once sat at the head of the dining-room table and had, indeed, been Mofad's only comfort, he turned it over and sank down.

Click. "The frequency modulation of point seven two betas—"

The man jumped up out of the chair as if he had

been shot. But then he smiled, and then he laughed. And then he couldn't stop laughing.

Where was a good place for a Terran to look but a Sirian to overlook? What might a tired Terran do when he reached here: chair and stool set up, inviting . . . but *when you're guarding against a race that was incapable of sitting down!* A simple matter for a genius like Mofad to rig the recorder. Treeg could have torn the chair apart without noticing the tiny minirecorder—but he would never have pressed hard on the seat!

Mofad's voice droned on, telling those precious formulae and figures that would win Terra the war. The Terran agent, still laughing, slit open the seat of the chair and dug into the wooden frame structure which Mofad had built as his recorder's final resting place. Only heavy pressure on the center of the seat would have made it begin playing.

The agent removed the recorder and shut it off. He then walked out of the bedroom, down the stairs, and into the main hallway. He took from his pocket a small control box, on which were two buttons. Pressing the red one, he disappeared.

And the last ghost of Hankin House vanished into time. ☆

Salty's Sweep

Arsen Darnay

In the summer of 2312, Hamsters Dugout, the venerable archivist of Plutonium, joined Godbod in eternal bliss. He had sickened in the spring but had lingered on in a state of delirium. During this time, by the abbot's special dispensation, he lay on a cot in the caverns below the seven-podded monastic fortress, in an area where Godbod's magic emanations had not yet been closed off by lead in accordance with the New Theology.

The abbot had approved the arrangement because Dugout was the last adherent to the old theology, the last monk who felt a compulsive desire to be near Godbod, to feel the radiations from His many forms: liquid, solid, semisolid, and gaseous. A strange Old Order mystery, once installed in Plutonium's Vigilance Pod, had created that compulsion in days gone by. The mystery had been destroyed forty years earlier, thus transforming the Permanent Priesthood, reducing its numbers and changing its theology.

The entire brotherhood, some five hundred men, turned out for the funeral. Word had spread that the abbot would make a special announcement.

A klick and a half from the fortress itself, in a westerly direction, was a rise in the ground—a domed formation, its one side covered by trees like a balding

36

man's head with hair. The brotherhood went there because it was a burial ground. Tradition had it that the
monkish spirits would rest well up there, able to see in
the distance proud Plutonium—a massive structure on
flat terrain, seven pods of painted mud held by inter-
laced thatch, each pod with many levels, pennants
cracking in the wind at pod tips.

The monks crowded about the gravesite. Those in the
back craned their necks, although there was nothing
much to see: a fresh mound of dirt, rope laid across the
rectangular hole, Dugout's body wrapped in straw.
Prayers and songs preceded the lowering. Then two
monks shoveled on the dirt. No one felt very sad. Dugout had been a recluse, hard of hearing, and very old.
He had survived his friends and acquaintances.

Several weeks before, a group of sweepers had found
a Golden Age mystery on wheels. The scholarly among
the brothers had a name for it: automobile. Few such
items could be found and fewer were still well preserved
enough to transport. This item had been pulled from a
gully. Oxen had dragged it to Plutonium. Near the
graveyard, almost safely home, one of its axles had broken. The artifact was temporarily stored among the
graves, safe from the curious country folk and wandering smiths. People didn't cherish commerce with ghosts.

After the last clod of earth had fallen on Dugout, the
abbot walked over to the artifact and climbed up on its
roof. Doing so, he disturbed some carry-crows who had
already found a nesting place within the thing. They
flew out through the windows in a panic and winged
their way to the south and west, in the direction of the
badlands of Socal.

The monks had shifted their position and stood in a
half-circle around the object, eyes on the abbot.

The abbot was a thin, tall man with a pinkish face
and light, straw-colored hair. Like all other members of
the hierarchy, he wore the traditional garb of the priesthood, unchanged since the Golden Age: trousers,
jacket, a white shirt, and tie. Once all the brothers
had worn such suits, but now hard times had come for

Plutonium. Common monks dressed like ordinary folk, in strips of cloth wrapped tightly about legs and trunks, secured by leather thongs; on the top they wore ponchos made of blankets.

The abbot waited for breathless silence. Then he spoke:

"Priests of Plutonium," he said, "we've buried Hamsters Dugout this morning. He was the last of the Old Guard. I am sad but also much relieved. Old and New had many, many bitter fights. Slowly we have won out. The New Theology rules over our seven-podded roost. The past is past. The future beckons. Men like Dugout were fundamentally different from us. They worshiped Godbod in the flesh rather than in spirit and in truth. They refused to see that Godbod's earthly emanations kill and maim. 'Lead' was a curse word for them. They could never understand our view: that service means *shielding;* that love of Godbod is *enclosure;* that Plutonium is a shrine of *protection;* that Godbod's will for man and monk is *life,* not death—*health,* not sores— vigilance, not *contact.*"

On the outer edge of the half-circle of brothers, Forkies Salt listened to the abbot with a bemused expression on his darkish face. Forkies Salt—or Salty, as his companions called him—had joined the Order five years before, in the autumn of the Year of Hunger, when the skydust had been thicker than in several decades and the crops had failed. He was thirty years of age, old for a novice, and a little less than devout. The hierarchs had doubts about him. But they let him stay because he was a very skillful sweeper. If, in the course of his excursions, he visited his two wives off and on, the leaders closed an eye. Salty had found things no one else had found. The "automobile" on which the abbot stood, for instance, had been one of his achievements.

Now Salty looked bemused. His black eyes sparkled. Dimples formed and disappeared on his cheeks. His black hair half covered his left eye as it fell across his brows, and consequently his left eye squinted slightly. On his right cheek was a longish scar.

He was bemused because the abbot was putting down the Old Theology. Salty wasn't old enough to remember how it had been back then, but he had heard the stories and could see for himself.

Nowadays Plutonium was nearly empty. The brothers occupied part of one pod. Six others were slowly gnawed by ruin—the home of bats and rats and carry-crows. Five thousand monks had once filled the coiling corridors in a day, hotdamn! Five thousand men! The Old Theology had something going for it. Troubles John, father of Salty's Oneish, could tell tall tales about Plutonium's power and might, back when the brothers had had the Godbod compulsion, back when they went into holy fits in the presence of radiation. Yessir! They died like flies, of course. But new novices came, thick as a flock, called by the Mystery mounted on the roof of Vigilance. Well! Forkies Salt knew this much: The Old Guard could be proud of something. They had had the power. Plutonium had made the presidencies tremble. Nowadays the brothers were sent begging, as likely as not.

"But this is no time to scourge the past for its follies and its ignorance," the abbot was saying. "Darkness has beclouded the Earth for centuries since the Holocaustic War. Up there," he said, pointing to the murky, dusty sky, "and down here." He pointed at his own head.

"But past is past. The darkness is lifting. The light returns. We're making progress. One or two centuries more, many diligent sweeps, hard work and sacrifice—all this, my fellow brothers, will bring back the Golden Age. We must, my brothers. We must assemble what's been lost. We must collect the mysteries, the books. We must discover again the *principles* that made these objects work."

He paused to catch his breath, to let the words sink in, to prepare the priesthood for his next pronouncement. Then, tapping the roof of the object on which he stood with a toe, he continued: "Progress has been made. This object here, this *au-to-mo-bile,* is a sign that much more can be found, well-preserved mysteries, large and small."

Several monks turned about and looked at Salty. Salty quickly wiped bemusement from his features.

"This object here is magnificent. We shall take it apart and study it. We'll meditate on every part and fragment. It's magnificent, as I have said—but, brethren, but . . ." He paused to rivet their attention. "But," he continued when he had them, "it doesn't work." He paused. "It's dead, lifeless, useless. It's essentially a piece of junk. We cannot understand its workings. It's too complex, too elaborate."

Once again monks turned to Salty. He made a face so that the others smiled.

"Brothers of Plutonium," the abbot said, "we must have a *working* mystery. And to get one I'll make you a firm offer. . . ."

Late in the summer of 1975, shortly before the fall term began at George Washington University, Professor Tristan Benholz invited a select group of friends to his spacious mansion overlooking Lake Barcroft in Annandale, Virginia. Benholz was a scholar of some cleverness, combining an interest in history and science. The two books he had published to that time had earned him a modest reputation which would grow in time. *Energy Trade-offs in Medieval Agriculture* dealt with the role of technology in a nontechnological age. *Clio and Daedalus* introduced a theme he had developed in a series of books: that science and technology had a far greater determining effect on culture than did political associations; the latter, he proposed, were merely necessary consequences of the former. The theme was not terribly original, but his treatment of it was, and consequently, by 1985, he became known as the Marx of technocracy. In 1975, however, he was still relatively unknown.

During dinner his oldest daughter played the sitar for the guests. His wife was in Connecticut at a lib convention, and the dinner was stag. After dinner he took the group out on the deck. Lake Barcroft lay still below, visible through trees and bushes. After cognac had been offered and poured, cigars and pipes lit, the guests settled, Professor Benholz began as follows:

"Gentlemen," he said, "you'll all agree with me that this society does very little good long-range planning. You might say, consequently, that we excercise a—how shall I put it?—a kind of intertemporal dictatorship over unborn generations. We deny them values by our lack of foresight; we close off options by our current choices; we make no provisions for predictable contingencies."

This introduction finished, Professor Benholz paused and looked about. His guests regarded him with concentrated interest. They realized, for the first time that evening, that each man present was an expert in one or another branch of knowledge. And by his manner and his deliberate, lecturing tone, if not necessarily by the content of his statements, Benholz had hinted at a revelation or proposal.

"Time and time again in history," Benholz resumed, "periods of progress, of efflorescence, have been followed by the sensuous stupors of decadence, by times of mindless expansion, of monotonous repetition. And then, from time to time, have come ages of total darkness—as if society were a living organism that must die and be born again. While science was an art, closely linked to craft, ages of darkness have little impeded the orderly ascent of man, as Bronowski calls it. But now our science has become a far more perishable commodity. The lever, the catapult, the waterwheel are one thing. Even steam power is simple. Cyclotrons, computers, silicon chemistry are quite another matter. Not to mention fusion power. I think you all see what I mean. If darkness strikes us now, in as few as three generations we could lose the whole ball of wax. And then it may take millennia to recapture once more this beachhead of evolution."

Professor Benholz had been speaking with fingers tented, comfortably reclined in a padded lawn chair.

Now he collapsed the tent, roused himself, and walked up and down on the wooden deck in front of his guests. He passed through clouds of smoke, suspended in the still, warm air.

At last he stopped and turned.

"Based on what I know about history," he said, "which is sufficient for our purposes and"— he grinned— "you know I don't suffer from an excess of modesty. In brief, I think that current cultural patterns, and the growing structural imbalances worldwide, suggest the strong likelihood of a devastating collapse." He paused. "That's why I have called you all together."

Contrary to his usual custom, Forkies Salt did not abide long with either Oneish or Twodie. Heading out on this sweep, he felt a sense of hurry. For once he had a strong incentive to perform. Salty stopped just long enough to give each woman coils of red metal he had filched from the brothers. One coil had come from the storeroom. The second one he had taken from that wheeled mystery one night. Salty, for one, was unafraid of ghosts. The metal would feed the women —and the eight little screamers they had between them—for a month or two. Wandering smiths paid handsomely for "red." It made wonderful pots and pans and ornaments. He had found time enough for kissing and the like as well, but for little else. Then, a carry-sack of dried meat over his shoulder, rope around his waist, implements suspended from the rope, Salty headed for the badlands of Socal.

He went off Californica way not because he cherished the prospect. He knew the Earth as well as most sweepers—had even been far to the north where the ice starts, to the east as far as the Miss-a-sip, and a good ways south as well. Nowhere had the Holocaustic War left the destruction it had wrought in 'fornica. Craters upon craters—some of them dry and glassy, most of them filled with water. In the old days sweepers had loved the badlands. They had grooved on Godbod's unutterable touch. Not so Salty or others of the New Theology.

Nevertheless, or for that very reason, Salty headed south and west. There were no people in Socal. You might run into bands of mutants here and there—and, rarely enough, a mutie hunter looking for people-shapes. You could see whole herds of Harvey hares: huge, white, slow-hopping beasts. But no settlements, no foragers, no wandering smiths. If a man hoped to find a *working* mystery, he would find it in those empty reaches and nowhere else. Let others waste their time digging about old mines. Salty would go where no feet had trod. He had no fear of ghosts, but those long nights out there would be something else.

So thinking, he set out on foot, hoping to catch a wild horse in a day or so.

Several weeks later, far to the south and west of Plutonium and Shashtuk country—New Mexico in the Golden Age—he settled for the night atop a hill in rolling, empty country. Two horses, each roped to a nearby bush on a longish tether, nosed about in knee-high mutagrass seeking the soft gray shoots of autumn. Salty himself sat with a strip of tough meat in his hand, but he didn't feel like eating. His mouth was dry. Endless travel had covered him with grime. His black hair had a reddish look from the settling dust. His wrapping rags were dark with wear, his poncho torn by prickly bush, by masonry and steel. He sat unmoving and stared at the rusty sunset, wondering if he should go on.

"Shin and shinola," he thought, speaking the words aloud. "Bells mells. Who wants to be deputy abbot anyhow!"

He sat for a while in a brown study, listening to the echo of his words. Then he slapped his knee with force.

"I do, hotdamned," he cried out. "I do!"

He threw himself down on the ground and stared up at the sky. A storm had passed over this region a few days ago, and the sky was clear enough to see a star or two. But the moon, already up over the horizon, was just a blur of light.

Salty wanted to be *abbot,* not *deputy* abbot. Still, a step was as good as a leap, and the abbot had made his promise. A simple thing could earn the position—and all that it implied. *One* working mystery. A single *one.* Cheesus Criez!

"Look here, Salty," he addressed himself—mono-dialogue having become a habit. "You ain't found nothing yet and you ain't gonna find nothing now. Not in this hotdamned no man's land."

One of the horses blew air through its nostrils, a low, rumbling sound.

Salty reflected gloomily on his progress to date. He had found and searched scores of ruins. Some he had had to dig up. On three occasions he had been down into tunnels, very far below ground. The Golden Age had traveled through those caves of darkness on automobiles that ran on rails of air—or so the scholars would have you believe. Nothing. Just walls oozing with water. Drip, drip, drip. He had found enough goodies to keep Oneish and Twodie for a year or more—with enough to spare for the storerooms of Plutonium. But this time he wasn't after goodies.

He wanted to be abbot—or deputy abbot at the least. Wasn't gonna get there at this speed. Hotdammit anyway! He needed luck. Yessir, he needed some luck.

In due time he fell asleep. The meat fell from his loosened grip. In the night a carry-crow landed in the darkness, hopped closer and closer, jerking its head as it observed its surroundings. Then it was close enough at last. It snatched the meat with a pointed beak and flew off swiftly. Salty mumbled in his sleep and turned on his side.

In the fall of 1986, Fred Herring, who handled the Eastern Region for Timex Corporation, had a call to visit Professor Benholz at the professor's George Washington University office. Puzzled by this request, Herring stopped by on one of his periodic trips to the capital to see what the professor wanted. After some preliminaries, Benholz said he had need for a thousand

Timex watches, of such and such description. —No problem, Herring said, still puzzled. —The watches would be used in an experiment. —Oh, said Herring. —Yes, Benholz said. The project would serve the cause of science and . . . —Yes, Herring said. —And, well, Benholz wondered about discounts that might be available, considering . . .

At this point a buzzer sounded. Benholz apologized and turned to the small visiset on his desk, punched a button. The screen remained blank. A woman's voice said that Dr. Perkins was calling on an urgent matter.

Herring could see that Benholz was electrified. The professor gave him a quick sideways glance. "I hope you don't mind, Mr. Herring, but . . ."

Herring gestured his assent and leaned back on the couch. He studied the professor's office, noting bookshelves in a state of professorial chaos; framed certificates on the wall, hung askew, dusty; a bullfighting poster with scores of signatures; African statuettes clustered on a table in company with a single bottle of beer; suspended from the ceiling a mobile made of seashells, clumsily, fashioned by a child—the usual scholarly clutter. It would drive Herring right up a wall to live here.

The only object he found oddly out of place was a map of the U.S. It hung on the wall opposite the couch and resembled a commercial map of plant locations. Neatly placed on its surface were circles and solid dots made of red plastic. The points were in remote locations—the Rockies, eastern California, Alaska, Montana, west Texas. Most of the points were circles; only three were dots.

Herring made a note to ask about the map. But at this point the visiscreen lit up and Dr. Perkins's face appeared.

"Tristan," he said. "Can you talk?"

"I've got someone in my office, Bernie," Benholz said with the barest flicker of a glance in Herring's direction. "If you like I could—"

"Never mind," Perkins interrupted. The man was

clearly wrought up and agitated, but with pleasure rather than misfortune. "The syn-neuron project," he said. "Need I say more?"

"You mean . . ." Benholz said. His face had suddenly turned red.

"Yes," Perkins said. "I think you'd better get up here in a hurry. Still time to catch the shuttle if you hurry. And notify the others, will you?"

"*Eureka* is not the word, is it?" Benholz said.

"No," Perkins said. A smile lit up his face briefly. "Too mild. Far too mild. See you tonight?"

"Tonight," Benholz said.

With a flick of his finger, Benholz made the face of his caller disappear. It collapsed toward the center, became a point of color, faded.

The professor rose quickly, hesitated. Then he advanced toward Herring. He rubbed his hands slowly. Joy mingled on his features with the first hints of polite regret.

"Mr. Herring," he said, "I *do* hope you don't mind terribly if—if we postpone our business until another time. I— Please forgive me, but I must get out of town at once."

Herring had risen. He was a salesman with well-developed instincts. He could sense success in the air and inferred that his product might have some connection with the project. And if not, some of the glory might rub off.

"Professor Benholz," he said, shaking hands, "about that discount you mentioned. The company will be pleased to provide the watches you require. At cost. We also believe in supporting science where at all—"

"Yes, yes, yes," Benholz said. "Very nice, very nice. Thank you so much. Marge," he cried—they had passed through the door and were in an outer office— "the shuttle schedule. Quickly. I'm going to Boston. Good-bye, good-bye," he said to his guest. Then he turned and rushed back to his desk, leaving Herring standing alone.

Herring got his coat and left. He was determined that

Timex and not some other company would participate in the experiment.

Morning came over the badlands of Socal. The sun rose up—a dirty brown at first, then a red diffusion in the dust, finally a yellow brightness in the sky.

The horses were feeding again.

In the valley down below, the westerly direction from whence Salty had come—and where a trail of trampled mutagrass still marked his uphill progress—a herd of peaceful Harvey hares had arrived during the night. They also fed. From time to time the huge white beasts rose up, ears erect and pink inside. Then they went down again to munch.

Finally Salty woke up.

He did so with a start. The sun was high. He couldn't understand how he could have snoozed so long. He had always been an outdoors man. Herding, farming, smithying a bit on the side had been his occupations. He awoke with the birds and turned in with darkness. The night before he had gone to sleep hungry. This morning a breeze had sprung up. Harveys had arrived down below. The horses were moving about. Yet he had slept, slept—right through it all.

Salty shook his head to clear his senses.

He had been dreaming. He had dreamed about a music. Not the ordinary thing, of course, fiddled or picked or sung. He had dreamed about heavenly sounds, a lulling and a humming so peaceful he hadn't wanted to leave it.

A dream?

Salty held his breath and listened. His black eyes stared with unseeing concentration. Outwardly he was completely still. Inwardly he felt the first signs of intense excitement. He had to breathe again, took a breath or two, held the last one, then listened again. He could swear he heard it still. It was some kind of vibration, not music at all.

Abruptly he threw himself down on the ground. His motion startled the Harvey hares. They rose from the mutagrass in huge leaps. Landing again, they watched the hill, white rabbit statues with pink ears erect.

Salty paid no attention to them. He had his ear to the ground. Then he tore out the mutagrass until only the bare earth was left. It felt cold against his ear. Next he listened standing up, waiting for a quiet spell. The breeze rustled the mutagrass.

Several further tests, at this and other spots on the hilltop, convinced Salty that he had really heard a hum. It came from beneath, right out of the hill, and it wasn't caused by wind or beast.

"Man alive," he murmured to himself. "Salty, you'll be an abbot yet—or at least a deputy for sure."

He ran to the spot where his packs were laid. Three carry-crows flew up and away. They had been pecking at his carry-sack where the meat was tucked away.

The carry-crows made him think. Three of these boys had flown out of that mystery when the abbot had climbed up on its roof. Salty saw that as a sign. Not that he held much by signs. Nevertheless, he felt elated. Armed with a spade, he returned to the spot where he had slept and began to dig.

The taping sessions began in 1992 and continued until 2006. (When Congress approved the Russo-Chinese Intervention, the Benholz cabal dispersed, never to meet again.) The group assembled once a year for a day of taping and four days of unimpeded discussions. As a rule they chose the Fourth of July weekend. One of the members, a distinguished geologist and planner, owned land near a hot springs in the vicinity of Gunnison, Colorado. Here a geothermal power plant had been built and, thanks to an intricate land-lease deal, the cabal could tap into its lines for unlimited power. Thus the conditions were ideal for *Project Transtempora:* isolation and a plentitude of power.

Toward the end, especially after the Nine Weeks War—also known as the Palestine Insertion Operation, which engendered the Israel-China Axis—the group devoted more and more of its planning to security. How to control the initial contact between the high sophistication of the twentieth century and the presumed savagery of some barbaric succession? That was the question. "For surely," as Benholz put it, "the last thing we want is the destruction of our silos by some primitive beast looking for a rag to cover his loins."

An excellent solution was devised, tested, and installed in the three silos that were operational. Then the Intervention deteriorated into the Holocaustic War.

Fall had become winter. Snow covered the badlands. Salty lived in an earth hut covered with packed snow. He had killed the horses long ago and survived now by hunting Harveys with bow and arrow. They gave him food and fur. Harvey hunting was an ordeal. The giant rabbits, as Salty would soon understand, were telepathic. In times of distress, they communicated to their hunters cloying emotions of love and affection. The hunter had involuntary visions of baby rabbits, of children, of his wives, his mother, and of other symbols of tenderness. Only the toughest, the least sensitive, the most determined, and the most hardboiled of hunters could close in and kill under those circumstances. Salty met these tests and consequently both ate and kept warm.

On a clear but excruciatingly cold day—Salty guessed it was just before or after the Feast of Superstar—he finally found the door.

Since that first day when he had started digging at the spot where he had dreamed of music, Salty had uncovered a massive concrete dome, deep underground. He guessed, correctly, that the structure had been buried even in the Golden Age and not, as most ruins, been merely covered over by the settling of atmospheric dust. He had bared the dome in strips. Most of it was still blanketed with earth, vegetation, and snow on top. Of late he had worked around its base, and in the process he had found the entrance.

During the passage of weeks, Salty had become used to the notion that he might be much too late to win the

competition. This sweep had lasted months. No one
ever swept in winter. Since the Golden Age, or so the
people said, the weather had cooled. Up north where
the ice was, they had had cities before the Holocaustic
War. A man still wandering after August or so was presumed lost. By now some monk might have returned
with a working mystery and would have assumed the
suit-and-tie of the hierarchy. That was fine with Salty.
He guessed this dome contained enough working mysteries to buy *eight* deputy abbot positions. He knew
enough about barter and trade to make the most of it.
The more he dug the more he heard the music. And
when at last the door was uncovered, he put his ear
against the frozen metal, his heart a-throb with unnatural excitement. The music hummed clearly, distinctly. It
hadn't been delusion caused by loneliness or Harvey
thoughts.

The door yielded to his spade blows with surprising
ease. He entered a narrow corridor, just barely wide
and high enough to let a man pass. A pleasant warmth
surrounded him and made his frozen ears tingle. Hands
outstretched to feel the walls in total darkness—the rec-
tangle of light behind him grew ever smaller—he went
ahead and found that the passage grew smaller with distance. After a while he had to crawl forward on elbows
and knees.

Salty grew anxious. What if the passage became too
narrow to let a man pass? He was already on his belly,
moving like a snake. Then his anxiety passed. His mind
had a natural gift for strategy and tactics, and he realized why the corridor had shrunk into a tunnel. No man
would be able to assault this place, much less a group of
men. Defense. A military installation?

The tunnel stopped abruptly, closed off by a hard,
flat surface. Salty felt the entire surface, barely able to
move or breathe. Traces of panic touched his mind.
Thoughts of suffocation plagued him. The passage was
so narrow, he couldn't possibly force this door. Only a
midget would have room enough to work, and even a

midget would have to be lying down. Salty was a husky man, nearly two meaties high.

Then, inexplicably, the blocking surface slid aside with a hum. Beyond it Salty sensed a wide expanse.

"Hey," he yelled. "Anybody home?"

His voice echoed in the cavern up ahead. He crawled forward. The confining walls on either side were gone. He rose to his feet gingerly, one arm stretched up to find the ceiling. But there was no ceiling. The music hummed.

Salty thought about a torch. Back out again. Build a fire. Explore. He turned just as the panel slid back across the opening he had just negotiated.

"Hey!" he cried, in genuine panic, feeling like a beast trapped by a clever hunter. *"Hey!"* he yelled again. And then the program kicked in.

Lights began to flash in monotonous rhythm, spirals of light, multichromatic, on all sides and above.

"Calm, calm, calm," a voice intoned slowly but in cadence with the flashes. It was a woman's voice. Soothing.

"Relax, be calm. You have nothing to fear. Be calm. Relax. Start to feel a pleasant, calm sensation. You already feel it. Your breath is slowing down. Pay attention to your breath. Feel it going in . . . coming out. Sloooowly. Caaaaalmly . . ."

Salty understood the words although they sounded a little odd, as if the speaker came from another region—the north, say, where the ice started.

He grinned briefly. Have it your way, sister, he thought. The scholarly among the brothers had told him about Old Order mysteries that could capture the voice. He had already found himself a working mystery. And those lights! They flashed at him even while he closed his eyes.

The voice told him to sit down, and so he sat down. The voice told him that he would now fall asleep but still hear every word. He went to sleep and heard every word.

Salty didn't *have* to do it. But he wanted to. He would play along until he knew his way about this place. Then he would take what pleased him—and make the deal of his lifetime.

The lights stopped flashing. A brightness spread. Salty knew this although his eyes were closed. He didn't open them. The voice had said he shouldn't. Nevertheless, he saw an orange glow on the inside of his eyelids.

The voice told him to rise and move to his left. It assured him that it was safe. He wouldn't fall. Salty trusted the voice and did as he was told.

"You may open your eyes now," the voice said. "When the bed comes out of the wall, you'll lie down on it, your head toward the wall. If you're wearing a hat, you'll take it off."

Aha! said Salty deep inside himself. So they can't see me, can they. He wore no hat.

Eyes open now, he faced a wall unlike any wall he had ever seen. It was bestudded with glowing jewels—red, yellow, green. Silvery metal frames enclosed tiny boxes of glass. Thin spiderlegs inside the boxes oozed fine traceries of color on spinning drums.

Despite the voice and its instructions to be calm, Salty felt a powerful surge of excitement. Hotdamned! Mysteries upon mysteries. All of them working.

Underneath the jewels and the boxes, the wall suddenly slid aside and a narrow cot came out, startling Salty. The voice told him that he need not fear. He relaxed again and laid himself down as instructed earlier. He *liked* the woman behind the voice.

On his back now, he could see the entire cavern. The ceiling was a mass of light—a mild shining like daytime on a hazy day. He saw more walls like the first one, and opposite him was a vast structure of shelves. The voice interrupted his dazed examination.

"Place your hands next to your body. Close your eyes again. What you will now experience is pleasure and serenity. You will accept it all with calm and joy."

Salty obeyed.

Then, abruptly, accompanied by a whirring noise and

a metallic slap, tight bands shot out of the side of the cot, crossed over his body, and locked in place.

Salty jerked out of his trance with a yell.

Pleasure and serenity be damned! Calm and joy go hang!

"Hey!" he yelled, struggling. The bands held him tightly. His mind raced. His veins bulged with exertion. "You!" he yelled, meaning the woman behind the voice. "Hey, you!"

The voice had fallen silent. Salty felt a prickling sensation in his arms. Then came a sharp pain. From below, rising up toward him with a rush, came a blackness. It enveloped him.

When his consciousness returned, he found pictures in his mind, new words—a forest, an ocean, an empire of concepts.

From the brain beneath the cavern, riding on a billion synthetic synaptic links, knowledge flooded his own awareness, knowledge so strange he could barely believe it; and yet he had no trouble understanding any part of it.

The brain, of course, was bathed in liquid helium. Naturally. It consisted of molecule-sized synthetic neurons in a maze of copper afferents and efferents so thin that microscopes were barely good enough to see them. At the cryogenic temperatures of liquid helium, superconduction was possible. Electropulses traveled without resistance.

How clever! Salty thought. How deuced clever!

He admired especially the holographic image-storage using the simple polysac-based branched polymer Perkins had synthesized. Compared with natural neuron chemistry, it was a crude construct. Hence, of course, the storage chamber was a hundred-meter cube. Of course it stored the contents of nineteen brains, but still . . . For a *storage* vessel, it was magnificent! The war, of course, had stopped development of self-generated thought routines. Also some trouble with vital functions. Vitality. *Élan vital*. Bergson. Poor hypothesis, some said. But the brain, alas, had no instinctive drives. So it just lay there, inert. A library of . . . must work on that. In the meantime, friends, we've got us the foolproof transtemporal know-how device. And will teach your daughter skating for sure. I'll guarantee it. Bet you a box of cigars. . . .

Hour after hour, day after day, relentlessly, the vast storage chamber in the silo disgorged its contents and filled Salty's brain. He came to understand the Benholz plan—to transmit the knowledge of mankind, or as much as would readily stick, from the past into the future. Salty consumed the knowledge avidly. Even in those early hours, he knew how he could use it. The fervor of the cabalists, implicit in the messages, escaped him altogether. Salty was a man of action, not a seeker.

Finally, after a hundred hours without sleep, the reticular formation in Salty's brainstem rebelled at last. Impulses traveled from his brain by invisible wiring back to that other brain. Synapses fired. The flow grew thin, stopped. Salty slept. Not even hunger could keep him awake. The music hummed. Now it was wired right into his shaven skull.

Salty waited for the thaw of spring. He had plenty to do, and life was a good deal easier now. Pleasantly warm in thermal underwear, an arctic parka above his hunting suit, butane heaters inside his mitts, armed with a high-powered, scope-equipped rifle, even Harvey hunting was a snap. He could just pick out an animal, put the cross hairs right on its head, and squeeeeeze off a round. The Harvey would leap three meaties into the air and drop. At that distance, no cloying telepathic attack. Scourgehill, the biologist, would never have believed these Harveys possible. The twenty-third century knew things about genetics and mutation—in an empirical, pragmatic way—the twentieth couldn't possibly credit. Take stump-walkers, for instance, birdmen, beemen . . . Well; as Benholz knew, war is the mother of all things. Some mother!

Salty spent most of his time below ground. He knew the silo as if he had built it himself, as if he had personally selected every mystery stored there for posterity. And in a way he had. At least he possessed the memories of all those who had. He carried out a meticulous inventory. Then he set to work on the security system.

By now all sense of hurry had left him. He knew he would become the Abbot of Plutonium, one way or the other. It amused him to recall the superstitions that governed the brotherhood. Godbod! Godbod was nuclear waste. The priesthood worshiped garbage, as it were! The present site of Plutonium had been a rad-waste storage depot in the Golden Age. He knew that because the cabal had been most interested in the project. It had been another attempt to plan far into the future. Plutonium, with a half-life of 24,000 years, needed *real* long-term storage. How the organizers of the priesthood had contrived to keep the brotherhood going right through the Holocaustic War remained a mystery, but Salty meant to find out.

Plutonium no longer worried him. He felt he was its master already. Not a bad institutional setup for a man with Salty's knowledge and ambitions. Not bad at all. But Salty had no wish to grapple with competition.

No man had ever found a treasure quite like Silo 3. Not in this day and age. He meant to ensure that no other man ever did. With that thought in mind he made changes in a number of the security parameters. The next visitor to this ol' dome wouldn't leave alive.

He chuckled himself, thinking about it all, while cutting plates for a trapdoor with a laser torch. He, for one, didn't share the cabalistic view of science. Nice, yes. Bloody goddamned useful, too. But as for knowledge for its own sake—hah! Any man who had made it through the Year of Hunger would laugh at that. And in this day and age, it might take generations to build it all back up. Salty had only one life to live, and it was halfway spent already. Look out for Number One, yes sir. Looking out for Number One meant welding these plates to hinges, face mask on, sparks flying. It meant securing the other silo before some clever guy found it. It meant some rough-and-ready maintenance on the clever breeder reactor that powered this place—it was almost ready to go. It meant bulldozing the dirt back on the mound and hoping that the mutagrass grew back in a hurry without leaving telltale signs.

Thus he occupied himself.

Then came spring. For days on end the sky was dark with geese in migration. Salty could just aim his rifle up, any which way, jerk the trigger, and one or two birds would drop down. The microwave oven roasted them before you could mutter "Forkies Salt."

One day—the air was mild and full of scents—Salty knew the time had come to leave. His hair, shaved off by the machine, had grown back out. His work was done. The mutagrass had sprouted on the scars of earth his spade had made in the fall. He put on his old clothes, washed to a sparkling clean in a Maytag that had worked like new because, in a manner of speaking, it was. At last he stood among the shelves upon shelves, racks upon racks whereon machines and gadgets of every possible type were lovingly stored by the clever foresight of the cabal.

Salty searched for just the right item—something small enough to carry without attracting attention, something whose purpose the abbot would readily understand and appreciate, something that evidently worked.

Pondering his future plans, Salty had decided to move ahead by easy stages. He had to secure the other silo—the third one was under the icecap in the north. It would take another sweep to do that. He couldn't well zoom about the land in an electric rover. Not yet. So horses would have to get him there. Therefore, this time around, he needed a small thing to keep the abbot occupied for a while. And something for himself as well, something special.

After much thought, he chose from a box that contained yet other, narrow boxes three self-winding Timex watches.

As for himself, he took the smallest Geiger counter he could find. After all, what good was a deputy abbot without his personal Godbod sniffer?   ✣

The Book of Padraig

Mildred Downey Broxon

In the twilight of his life Teval landed at stone-bleak Aran, flew to Shannon Airfield, "Gateway to the Gael," and took the hydrofoil up the river. He enjoyed the leisurely pace of surface travel, skimming between green rolling banks. It was good to revisit the scenes of his youth. He was ready for death, but he had errands during the brief time that remained, before grayness claimed him.

He had been summoned from his obscure cataloging by the Curator of the Museum of Ripar. After all the years, all his education, Teval was but a functionary in a routine job. But he was home on Ripar; and in the museum, surrounded by beauty and history, he was at peace.

The Curator's office was black save for one area, yellow-lighted. And in it—

"You collected this, Teval," the curator said. His voice was faint and raspy; it fluttered with soft sounds. Teval wondered to what planet he had been adapted in *his* youth, that left its mark on him as Earth had on himself.

In the dark Teval stood, proud. He was being noticed. "I collected it myself, indeed. I carried it with me until my return, then I donated it."

"Primitive," the Curator interrupted. "Two-dimensional. We have recorded it for reference, in the event"—
he was disdainful— "it is ever required."

Teval reached out. "I worked on it myself. You have
no idea what it was like there—only I know."

"It is yours, then. You have no further need of possessions; return it to the natives, if you will."

Teval was dismissed. And so, in the twilight of his
life, Teval returned to Ireland. And the Gael.

The countryside had changed. He noticed the ruined
castles first; they stood shattered on hilltops or crumbled in pastures, stone wrenched from stone by the
force of time and the fortunes of war. None of them had
been built when last he walked this land, centuries before the Norman invasion. These people lived so fast:
Generation trampled generation, and war followed war.
All he had known were now dusty molecules.

Over the microphone the tour guide spoke, first in
English, then in Gaelic. "Ladies and gentlemen, ahead
we see Clonmacnois, founded in the sixth century by
Saint Ciaran." Teval stared, overwhelmed by the evidence of time.

The Shannon still flowed broad and reed-rimmed
here, but on its banks so many buildings stood—
roofless ruins, built since his last trip. The wooden
structures all were gone; the small stone church alone
remained. New at his first arrival, it stood crowded in a
graveyard.

"The oldest building here," the guide said, "is Saint
Ciaran's Church, *Teampul Ciaran,* dating from 800 A.D.
In its time Clonmacnois was an eminent center of learning, one of *the* universities of Europe."

Gaelic, Teval noted, had changed over the centuries;
he could not tell about English, as his was newly
learned.

The hydrofoil coasted toward the dock, settling back
onto the water. The passengers rose to disembark. Still
Teval sat, looking out the window, aware of the weight

within his llur-skin backpack. *An eminent center of learning . . .*

He had been young then, and one of his tasks, or privileges—in Teval's language the concepts were identical—was to examine and appreciate alien cultural development. His group was chosen to see Earth. They were cosmetically humanized and scattered over China, Arabia, India, and Abyssinia, sent to the Mayans, the Inca, the Aztecs, Eskimo, and Norse. Three fourteens of them there were—but Earthfolk counted to base ten, Teval knew. His new hands were awkward.

Teval, one of those assigned in Western Europe, was sent to the Irish monastery at Clonmacnois. He found it not too difficult to blend in. Amid the babble of tongues, the variance of dress, the confusion of customs, he was merely another foreigner, an alien amid aliens. From all parts of Europe students came. Here books were preserved, here reading and writing yet lived, here survived the learning of those who had flourished before barbarians overran the known world. Seeking scarce knowledge, folk flocked to Clonmacnois.

Teval longed, in that fog-and-rain-enshrouded land, for the jeweled nights of Ripar's star-rich sky, for perfumed drink and aromatic food, for the company of his kind, for ease and entertainment and luxury, skin-music and mind-colors. Life at Clonmacnois was dull: gray toil, rough clothing, plain food, and far too much silence.

Such a short time they have to live, he thought, in his youth, *and how they waste it for this religion of theirs.* But it was the religious at Clonmacnois who had the learning and kept the books; so the young nobles and the half-tamed barbarians disciplined themselves to monasticism. Up early, pray, work in the scriptorium if skilled enough (if not, practice on wax tablets), more prayer, a scant meal of porridge "lest the stomach be burdened and the mind confused," then prayer and silence and meditation. Bend over the books carefully, carefully, not touching or marking them. Listen to readings, go to bed at sundown when the light fails and rise in the darkness to pray—to Teval it was only an episode, an interlude during which he would learn patience. It was not his nature to complain.

Time stretched on, and he stayed. Finally he took monastic vows and received the Celtic tonsure; his head was shaved back halfway from his brow. What was the pledge of one human lifetime to such as he? He was to learn all he could, until his group was summoned home. His body, of course, would bear the mark of Earth forever. The rhythm of life became natural to him: the wheeling of the seasons, the joy-to-sorrow cycle of church festivals, year after flickering year.

When his hands became skilled he was permitted to work with ink and vellum in the scriptorium—he who had learned to write with coded light! He whittled goose quills and mixed brown-gall ink; he copied page after page, leaving the color work on the glowing illuminated capitals to others, doing instead the work any printing machine could have done. But machines were far in this world's future—writing itself was a rarity, and a book was a treasure beyond price.

His book. Recorded, then discarded—had custom not demanded the donor be told, it would have been destroyed. His book!

In the hydrofoil, Teval hefted his backpack and rose to walk down the aisle.

Brother Padraig had loved books. Amazing how many monks were called Padraig. This particular one was chubby, blond, and had a tendency to complain. He was a younger son of a chieftain, destined from birth for the church. But he had never quite resigned himself to the monastic life; the rule of silence was one he could not keep. Padraig was most at home in the scriptorium, where he painted designs of such imagination and intricacy that even Teval, who had played with Ankharian holograms as an infant, could only watch in awe. Part of the time, of course, Padraig spent digging in the garden as penance for his many transgressions, digging and complaining to the carrots and cabbages.

Perhaps as much to restore the blessed silence of Clonmacnois as to broaden Padraig's horizons, the old Abbot ordered him to deliver a book to the monastery at Kells. Padraig asked if Teval might accompany him; the Abbot, doubtless thinking Teval a steadying influence, agreed.

Teval was surprised to be invited, but he was here to learn.

"I have seen you admiring the drawings, Teval," said Padraig as they set off on foot. "I thought you might appreciate the treasures at Kells."

Teval nodded. Silence caused few problems.

The road to Kells was long; they received hospitality on their way, as was the custom in the land. Wherever they lodged, Padraig took pains to keep the book dry and safe, for it was a great treatise by Galen.

Galen. Of what use was Galen? Teval himself had helped scribe the book, biting his tongue to keep silence as he copied page after page of misinformation, setting down wrong anatomy and useless herbals, all in a clear round uncial script.

Away from the monastery Padraig came into his own, singing snatches of bawdy songs, telling tales of Maeve and Cuchullain, guzzling ale, smiling at women, neglecting his devotions. Rarely did they lodge at monasteries, but rather sought accommodation in chieftains' stone-walled *raths*. Padraig did, however, stop one Friday at Clonard, "so the brothers may be released from their fast for the day."

They took more time than necessary to reach Kells, or so the brothers there implied. The Abbot accepted the copy of Galen with gratitude, though the tight-lipped Brother Librarian sniffed at it for crowding too many lines onto the page. He then showed their own library and, in triumph, escorted them to the church, where he displayed the great gospel book the community had carried from Iona when it fled the Viking raids.

Teval, awestruck, stared at the jeweled and golden

cover, at the intricate designs, the glowing multicolored inks. Unusual for him, Padraig said nothing.

For the rest of their stay at Kells, Padraig kept his silence. He observed the work in progress in the scriptorium, scrutinized the volumes in the library, and somehow made off with the brothers' secret recipe for black ink. At last Padraig and Teval headed home to Clonmacnois by a circuitous route.

Padraig seemed determined to stop at every *rath*, speak with every bard, sing late every night. One evening when the ale was stronger than usual he began to tell Teval of a project, but he quickly stopped and said no more.

The weather grew cold; a stiffness of the limbs troubled Padraig on damp mornings, and he coughed at night. He remarked to Teval that it must be wonderful to be young and strong again; Teval smiled and said nothing. *Have I lived here so long?*

At night, sleepless as usual—his kind required little rest—Teval would step outside to search the stars. Even if only a few wisps of cloud sped across the sky, he could never find his own sun. It was too dim, and too far away. *When will they come for me?*

With the first hard frost, Padraig and Teval returned to Clonmacnois. Within the year the old Abbot died, and Padraig, who had been strangely quiet of late, was elected to his place.

Teval stepped onto the dock and felt the chill wind's bite. He had forgotten how cold, even in summer, this part of the planet was. The Shannon, glassy-green, flowed by as ever, bearing in its waters chemicals unknown when Teval last trod its banks. He shrugged his thin shoulders under his llur-skin backpack, feeling the bulk and heaviness inside. Across the dock flapped sad little banners proclaiming the tenth anniversary of the Gael.

Ulster had first joined Scotland; when Wales and the Irish Republic demanded entry, the Gael was born. England, crumbling economically, made feeble protest.

But England's problems were shared, and internal rivalries were yet strong. A Celtic nation seemed ridiculous in the modern world. Who cared? With starvation and war and daily ugliness, what was the use of being a "nation of bards and artists"?

Teval had studied well for his return. The banners, he saw, were in uncial script, but they were written in English.

"Clonmacnois," the guide was saying, "was repeatedly sacked by the Vikings. Its treasured manuscripts were scattered or destroyed. The round towers are thought to date from the time of the raids—"

A little after they began, thought Teval. *For they were not here in my time, and I left when—but first there was the sickness.*

Antibiotics would have cured the plague; with decent medical care most of the stricken would have survived, but it was not Teval's place to tell the monks that their herbs and infusions were worthless. He himself was immune to disease, as he was almost immune to time, so he helped in the infirmary, nursed the sick of the community, the students, and the local farmers, for after all a monastery was bound to help in time of need.

When even the Brother Infirmarian grew ill, Teval alone carried water, changed linen, administered useless medicine, and gathered herbs from the garden. All work in the scriptorium was suspended.

Padraig, who had been Abbot now for years, was not spared. When he grew ill he babbled of some secret book, some masterwork he was scribing, and Teval recalled the almost-confidence of years before.

When frost chilled the river mist and gleamed silver on the reeds and grass, those who did not succumb to the racking autumn cough recovered. Pale and weak, they rose from their pallets and went back to work.

All but Padraig. His hands shook, and he coughed continually, so that he could no longer hold a pen. Moreover, his eyes had grown dim, and a novice now had to read aloud to him. Toward Easter, when it became obvious that his was no temporary infirmity, he called for Teval.

Teval stood in the dim-lit cell. Padraig, no longer plump, lay propped on sheepskins, a woolen shawl about his shoulders, his hands fluttering on the bedcoverings, restless, useless, uncontrollable now, spotted with age as once they were with ink. Teval, time-spared, looked at him in pity.

"Teval," Padraig said, "I remember—you cared for me when I was ill, did you not?"

"That I did," said Teval.

"When the fever was on me I spoke of a secret project; you must have heard me, and thought I knew not what I said."

"Men speak, in fever, many things," said Teval.

"I spoke of a book, one I scribed myself, one finer than the great gospel book of Kells. Remember the old librarian?" Padraig smiled. "If pride is a sin, he burns, though his was only the keeping of the Book, not the making of it. But I have scribed this book myself, and it is no copy." He tried to sit up. "In it I recorded the songs of the bards, the ancient pagan tales, the stories of the gods who went before . . ." He coughed. "And I wrote it in our own language, not that of the Romans. I wonder now if I did wrong."

"You, the Abbot, ask me?" said Teval.

Padraig coughed again. "I never wanted to be a monk, let alone Abbot." His milky eyes were sad. "Life is short, but which of us can decide how he will spend it? Promise me this, Teval. On my death you will take the book and keep it. I fear the barbarians who struck Iona will strike here; all our books will be burned and all our learning forgotten. For years I have worked, waking nights, telling no one. It will not be finished, now." Padraig looked at his palsied hands. "And still I had stories—"

"I am no artist," Teval said, "but a fair scribe, and silent."

The Abbot stared. "And you, a monk, would do this thing?"

"I would," said Teval. "Speak, and I will write."

So I did, Teval recalled. *And never, by my promise to Padraig, told I any man. But I completed it, and kept it safe.*

A day of swords followed a night of fire. Dragon-prowed ships sailed up the Shannon to plunder and slaughter. Teval watched and knew his time here was measured in hours; this was the end of his life at Clonmacnois. Younglings were always removed from danger, and the situation here was dangerous indeed.

The raiders struck the library first. Hooting, they carried forth the volumes, stripped off the gold and jeweled covers, then set the glowing pages to the torch. Any who cried out for his lifework was flung onto the pyre as well. Teval said nothing; his meekness enraged the raiders, who spoke to him in a language he'd not learned. They bound his arms, struck him, and threatened him with the sword.

If the monitor is working, he thought, *they will be coming for me soon.* He was marched toward the fire, to where the books were burning, *his* books. He saw Padraig dragged forth from his burning hut, his ancient bones cruelly jostled, his face twisted in pain, his near-blind eyes staring at the fire.

With a yell of rage Teval burst his thongs. He knew he should not display his strength, but he was young, and forgot. He rushed toward those who held the Abbot. The raiders laughed and put the old man to the sword, a soft sound, brightness into crimson. Then they turned on Teval.

The leader, a huge man, stepped forward, holding his still-dripping sword. "You next, coward-with-strength," he said in broken Gaelic. "Mine will be your killing, and it slow."

The earth shuddered. Monks and raiders alike looked up at the shape that descended from the sky.

Teval—evacuate. The voice of the monitor was cold inside his skull. *NOW!*

The raiders stood frozen. Teval pushed past the leader and ran toward Padraig's hut. The burning thatch dropped chunks of fire onto the rush-strewn floor and straw bedding.

The book!

He looked back at the ship one moment as it touched down. He was disobeying. He plunged into the hut, pulled aside the flaming bedding, and scrabbled for the book. Its leather cover had protected it. He clutched it to him and ran for safety.

Not until later—much later, shipboard—did he notice that his hands were burned.

"Early Christian grave-slabs are displayed on the walls of the gallery," the guide said, gesturing at a stone-walled corridor. Teval looked down its length. For one moment he blinked, thinking he saw—but no, it was centuries past that his ship had rescued him, and this tapering structure was built of stone. The entrance was partway up the wall; that, and the usual small windows—he smiled and shook his head. Someone had survived to tell stories, and someone else had remembered and built. He hefted his backpack and walked down the gallery, looking at the weathered slabs set in the wall. Centuries of wind and rain had scoured the lettering, dulled the carving; the stone was porous now, lichen's-home. He read no familiar names.

I have brought your book, Padraig, but where are you? Where are they all?

Beyond the gallery a great crop of gravestones had sprouted in the enclosure, the dead crowding onto what they hoped was holy ground. *There* was where the Norsemen had built their fire; on *that* spot the herb garden once grew. All was covered now with centuries of stone and history.

Teval stood looking at the two round towers. All over Ireland they and others like them stood. Bell towers? Places of refuge? Refuge, perhaps. He smiled. *They are crumbling while I yet live. For a time.*

He wandered away from the group. Stones erected

centuries since his time were tilted, their inscriptions erased.

I have lived long enough, and traveled far, Teval thought. *In all that time I have treasured this book, and shared it with beings stranger than any in Padraig's mythology. But when I wished to leave it for the ages—the ages will have it yet.*

He looked at the towers, stone rockets pointed at the sky. His monuments, and they already old. He climbed back into the hydrofoil and sat, watching the river flow, waiting for the tourists to return.

The library at Trinity College was dim; dusty centuries slumbered on the shelves, and two rows of marble busts stared down at the line of visitors. Teval shuffled forward, a few steps at a time, his pack still heavy on his back. The line was long, as usual. No one hurried; after all these centuries the Book of Kells was still worth perusing. Eyes used to dull printed pages and flickering holovision paused a while to appreciate the colors, vivid after centuries, the swirling, surreal patterns, details too small to be seen without magnification: the essentially Celtic riot of design and color, adapted to a Christian gospel book.

It lay encased in glass, in a filtered atmosphere. The fumes of modern Dublin would corrode the pigments. The pages were now turned by mechanical means; in years past, a card said, the case had been unlocked that a gloved librarian might turn one page a day. But now the Book sat guarded like a jewel, untouched by human fingers, breath, or life.

Teval had touched the Book once—after washing his hands, of course. But that was many years ago, in Kells. Kells Priory itself was ruined now, all that stood there at his time destroyed. In the modern church was a facsimile of the Book—the Abbot had sent the Book itself to Dublin for safekeeping, in Cromwell's time.

He leaned forward and looked. The gold-and-jeweled covers were gone, lost in a raid; he'd read of that. And a few beginning and end pages were missing. The

pigments were ever so slightly faded, and some of the
vellum was turning brown. He looked at the brush-
strokes forming the capitals. He had always wanted to
indulge his fancies, create beauty, but he had no talent
for art, not with his human hands. He stood for a long
moment, saying good-bye. A pair of giggling school-
boys followed him; they grew silent, looking at the
Book.

"Is that in Gaelic?" one of them whispered.

"No, Latin," said the other, educated and superior.
"They didn't write Gaelic then. Nobody did."

Some of us did, Teval thought.

At the end of the line people wandered off to stand
before the glass-fronted cases of special exhibits. Some
stared at Brian Boru's harp, its frame time-blackened,
its strings slack. Many were herded out to other attrac-
tions.

Teval followed them into the corridor and up, not
down, the stairs. He was correct; here was the familiar
dismal dustiness of cataloging rooms and stacks.

One office, the door ajar, was particularly cluttered,
almost homelike. Boxes and piles of books were strewn
over table and floor alike. An elderly man was bent
over one page, examining it through a magnifying glass.

Teval could move very softly when he chose. He
opened his pack—the bright-blue scaly leather rustled
only slightly—and pulled out the parcel. The water-
proof wrapping was offworld, and must be removed. He
hefted his burden one last time.

One quiet step into the room, reach out slowly, set
the book atop a stack; done, now. One more step out,
back down the hallway. A guard appeared behind him.

"Sorry," he said, "this area is off limits to visitors."

"I apologize," said Teval. "Trespass was not meant. I
was separated from my tour, and thought—"

The guard considered him. "I'll be needing to check
your parcel, you know." Treval proffered it.

He looked inside. "Ah, naught but a bit of plastic
wrap in here. Sorry to trouble you, but—"

Teval nodded. "I would not wish you to be less than

careful," he said. "It's your job, of course, and all those lovely books—"

The guard smiled. "Ah, they are that." He paused, evidently considering another possibility—but who would bomb a library? Those times were surely past.

Teval returned his gaze with all the innocence of centuries. The guard began to speak, then thought better of it. "I'll be showing you the stairway, then," he said. "Mind you don't miss your group. They'll be waiting for you out to the right, you know."

Teval's pack was empty now, uncomfortably light. He went down the curving marble stairs to the gift shop, where he bought a full-sized plastivellum facsimile of the Book. The weight was about the same; he would carry it until he needed no more possessions. *Soon*, he thought, *there will be another Book available. I'll never see it. But Padraig would have been happy. His is the more beautiful. And I took better care of it than could the monks at Kells.*

He stepped out into the cobblestone courtyard of Trinity. Tattered festival banners hung overhead, proclaiming the tenth annniversary of the founding of the Gael. They flapped, sooty and draggled, in the gray Dublin breeze.

The Gael. Still searching for its history, the history not of war and betrayal, but of song and beauty—and it was gone, so much of it was gone.

But now they have the Book of Padraig, and the old tales, told before the divisions, then lost or suppressed. He was tired now. A biodegradable newssheet, already lacy and half deteriorated, flapped against his ankles. He looked down at the stone-gray, battered print, and smiled. The round uncial lettering of Padraig's book— *and his*—was yet clear and dark. Centuries had passed. It was time to return to Ripar, the last trip home.   ✰

When You Wish Upon A Star

Gene DeWeese

The Return (1)

Jason Holman came awake abruptly, before the first buzz of the phone's nightcall died away. He jabbed at the audio button at the head of his bed as the second, slightly louder buzz began.

"They're back, Jase! They're back!" The familiar staccato voice of the Agency Director burst from the speaker.

Deep within Holman, something exploded, tearing viciously at the pit of his mind, battering its way furiously toward the surface. "It's over!" the explosion screamed at him. "It's all been for nothing! *Nothing!*" And the light from its flash showed him once again the monstrous, stillborn corpse, its billions of swarming cells now chained forever to the overflowing, rotting womb of Earth.

But, except for a momentary glazing of his eyes and a split-second hesitation before he replied, the destruction remained internal, totally contained.

"Where are they, Carl?" Holman asked. His well-modulated voice reflected the proper amount of excitement and surprise and relief while his mind clamped down on its inner chaos and began exploring the possibilities of what could be salvaged from the program. "How far out?"

"A billion kilometers, give or take a few hundred

million, they told me. Number Ten picked up their signal a few minutes ago."

A billion kilometers. They would be in Earth orbit in three days or less.

"What did they say?" Holman asked, knowing that there could not possibly have been a message. There was only one message they could have sent, and if that message had been received, Carl's voice would have been displaying an emotion far different from the elation it radiated now.

"Not much, Jase, but it's enough. Just a short loop, on automatic, with their identification, followed by one word." The director's voice paused, as if he were savoring the moment. "One word, Jase: *Success!*"

Impossible! The word began to form on Holman's lips, but he cut it off sharply.

Could it be a trap? Had Carl, or some other Agency executive, somehow become suspicious? Was the director simply trying to jolt Holman into revealing something? Something solid enough to let them crank yet another delay into the FTL-2 launch schedule? Something solid enough to let them cancel the entire FTL program? Or turn it over to someone else—which would be the same as cancelling it.

Holman forced a laugh to indicate his high spirits. "What did you expect, Carl? A failure? Now perhaps we can get on with the final phases of FTL-2 and 3. Maybe we can even get them to cut loose the funds to start 4 and 5."

"Anything's possible now," the director said. "At least for a while, until the glamor wears off. Of course, a lot depends on what FTL-1 is bringing back, if anything." The excitement faded, replaced by a dull apprehension. "If we don't get something pretty damned practical or exciting out of these first few, we could be right back where we started in a few years."

Where we will stay forever, Holman thought as that Earthbound corpse floated before his eyes once again. Instead he said: "We'll never be back where we started.

We will have been there, no matter what happens afterward."

"That's the spirit!" The vigor and enthusiasm was back in the director's voice. "And that's what will get us more money, at least for the next few months, that kind of talk. And speaking of such mundane matters as public relations, you had better get down here, fast. As soon as I let the President know what's happening, I'll be letting the media in on it. They'll want to talk to someone who can come up with answers that are more intelligent than their questions. Can you be ready in, say, an hour?"

Ready for what? Holman wondered. "Certainly," he said. "Isn't this what we've spent the last two years getting ready for?"

The director chuckled. "Yes, I guess it is. See you later."

The speaker fell silent as the connection was broken at the director's end.

Jason Holman sat motionless and silent on the edge of the bed for several seconds, then began punching Almeda Sorrells' number into the phone.

The Departure (1)

MEDIA: This tall, handsome gentleman is Dr. Jason Holman, the man behind the scenes, so to speak. He has been in charge of the FTL Project since its inception nearly— Just how long ago was that, Dr. Holman? Or may we call you Jason?

HOLMAN: Certainly, Don. That title—Doctor—has always made me just a little nervous anyway. Jason, or Jase, is fine with me. In answer to your question about the Project, it started officially only four years ago, but unofficially it had been going on for quite some time before that.

MEDIA: How do you mean, unofficially?

HOLMAN: Perhaps I should have said the program was uncoordinated, not unofficial. There were many people, myself and Dr. Sorrells included, who had been thinking about and experimenting with approaches to the problem of faster-than-light travel—or FTL, if you will—for decades. But they had all been involved in individual efforts, funded from different sources, each one approaching the problem from a different angle.

MEDIA: I see what you mean. And of course it was one of those individual—independent—efforts that finally paid off.

HOLMAN: Very true. Without the individual contributions, there never would have been a unified FTL program—or an FTL drive. Remember, the FTL drive—or, to be more accurate, the discovery that led to the drive—came long before the FTL Project itself. All the Project has done is mechanize that discovery. Translated it from a lab experiment, a theory, into reality, into actual hardware. The real hero of all this is Dr. Sorrells. Without her, we wouldn't be standing here today, only minutes away from the departure of the first starship.

MEDIA: That brings up an interesting point, Dr.—Jase. I suppose you get this question all the time, but I feel compelled to ask it anyway. Didn't Dr. Sorrells' discovery come in the nick of time, so to speak? Wasn't the timing just a bit dramatic, even a little melodramatic?

HOLMAN: You could say that, Don. In fact, as you suggested, it *has* been said—many, many times. But if you look at history, you'll see that many important discoveries seem to have been made in the nick of time. Atomic power, for instance, in the nick of time to replace dwindling fossil fuels. Then solar power in the nick of time to replace an increasingly dangerous atomic power.

MEDIA: I see. But let me attack the question from a different angle. Until Dr. Sorrells' discovery, interest in interstellar exploration was declining so badly that funds were being cut drastically every year. In fact, according to most authorities, Project Long Haul was in danger of being phased out altogether in two or three years.

HOLMAN: I see you've been doing your homework,

Don. Yes, what you say was quite true. *Was!* But there's no guarantee as to how long the situation would have remained. You, if anyone, should know how often national and international priorities and interests change. Project Long Haul might have gone into hibernation, and the ships might have gone into mothballs for a few years. But I'm positive that everything would have worked out eventually—over the long haul.

MEDIA: You think, then, that the Long Haul ships would have eventually been launched even if the FTL drive had not been discovered?

HOLMAN: I'm sure of it. They wouldn't have been launched this soon, but they would have made it sometime, somehow.

MEDIA: One more thing, Jase, and I'm sure it's another question you've heard a thousand times. What is it that—

HOLMAN: What is it that we expect to find out there? Yes, Don, I've heard that a few times, but it's a question I never tire of answering. And the only honest answer is, I don't know. I don't know what we will find or what we will gain.

MEDIA: But if you don't know—

HOLMAN: If we already knew what we were going to find, what would be the point of going? Seriously, I think our position can best be illustrated with an analogy. I first heard it about the time I started to school, more than thirty years ago, but I'm sure it's been around at least a century, since the first Lunar flights or even before. But it's more apt today. Think of our solar system, with its planets and satellites, as a house. One single house, in a city of billions of houses, in a world of billions of cities. Here we are on Earth, confined to one tiny room of that single house. We have lived in that room for millions of years. Until a few centuries ago, we didn't even know that the rest of the house existed, let alone the rest of the city or the rest of the world. Then, a few hundred years ago, we started peeking out through the keyhole of that room with our telescopes, even got a few looks out of a window at the rest of the city. We saw that something was out there. Then, last century, a door to that room was opened a crack—just a crack—and a few dozen people and a few hundred machines crawled out of the room and took a closer look at the rest of the house: the Moon and the planets of our own solar system. Not a really good look, you understand. No one stayed long enough for that. Certainly no one stayed long enough to set up housekeeping. So we continued to live out our entire lives in this one room. Now, for the first time in history, we have a chance to open the front door of that house and step outside. To step outside and see what our neighbors look like. To see if we *have* any neighbors.

MEDIA: An intriguing analogy, but—

HOLMAN: But not realistic. I know that many feel that way, Don. But think about it for a minute. And then look up into the sky on any clear night. If you do, you'll see over two thousand of our nearest neighbors. And then think that, for each one you see, there are millions more that you can't see. Literally millions.

MEDIA: That's certainly an impressive analogy, but surely even you can't imagine that we could ever reach them all.

HOLMAN: Not in the foreseeable future, certainly. Even with the FTL drive, we'll be lucky to reach a hundred systems in my lifetime, very lucky. But in the future, who knows? And who can say what we will find once we get out there? The possibilities, believe me, are infinite, simply because the universe itself is infinite.

MEDIA: Thank you, Dr. Holman.

The Preparations (1)

Jason Holman had always known that man must someday go to the stars, or someday die. He knew it in the same way that most men know that to live they must breathe. He rarely talked about it. What was the point? How many people talk about the need to breathe? He simply went about the everyday business of breathing—of moving man toward the stars.

He did, that is, until the day Project Long Haul died.

At the wake—officially designated a staff meeting to determine what would be the impact of the latest budget cut—the billion-faced corpse showed itself more clearly than ever to Holman. It stared at him from every page of the Agency's endless report printouts and from the faces of his staff as they filed, one by one, into his office.

When the last of the walking dead had straggled into the room and settled quietly into chairs, Holman forced the picture from his mind and stood up. Slowly and deliberately, he picked up a foot-thick printout from his desk and dropped it with a thud into the recycler chute. A couple of raised eyebrows were the only visible reactions.

"So much for our schedule," he said flatly. "The word came down a few minutes ago. They have, once again, reordered their priorities."

The news was greeted by general sighing, but no one said anything. It was not as if the verdict had been unexpected. From some of the expressions, it was difficult to say if the outcome was even unwelcome.

Finally, when the hum of the recycler died away, Chet Crescska of the communications group spoke.

"What the hell did we lose out to this time? Or does it matter?"

"It wasn't anything specific," Holman said. "Nothing that could be argued about, at any rate. From the questions the committees have been asking the last few weeks, I suspect they have only now awakened to the fact that Project Long Haul is really a long-, repeat *long,* term investment. I get the feeling that they hadn't fully realized, until now, that they won't get anything, not even a progress report, from this investment for nearly fifty years."

"But surely they've known that all along!" Jenkins of the propulsion group objected. "They've been told often enough."

Holman shrugged. "Of course they have. But knowing isn't the same as realizing. Knowing you're paying for a fifty-year project is one thing. Realizing that there's a damned good chance that you won't be alive when the first ship comes back is something else."

"So," Jenkins said, "where does this leave us? How much did they amputate this time?"

"For right now," Holman said, "it's a straight twenty-percent cut. You tell me what it means. How much of a delay will this cause each of you?"

"Simple enough for me," Jenkins said. "Double the time in every schedule." He shrugged. "Not that it's going to make any difference. How many more cuts before we're out of business altogether?"

"And when *is* the next cut?" Horton of life-support asked.

And so the meeting went.

The wake disbanded a few minutes later with everyone promising to have a documented estimate ready by the end of the week.

Long after everyone had gone, Holman sat, leaning back in his chair, and a realization came to him, much as it must have come to the various committees. Time was running out. He had known for months, perhaps years, that it would, but until that moment he had not fully realized all the implications.

Time was running out, for him and for everyone.

If Project Long Haul died, as now seemed certain, it would never be revived. Those gigantic shells of the ships would stay in orbit forever, and as the years went by and it became accepted that they would never be used for their original purpose, they would be taken over and converted to other, more mundane uses. Orbiting cities with entertainment centers. Orbiting labs. Orbiting factories. Perhaps even, if the Federation disintegrated again, orbiting war machines.

Just what they needed—another set of orbiting sentinels, observing the slow, ever so slow but inevitable death that spread below them. Observing the death, but not seeing the corpse.

But what could he do? What could Jason Holman, alone, do?

He was not the same man he had been ten years before. Then there had been hope, and there had been things he could do.

He had started at the Agency only months after graduation, and within weeks he had gotten himself an assignment on Project Long Haul, an old, established program even then. Conditions, of course, proved intolerable in short order. He had been prepared for inefficiency; he had even expected it. He was, after all, not naive. His mandatory three years in Public Service and his six years in college had shown him what to expect from any kind of government.

He had even been prepared for delays and frustrations. They were, he knew, built into any large organization. The endless chains of approvals and initials and pseudodecisions had always been a part of the game and always would be.

But that was a game he had been prepared to play and win.

What he had not been prepared for—and what forced him to take matters into his own hands more rapidly than he had wanted—was indifference. It lay like a haze over everything. With very few exceptions, it ran from the lowest tech to the highest executive. They were all simply doing their jobs. The fact that the jobs were part of sending two hundred men and women to another star was of little or no importance. There were many, isolated in their own tiny areas of responsibility, who didn't even seem aware of what the overall goal was.

Six months after he joined the Agency, Jason Holman became the manager of Project Long Haul.

And now, a decade later, he realized that it had been for nothing. Despite his efforts, despite his finding a nucleus of at least marginally enthusiastic people, the Project was still dying. It had somehow lasted ten years instead of two, and there were three orbiting shells instead of one, but that was all.

Death had been delayed, not prevented.

Unless he could do something.

Unless . . .

Abruptly, in the silence of the night that was deepening outside his window, something flickered in Jason Holman's mind, and he laughed.

It was a vague and impossible something.

Something that would not fight the bureaucracy and the indifference, but would make use of them.

Something that was totally insane and would, almost certainly, involve his own ruin and that of anyone foolish enough to help him.

But it was something that was, he knew, better than the slow death that faced him now. . . .

The Return (2)

Almeda Sorrells swam awake slowly, the buzz of the phone's nightcall still echoing in her ears. Frowning in the dark, she brushed the sleep from her eyes as she reached for the audio button.

"Sorrells," she said indistinctly.

"Jase, Almeda." Suddenly she was awake, a sinking feeling pulsing through her as she recognized Jason Holman's voice.

"Yes, Jase, what is it?" Her voice was steady, but just barely. She was glad she was sleeping alone for a change tonight.

"Carl just called. They picked up a message from FTL-1. It's a billion kilometers out, on its way back."

So that was it. She let her breath out in a sigh. The sinking feeling was replaced by a kind of numbness.

"We've had it, then," she said. "Well, it was fun while it lasted, and all for a worthy cause. What now? Do we surrender to our friendly, neighborhood Agency representative?"

"Not necessarily," Holman's rocklike voice said. "Until I find out more, I'm going to play it straight. What about you? Do you feel up to bluffing it out a few more hours? Or days?"

"Why not?" She laughed harshly. "Maybe we can say the drive malfunctioned."

"It's a thought. You invented the thing. Could we get away with it?"

"Not likely. But, as you say, it's a thought." She paused. "There's no chance of getting number two or three sent out without a lot of testing and investigation, no matter what we say. And you know we can't stand anything like that."

"I know. Well, think about it, just in case . . ." He paused before going on. "But there's something you should know, Alma. The message."

"Message? But I assumed—"

"Assumed what?"

A new fear struck at her, piercing the shell of numbness. Her voice was sharp as she replied.

"Jason, what the hell are you playing at? Do you have some new game going that I don't know about?"

He wouldn't try to bail out now, she thought. No, there was no way he could, even if he did have the inclination. There was no way he could get away with it.

"No game, Alma." There was no emotion in his voice. "I only asked what you assumed about the message from FTL-1."

"What is there to assume? They're back after only two years, so they obviously turned back when they were a few light-weeks out. Whether they caught on to what was happening or Martin's detectors went off— does it make any difference? One way we're dead right now; the other way, we may be able to bluff it out a few more weeks with a malfunction story. Maybe."

"That's what I assumed, too. But I was wrong. The message from the ship was just one word, according to Carl: *Success!*"

She was silent for a moment. "Now I know you're up to something, Jason," she said finally, flatly.

"Not me," he said. "If anyone is up to something, it must be Carl . . ." He left the words hanging suspended in midair for her to inspect.

She wasn't sure if she should feel relieved or not. If what Jason was suggesting were true, the certainty of immediate failure and exposure was at least postponed, but . . .

"You think Carl's trying to trick us into something?" she asked.

"It's the only answer I can think of," Holman said. "But Carl said he was going to call the President, and the media. So we have to act as if we believe him and be prepared to be puzzled as hell when we get to the Center and find out that no one has been notified after all." He paused, and then went on in a concerned tone. "You can bail out if you want, Almeda. Turn state's evidence. Claim your conscience got the better of you. It might help."

"Help what?" she snapped. "If Carl is trying to trick us into something, that means he doesn't know for sure. And if he doesn't know for sure, that means we still have a chance to get FTL-2 off. Not much of a chance, but a chance."

Damn you, Jason! she thought. You know just when to offer me a way out, knowing that I won't take it. That I can't!

"Just what I thought a few minutes ago," Jason said. "See you at the Center. We'll know more by then. Just be prepared for anything. And I do mean anything!"

She hung up slowly, fighting down the irritation she felt at the way he had fed her the information a piece at a time, checking her out. But the irritation wouldn't last, she knew, because she was sure that, in Jason's place, she would have done the same thing. Besides, there were too many other things to think about now to waste time on petty angers.

Abruptly, her mind moving ahead toward whatever was coming up in the next few hours, she threw back the sheets and stood up.

The Departure (2)

MEDIA: This lovely lady is Dr. Almeda Sorrells, the inventor of the FTL drive. I suppose this is a proud day for you, Dr. Sorrells.

SORRELLS: Of course it is, Don. I don't want to sound corny, but today is literally the high point of my life.

MEDIA: As it is for many of our viewers, I'm sure. Now, I don't want to put you on the spot, but do you think you could give us an explanation of just how the FTL drive works? Something that even a mediaman like myself could understand?

SORRELLS: I'll try, Don. In some ways, it's very simple, just as most discoveries are. As you no doubt already know, the speed of light was thought for a long time to be the ultimate speed. Or rather, the speed of light in a vacuum was thought to be the ultimate speed. That's an important distinction, and it's the basis for the FTL drive. You see, we've had particles traveling faster than light through substances other than a vacuum since the early days of particle accelerators.

MEDIA: But I was under the impression that the speed of light was constant.

SORRELLS: In any given substance, yes. But in many transparent materials—glass, for instance—light travels much more slowly than it does in a vacuum. Thus, if we accelerate a particle to, say, eighty percent of the speed of light in a vacuum—that would be about 240,000 kilometers per second, an easily attainable speed—and then pass those particles through some transparent substance in which the speed of light is only 200,000 kilometers per second, what happens? The particles continue at their original speed, even though light itself is slowed down. So, in a very real sense, we have FTL motion right there.

MEDIA: I hadn't realized that. How does this apply to your invention?

SORRELLS: It's just necessary background, Don. Light travels at different speeds in different mediums. Until recently, the medium in which it traveled fastest was a vacuum. But what if we could create another substance, another medium in which the speed of light was greater than it was in a vacuum? Well, in a way, this is just what the FTL drive does. It sets up a field, a very strong, very complex electromagnetic field. Within this field, for reasons we don't fully understand as yet, the speed of light is—well, it is at least thirty times what it is in a vacuum. We haven't been able to pin it down precisely yet. That's one of the things we hope to accomplish in this first extended trip. In addition to the obvious things, of course.

MEDIA: But what about the energy requirements? I understood that it was an energy limitation that was going to keep the Long Haul ships from reaching more than half the speed of light. If all you have done is take the speed limit off, don't you still need more energy than you have available?

SORRELLS: That would seem logical, I agree. But—again for reasons we don't fully understand, even though we have developed all the necessary mathematical equations to describe its action—we don't need extra energy. You see, we don't simply accelerate to our final speed, which, by the way, will be approximately three million kilometers per second, about ten times the speed of light. We accelerate normally until we reach what we call the critical speed, roughly 30,000 kilometers per second. At that point, we turn on the FTL field. When the field forms, the speed of the ship jumps abruptly—a quantum jump, you might say—to the other side of the speed of light. As I said, we don't come close to fully understanding the mechanism, but we do know that it works. For your viewers, we might compare it to light as it emerges from some substance in which it has been traveling at, say, 200,000 kilometers per second. As the light emerges into a vacuum, its speed jumps instantaneously from 200,000 to 300,000 kilometers per second. Mathematically, we can describe it, and we know that it always happens. But as to the basic reason, we can only speculate.

MEDIA: Isn't using something like that dangerous?

SORRELLS: There could be some danger, I suppose, just as there is in anything. However, that's the way it has always been. Take electricity, for example. It was in use—in fact, it ran most of the world—for a hundred years before we even approached an understanding of

its basic nature. Even today, in the area of supercon-
ductors—which, I imagine, make up a good portion of
that machine you are using to record this interview—
there are many things we don't fully understand. But we
can describe what electricity does, and we can control
it. So we use it.

MEDIA: I see your point, Dr. Sorrells. But still, in something as important as this, where the lives of a half
dozen crew members depend on its working— Let me
put it this way: Would you trust your own life to it?

SORRELLS: If you recall, Don, Dr. Holman and I personally conducted the test flights of the drive less than
two years ago. We were on board the test ship every
minute. So you see, I have already trusted my life to the
drive, whether I fully understand its workings or not.

MEDIA: Very good, Dr. Sorrells. Just one more thing,
and I'll let you get back to watching the FTL-1 as it
prepares to leave orbit. As you no doubt know, there
are those who have objected to your work, to your invention, on practical grounds. For one thing, they say
that no one has ever been able to duplicate your original experiments.

SORRELLS: I'm glad you brought that up, Don. It points
up one of the problems we in science have had for some
time now. You see, it's not a matter of not being *able* to
duplicate the experiment. It's a matter of not having an
opportunity to duplicate it. The fact is, there is only one
particle accelerator in which the experiment could be
performed, and its time is booked solidly with other,
equally important experiments for the next five years.
There are plans for another—plans, I might add, that
have been consistently delayed for the past ten years. If
we—

MEDIA: Thank you very much, Dr. Sorrells.

The Preparations (2)

"Well?" Jason Holman leaned back in his chair, his
explanation completed, and looked challengingly at Dr.

Almeda Sorrells. "Well, Alma, is it possible? Can you do it?"

Her broad, high-cheekboned face had been a mask for the last ten minutes. Now a grin broke across it, and she laughed. "Jase, you are absolutely certifiable, right this minute! You really mean it, don't you?"

"Damned right I mean it! Can you do it?"

"Hold up a minute, just a minute. This is pretty unbelievable, even for you. You're talking about fooling several billion people, including a few hundred who may actually know what the score is. This isn't a game."

"I know it's not a game, believe me. But before you ask the obvious question, the answer is *no,* I don't expect to get away with it—not for very long, anyway. Only until we get one or two or three ships safely on their way. After that, when the ships don't come back on schedule . . ." He shrugged. "I'll worry about that when the time comes. The important thing is, they *will* be out there, and they *will* come back, even if it is fifty years from now, or a hundred."

She shook her head. "I still don't— Look, what about the crew? You're obviously going to have to let them in on your little secret. What makes you think they'll go along with you?"

"I don't know. Maybe they won't. Maybe we'll have to find a new crew. Maybe we'll have to go ourselves. All I want to know right now, Alma, is if you can do it. Can you? Or can't you?"

"How the hell should I know?" she flared. "I've never tried to *invent* an FTL drive out of whole cloth before! But damn it, Jase, why me? Don't you have some tame physicists in your Agency hive who could do it?"

"Frankly, I doubt it. And there's certainly no one I would trust."

"And what makes you think you can trust me? Just because you knew me for a few months in school nearly fifteen years ago? If I turn you down—which anyone in her right mind would do—and you conveniently come up with somebody else's FTL drive next year, what makes you think I won't call you on it?"

He shrugged. "*If* you turn me down . . . But are you going to? And once you accept, you'll be in as deeply as I am. Besides, you think it's a good idea, don't you?"

She laughed sharply. "Sure, it's a dandy idea. It's just impossible, that's all. Why can't you face defeat gracefully like everyone else? Project Long Haul is dead, and we won't get out of the solar system until someone comes up with a *real* FTL drive."

"I'm not very graceful, in case you hadn't noticed. And, since you mentioned it, what *are* the chances of a real FTL drive being found? I haven't heard very many encouraging reports. What about your search for tachyons? Any progress?"

"That's fighting dirty, Jase. You know the answer to that."

"You're right on both counts. But this is still beside the point. All I'm asking is, can you do it? Can you invent an FTL drive that we can slip past the experts? That's all. Once you do that, there's time enough to worry about the other things. Who knows, we may never even have to use it. Maybe someone else will come up with a real drive. Maybe the momentum we pick up from your invention, even if we have to decide it's impractical, on a scale large enough to propel a ship, will carry us through to a point where we can get Long Haul started again. Anything's possible as far as I'm concerned. All I want now is a paper FTL drive, and you're my first choice to be the discoverer. Well?"

Almeda laughed despite herself. "Jase, you're a devious son of a bitch, you know that? All right, if that's the way you want it, yes. Yes, I think I can. I don't think it will do you or anyone else the least bit of good, but yes, I think I can do it."

Holman let his breath out in a controlled sigh. One down, he thought, and how many more to go?

The Return (3)

Martin Aronson's nightmare was little different from the last one, or from the last hundred. But this time at least it wasn't allowed to play through to its usual grisly climax. Before the coffinlike door of the ship opened to reveal its cargo of bleached death, before he felt his own flesh shriveling and then being torn away as if by a swarm of invisible piranha, before he tried to scream but found he had no lungs, no throat with which to scream—before any of this, he was jerked awake, pulled abruptly away from that shadowy, windswept landing field where he had died so slowly and so often before.

For long moments he lay still, forcing his middle-aged, overweight body to relax, unclenching his fingers from the tangled sheets, letting the cold sweat dry on his face and hairless scalp. Visions of his death and the death of a dozen others still pounded at his eyes through still-closed lids.

From a distance, somewhere beyond the nightmare landscape that still swirled around him, the raucous sound of the phone's nightcall repeated its ever louder summons. Still he remained motionless, pulling in deep, rasping breaths to loosen the painfully taut muscles in his throat.

Where was Edie? Why didn't she answer the damned thing!

But then, as the clamorous buzz pulled him further toward reality, the inevitable memory and the brief confusion that always accompanied it returned. She was gone, just like the others, and he couldn't—

Again the buzz came, now a deafening roar in his ears. With a final shuddering breath, he heaved himself sideways and jabbed at the audio button.

"Yes?"

"Martin, this is Jason."

Returning fear jolted through Aronson like a pitcher of ice water dumped on the small of his back. His heart, only now beginning to slow from the effects of the nightmare, spurted anew.

"Yes, Jason," he said, his voice unsteady but not quite shaking. "What's happened?"

There was a pause, as if Holman were evaluating Aronson's reply, his tone.

"Well, damn it!" Aronson almost screamed when the silence lengthened into seconds. "What the hell is it?"

The silence continued for another second, and then Holman's voice said: "Carl just called a few minutes ago. He said Number Ten had picked up a message from FTL-1. It's on its way back. It will be in Earth orbit in a few days."

The fear, the iciness around his spine, hit a shattering peak and then, surprisingly, as if a fuse had blown somewhere inside him, it was replaced by a kind of leaden relief.

It was over.

It was finished. They were all finished. The FTL Project and the dream of reaching the stars was finished.

It was as if someone had lifted the world from his shoulders, only to smash it to the ground in a million pieces. For the moment, the relief at the lifting of the burden overwhelmed everything else.

"So," he said, his voice unaccountably steady, "those detectors I insisted on paid off after all." What else, he thought, could have brought them back?

"Maybe, and maybe not," Holman went on. "According to Carl, the mission was a success."

Aronson blinked. He couldn't have heard right. "What? What did you say?"

"I said, the mission was apparently a success. The message was just one word, Carl said. One word: *Success!*"

"Are you—"

"I don't know any more than you do, Martin. Carl said he was about to notify the President and the media when he talked to me. That's all I know. I'm starting for the Center in a few minutes."

Aronson was silent, waiting for Holman to continue, not knowing what to think. Finally, when Holman said nothing, Aronson said, hesitantly, "Should I come down, too, do you think?"

"That's up to you, Martin. How do you feel?"

"Under the circumstances . . ." He shivered in the darkness. "I'll be all right. But damn it, Jason, what the hell is going on? What do you mean, success?"

"I don't know, Martin, I just don't know. But . . ." Holman paused for several seconds until Aronson was almost ready to ask if he was still there. "But, Martin, there is one possibility we can't overlook. A trap."

"Trap? What—" Abruptly Aronson fell silent as he realized what Holman had said. Yes, it was possible, very possible. With the ship a month overdue, rumors had begun to fly, and the old charges had started to surface again. And the Agency Director could hardly be expected to ignore them. He would have to do something, and this could very well be what he had chosen to do.

But did he want to fight it? Aronson remembered the relief he had felt only moments before. Did he want to trade that relief, and the certainty of failure that went with it, for another day of uncertainty? And another night of that endlessly repeating nightmare?

"I see what you mean," he said finally. "What can we do about it?"

"Right now, I don't know. It all depends on—well, on a lot of things. For the time being, we had better play it straight. Just remember, if it is a trick of some kind, we're not through yet, not by a long shot. As long as we don't panic, we can still make it. Okay?"

"I suppose," Aronson said, slowly, reluctantly.

"Remember," Holman's voice came again, "play it straight when you get to the Center, no matter what's going on. Take your time and be ready for anything. Okay?"

Martin Aronson sighed. What difference did it make? Another hour of pretense, or another day, it was all the same now. But he would follow Jason's lead, just as he had followed it the last six years. For better or for worse, he would follow it. There was really little else he *could* do, now. There had been a time when he had had a choice, when he could have pursued his dream in his own, ineffective way, free of terror and deception and nightmares. There had been a time . . .

But that was a time long past, a time before Jason Holman had forced his way into his life.

"Very well," Martin Aronson said. "At the Center, in an hour."

He switched off the phone and, slowly and tiredly, reluctantly and fearfully, got out of bed.

The Departure (3)

MEDIA: We are now talking with Dr. Martin Aronson. He is the man who selected the crew of the FTL-1, and who is even now probably working on his selection for later flights. I imagine, Dr. Aronson, that crew selection is extremely important for flights of such long duration. Could you tell us just what you look for in crew members? Compatibility, perhaps?

ARONSON: Yes, compatibility is important, of course, in more ways than one. Obviously the different members of the crew must be able to get along with one another, but—and this is something your viewers may not know—they must be compatible with the FTL drive itself.

MEDIA: I'm afraid I don't understand, Dr. Aronson.

ARONSON: We don't either, not completely, but we have found that the drive field makes a great many people— myself included—violently ill. Probably nine out of every ten people, actually. That is one reason so few of the crew originally intended for the Long Haul ships were used. They just weren't compatible with the drive.

MEDIA: I suppose those who couldn't go were terribly disappointed.

ARONSON: Many were, yes, but there was nothing to be done about it.

MEDIA: Once this basic compatibility with the drive is established, what then? What else do you look for?

ARONSON: Good health, certainly, but I assume you mean what do I look for psychologically. Well, one of the most important things, perhaps the most important single characteristic, is the ability to live in isolation.

MEDIA: Isolation? You mean as a group? The six members of the crew, isolated from the rest of humanity?

ARONSON: Partly. Because they will be, in reality, the first totally isolated group of men and women in all of history. Isolated not only from Earth, as were the crews of all our planetary expeditions, but from all contact with Earth. All contact, really, with the known universe.

MEDIA: You make it sound rather frightening, Dr. Aronson.

ARONSON: I don't mean to, but, in a way, it is frightening. Traveling faster than light, as they will be for most of the trip, they will have no way of communicating with Earth. Except for recordings they take with them, they will hear no human voices other than their own for the entire two years.

MEDIA: Yes, frightening indeed. I certainly wouldn't want to be put in that position.

ARONSON: And I wouldn't want to put you in it, Mr. Melton. Just offhand, I don't think anyone as socially oriented as a mediaman must be would ever qualify for an FTL crew, even if he did turn out to be compatible with the drive field.

MEDIA: I'm sure I wouldn't. I get upset if people don't talk to me at parties. But you said a minute ago that isolation as a group was only part of the picture.

ARONSON: That's correct. Even more important is the ability to survive completely on your own, in isolation even from the other crew members.

MEDIA: Isolation from the other crew members? I'm afraid I don't understand.

ARONSON: Forced contact with the same group of a half dozen people, with no other contacts whatsoever, causes greater problems than the group isolation. Or so my experiments and research, as well as those of many other researchers, have shown. To avoid this problem, to avoid the multiplying of interpersonal frictions and conflicts, each crew member has his or her own individual quarters, where they can have total privacy—or isolation—whenever they prefer. We have recommended that they spend at least fifty percent of their time alone, and no more than ten percent together as a group. As time goes by, they will, of course, work out their own schedules on a day-to-day basis. We feel that, with the total group getting together only occasionally, these group meetings will act, to some small degree, as a substitute, psychologically, for a return to Earth from the relatively greater individual and pair isolation.

MEDIA: And how do you find this type of person?

ARONSON: With great difficulty. But I assume you mean, what process do we use in determining who is suitable? Actually, it's fairly simple, if time-consuming. We take large numbers of volunteers who have passed the basic physical and mental tests—including, of course, the test for compatibility with the FTL drive field—and place them in isolation where we can closely observe their reactions. We have two orbital workshops devoted full-time to this work. The rejection rate, I'm afraid, is very, very high. We're lucky to find one suitable subject in each group of two hundred we send up.

MEDIA: That is a high failure rate. Could you tell me just how you determine whether or not a person is suitable? What, specifically, do you look for?

ARONSON: For one thing, he has to survive with his sanity intact. And to do that, for six months, totally alone in space, with no human contact, is not easy.

MEDIA: There must be more to it than that.

ARONSON: Much more. Their physical reactions are equally as important as their mental reactions. Many subjects deteriorate physically very rapidly, even though the stations are rotated to maintain near normal gravity.

MEDIA: So it's simply a matter of survival, both physical and mental? Is that what you're saying, Dr. Aronson?

ARONSON: Of course not. Everyone has survived, as you put it. We keep a very close watch on them, monitoring all their biological and mental functions at all times. If anything untoward begins to happen, the subject is brought back to Earth immediately. And a subject can terminate the procedure himself at any time by simply announcing that he wants to quit. Incidentally, that's how we lose more than half. They simply quit.

MEDIA: Fascinating, Dr. Aronson. I assume it gives you a great deal of satisfaction to be involved in this project.

ARONSON: Certainly. Travel beyond our solar system is something that all of mankind needs if it is not to stagnate entirely. It may even—

MEDIA: Thank you very much, Dr. Aronson.

The Preparations (3)

Dr. Sorrells brought off the discovery of the FTL phenomenon with remarkable smoothness, making it appear to be a serendipitous result of a small malfunction in one of her tachyon experiments at the Prospect Woods accelerator. Most of the general public and most of the high-energy physicists accepted it without question. A few holdouts objected that, even though her mathematical description of the phenomenon was faultless, the actual phenomenon itself was obviously impossible and should therefore be disregarded. Other than that, however, there was little skepticism, and rumors that the principle could be applied to an FTL drive were circulating freely within a month.

The problem, as it turned out, came from another quarter. As soon as the possibility of an FTL drive, no matter how remote it seemed, was mentioned, the Long Haul volunteers began unvolunteering. From numerous and roundabout conversations with almost every one of them, Holman discovered that very few, if any, would willingly take part in the sort of pseudo-FTL trip that he had in mind. There were as many reasons as there were nonvolunteers. But most of them came down to a simple: "Now that FTL is a possibility, I think I'll wait and see how that works out."

The problem, Holman realized, was that the wrong people were being deceived by the FTL discovery. The ones who would have to be fooled were the ones who would make up the crew. Such deception, however, was obviously impossible. They could be gotten aboard and launched, perhaps, but after a few months or a year at most, they would discover the truth and simply turn back.

And so matters rested until, about three A.M. one night three months after the FTL discovery had been announced, Jason awakened unexpectedly and remembered an entry he had seen several months earlier in one of the thousands of Agency reports that flowed past his desk on the way to the recycler chute. By four A.M. he was at the readout unit in his office, scanning the report summaries as they flashed across the screen.

By five he had found the entry he was looking for, a report on one in a long series of experiments on the effects of weightlessness and isolation on human biological rhythms.

By seven, after skimming through a series of reports that stretched over more than twenty years, he had the hazy beginnings of a plan, one that was, he had to admit to himself, even more insane than the pseudo-FTL drive had been.

By ten he had obtained, read, and recycled printouts from the National Files on every researcher mentioned in that series of reports, concentrating particularly on their personality profiles, and he managed to narrow the field to a half dozen.

By noon he had talked briefly with several friends and relatives of those six.

Shortly after noon, he placed a call to Dr. Martin Aronson.

Two weeks later, Dr. Aronson officially joined Project Long Haul and began a series of experiments, conducted in Earth orbit, ostensibly designed to study human reactions to total isolation and varying degrees of sensory deprivation.

Four months later, which was still several months be-

fore an official FTL program existed, Dr. Aronson
found the first possible candidate for FTL travel.

"It's the damnedest thing I ever saw!" he said to Jason. "I'm not sure I really believe it myself. It's as if the
man had gone into slow motion, literally."

"Everything?" Jason asked. "Biological rhythms?
Heart rate? Metabolism?"

Aronson nodded emphatically. "Everything! Even
his temperature is down a few degrees. And the heart
rate—my god! It was less than twenty per minute!"

"And still there were no ill effects?"

"That's the incredible part. No ill effects, no damage
whatsoever. During the entire month, every indica-
tion—and you know how many instruments were
hooked into him—was perfectly normal. They just
gradually got slower, as if he were gradually shifting
into another time stream."

Holman laughed. "Maybe he was. Or do you have
some more rational explanation?"

Aronson shook his head. "Not a damn thing more
than I did when we started. The only thing that's really
obvious is that the mind—in a few select cases, at
least—has one hell of a lot more control over the body
than anyone ever suspected before."

"What are the limits? Do you have any idea?"

"None. A few months ago, I would have said—in
fact, I remember saying so, to you—that the whole
thing was impossible. Until now. Well, we had never
gotten anything more dramatic than a few biorhythms
settling out at forty-eight hours instead of twenty-four."

Holman grinned. "But, then, you never set out to
purposely deceive the subjects, either."

"No, I suppose not. Not to this extent, at any rate."
A troubled frown crossed Aronson's face. "I sometimes
wonder—"

"So do I, believe me. So do I. And the main thing
I'm wondering right now is, how far can this thing
be pushed? How slow can someone be made to live?"

Aronson smiled weakly. "I have no idea. But I have

the feeling that we're going to be finding out in the next few years."

The Return (4)

By the time Jason Holman reached the Center, he had decided that, whatever was going on, at least it wasn't a trap. Not unless half the people in the country were in on it and were conspiring against him. All four of the all-night news-service channels had been repeating the announcement of the ship's return and talking around it at great length for the past forty-five minutes.

The minute Jason stepped out of the Transport Terminal at the Center, even before he reached the lobby of Building 98, which housed his office as well as the FTL Communications Section, a dozen mediamen were swarming around him. All the standard questions he had been fielding for the past month, reworded slightly to take into account the announced return, poured at him in a jumble:

"Had you given up hope, Dr. Holman?"

"Do you have any idea why they are so late in returning, Dr. Holman?"

"How soon will you be in direct contact with them?"

"How does this late return affect the schedule for the remaining FTL ships?"

"Are they all in good health?"

"How soon will they set foot on Earth again?"

"Will they be held in quarantine any longer because of this delay?"

"Have you ever had any serious doubts as to the merits of the FTL Project?"

As the swarm of voices battered at him, Holman forced his way through the lobby with the help of two Agency guards and pressed toward the private elevator at the rear. As he reached it, the doors slid open. He stopped just inside the elevator doors and turned to face the horde of mediamen. He looked around silently, picking out familiar faces, keeping his own features set and motionless, his eyes steady. Slowly the questions faltered and subsided into silence.

When it was quiet, Jason spoke briefly.

"At the moment, I don't know any more than any of you. I was notified of the contact with the FTL–1 only minutes before you yourselves were. Obviously, considering the distance involved, there has been no two-way contact as yet. I assume a message was sent to them as soon as their signal was identified. If they receive that message and if they respond immediately, we should have their reply in"—he glanced at his watch—"in somewhat less than an hour."

Abruptly he stepped backward, the doors slid shut, and the elevator flowed upward.

The Preparations (4)

"I must admit," said Almeda Sorrells, Director of Propulsions Development for the newly formed and newly funded Project FTL, "I must admit that things are going well. If I didn't know better, I'd be convinced there really was an FTL phenomenon."

Jason Holman, FTL Project Director, grinned as Almeda eyed him speculatively. Martin Aronson, Director in Charge of Crew Selection, looked uncomfortable.

"Incidentally," she went on after a moment, "now that we're officially committed to a life of fraud and folly—and we lambs have been, figuratively speaking, nailed to the payroll—would you mind telling us just how the hell you expect to get all this garbage built?"

"You can design it, can't you?" Holman asked. "Well, anything you can design, we can get built."

"Come on, Jase," she said, "I don't mean the drive. I know that's a simple matter. The hardware will produce all the fields that my equations call for, and that's what everyone will be expecting, whether they understand it or not. But what about the other gadgets? The ones that are going to have to do the real work? Like the ones that gradually slow down all the timing devices on board. Like the ones that will gradually decrease the acceleration. And god knows what else we'll need before we're through. How do we get all those built?"

Holman laughed. "Just wait until you've been around here a few weeks. You won't have to ask. Right, Martin?"

Aronson only nodded.

"Don't worry about it, Alma," Jason went on. "The people who design and build the hardware will do anything we tell them to, no questions asked. You tell them you want a box of a certain size which takes inputs of A, B, and C, and produces outputs of X, Y, and Z, and they'll give it to you. With a few very rare exceptions, they won't know or care where A, B, and C are coming from or what you're going to do with X, Y, and Z."

She shook her head. "You make this sound like an assembly line."

"It is. A scientific assembly line. It has been ever since the basement inventor passed away. Things are just too complicated for anyone besides a computer to design them in their entirety. So everyone designs and builds bits and pieces, and they couldn't care less about what the bits and pieces are used for. And if you have any doubts, just talk to some of the techs and engineers. I have. If you can find more than two or three who really know what they're building or designing, and just where it fits into the overall system, and what the system really does—" He shrugged. "If you can, you'll be doing a lot better than I've been able to do in the last few years."

She frowned thoughtfully for a moment. "But won't the FTL Project attract a few of the more alert types?"

"An egotistical thought, not unlike my own when I started on Long Haul. But totally unjustified. No, FTL may have turned on the imagination of your average man in the outside world—thank god!—but it will have damned little effect on your average Agency employee. Don't forget, unlike the public, these people have been doing all the nonglamorous, nuts-and-bolts work on Agency programs most of their working lives. They're used to it and they're bored with it. Besides," Holman added, "if anyone shows signs of digging too deeply, we can probably recruit him to our side. Or transfer him to another project."

Almeda laughed. "You've got an answer for everything, you bastard!" She stood up and started for the door, glancing toward Aronson, who had sat quietly through the entire exchange. "Well, Marty, we'd better get busy if we're going to design an FTL drive and find a suitable crew before somebody finds out what the hell we're doing and blows the whistle."

Smiling, she left.

Martin Aronson stood up slowly.

"Jason," he began, his eyes directed somewhat below the level of Holman's, his words slow and forced, "it's not going to be that easy."

Holman's face sobered. "Yes, Martin? Problems?"

"You might say that." His eyes flickered upward to meet Holman's briefly. "This whole thing is just too risky. The human mind, no matter what we're finding out about it, just isn't predictable enough for something of this magnitude."

"I take it you're having second thoughts, Martin?"

Aronson's ruddy face hardened, and his eyes met Jason's solidly for the first time. "You're damned right I am! We could be sending these men and women to their deaths, do you realize that?"

Jason let several seconds of silence pass before he spoke.

"Martin," he said finally, "of course I realize that. And I've been thinking what we could do about it, what we could do to guarantee that nothing will go wrong."

"Guarantee? How? How do you guarantee that, just because a person's biological functions have been slowed down for a few months, they can remain slowed down for longer periods? There's no practical way of testing it. And it *must* work! We can't leave any room for doubt!"

Again there was a lengthy pause before Jason replied.

"What if we check on them? Suppose we install a set of metabolic analyzers, anything you want, to check the actual rate at which they're living? It shouldn't be too difficult to sneak them in somewhere in the maze we're already putting together. Set up certain limits. Set the machines so that, if anyone's metabolic rates aren't slowing down fast enough or far enough, the machines will trigger an alarm—say an alarm that will indicate a malfunction in the FTL drive. Something that can't be repaired, something that will force them to turn back."

Aronson shook his head. "But what if— Suppose their functions slow down on schedule, and then start speeding up spontaneously? What then? What if this effect we've discovered, whatever it is, won't last more than six months or a year? Or ten years?"

"Do you have any way of finding out?"

"You know that I don't!"

"Yes, I do know. And I also know that nothing is one-hundred-percent sure. But look, Martin, even if worse comes to worse, it means only that they will age a little more than they expected. Don't forget, the ship is still a closed system, just as the Long Haul ships were planned to be. With everything recycled, they could exist the full fifty years at normal rates if they have to."

"*Only* age a few years more!" Aronson shook his head again and stared at Holman. "You're talking about ten or twenty or forty years! Do you realize that?"

"Of course I do. And do you realize what the alternative is? There is no alternative. It's this or nothing. Compared to the fact that, without this flight, we'll never get beyond the solar system, ever—compared to that, the slight possibility of an extra ten, even an extra fifty, years for six people is nothing. And compared to what the three of us will, in all probability, have to go through when the ships don't return on schedule, that's not too bad, either."

Aronson continued to protest and argue with Holman for another half hour and with himself for months, but he had known from the start, from his first acquiescence more than a year before, that it was no use. The combination of his own desire, seemingly reflected and magnified a hundredfold in Holman, and Holman's imperturbable self-assurance and steamroller practicality, gave his conscience little chance. If it was indeed his conscience that was bothering him, if it was not simply his own fear of facing up to the consequences that would inevitably come when the ships failed to return.

The alarm system was designed and, according to Jason, it was installed, although Aronson had no way of being absolutely sure.

Project FTL went on.

The Return (5)

Jason Holman stood alone at the back of the room. The half dozen techs, all but one pulled from an early-morning sleep, hovered over their consoles, waiting. Almeda Sorrells and Martin Aronson sat in chairs before two of the unused consoles, listening. Almeda sat tensely, her eyes roaming impatiently over the unlighted screens and controls. Martin, silent and subdued, glanced nervously and often toward Jason, then at the window in the back wall, through which a milling mob of mediamen could be seen. From a speaker at the front of the room, the same words were repeated endlessly:

"FTL-1, McCourtney, Hendricks, Davidson, Akito, Bennis, Calsor calling Earth. Success! FTL-1, McCourtney, Hendricks . . ."

Over and over, again and again. Each time, it seemed, the background noise grew less, and the voices became clearer.

The digital clock at the front of the room soundlessly flickered out the seconds and minutes, and every ear listened for the endless loop to be interrupted. Outside, listening to the remote speakers, keeping a sharp lookout for Project people, were the mediamen. Across the country and the world, billions more listened, waiting for the first real words to come trickling across space from the returning FTL-1.

Abruptly the voice cut off in mid-word, leaving only the background hiss and crackle. All conversation stopped. Every eye snapped toward the consoles.

There was a loud burst of static, and a new voice came through.

"You mean this damned thing is finally working?"

Again there was silence except for the background hash, and then a laugh, fainter and more distant than the voice that had just spoken. A feminine voice said, "Good going, Mac. Did you get that, Earth? The first words spoken by the first humans to return from interstellar space."

A billion kilometers away, someone cleared his throat, and the sound of paper crackling was added to the background noise.

"People of Earth," the original voice came through again, haltingly, "we of the FTL-1—" More crackling of paper, and then, "Oh, the hell with it! Ed, do you have the video carrier working yet?"

"It's been working all the time," a third voice said faintly. "It's just been a matter of getting the antenna lined up right. If the audio got through, there's no reason they can't pick up the video, too. All we can do is send it out and they'll let us know in a couple of hours if it got through. Okay?"

"Great," the first voice returned. "Earth, if you're really there, we're not going to waste a lot of time making speeches for posterity, telling you how fantastic it all was. We're just going to send you some pictures of where we've been. And maybe a few words of explanation as we go along. Ready, Ed?"

"Ready to try. How about you? If you're going to make like a mediaman and explain all this, you'd better get over here where you can see the monitor I set up."

More shuffling sounds came through the speaker, along with indistinct voices in the background. Abruptly the screens on all the powered-up consoles lit. An instant later a larger screen at the front of the room came on. At first there was nothing but multicolored snow, and then it became a greenish-white, flecked with dots of static as the carrier, still a billion kilometers weak, was picked up.

"We'll start with our best shot," the voice said, and the first image appeared. "This is one of the outer planets, a gas giant, almost 200,000 kilometers in diameter—and get a look at those rings! They make Saturn's look sick."

And they did. Six distinct bands, each a different and rather garish color, reached out a distance equal to at least the diameter of the planet. And the surface, multicolored and banded, swirled like a surrealistic Jupiter.

"There's another biggie in the system," the voice continued, "but this is the only one we were close enough to to tape. Aside from the one we landed on, that is. That's coming up in a minute."

In the background, just barely audible, came the woman's voice they had heard earlier. "Melodramatic bastard," it said, chuckling.

"We found four planets altogether," the first voice went on, "the two gas giants a billion or so kilometers out, a little one about half the size of Mars whipping around not more than forty million kilometers out from the sun. And the one we landed on."

On cue, a new planet appeared on the screens. At first it looked like Earth, a mixture of blue and brown and swirling white, but then, to the trained eyes in the room, it became obvious it was not Earth. The colors, though similar to those of Earth, were not the same. And the continental shapes, what little they could glimpse through the spotty cloud cover, wouldn't fit any part of Earth. A long thin neck of land stretched irregularly halfway across the planet's diameter before being swallowed up in clouds. And at what must have been one of the poles, there was only blue, not the glittering white of a polar cap or the uneven white of cloud cover.

"These are some of the best shots we got from far orbit," the voice crackled from the speaker again. "Usually there were a lot more clouds than this. It's the second planet out, right on the inner edge of that habitability zone you kept telling us about. It's a little over

11,000 kilometers in diameter, and believe it or not, it has an atmosphere a hell of a lot like Earth's. And there's no moon, so that shoots down that old theory about a large moon being necessary to keep a planet from looking like Venus. All in all, the planet is a few degrees warmer than Earth, quite a bit wetter, and has a lower percentage of oxygen.

"As for the surface . . ." The voice paused for a moment as the picture on the screens shifted to a surface shot. "There are practically no open, level areas. This area was as good as we found in several orbits, and it was pretty tricky. And look at the color of everything. It's not the camera. It's really yellow, occasionally blue. We don't know what it is; all we know is, it isn't chlorophyll that gives them that color or keeps them working. It's something equally complicated, but . . . As for animal life—like that greenish-looking thing peering out of the undergrowth there at the left of the lander. It looks to be carbon based, but that's where the similarity ends. Just how the atoms hook up to each other, we'll leave up to you. We've got plenty of samples in the freezer. We tried feeding a couple of them our food— unintentionally, but that's another story—but it didn't take. They ate it at first, but it didn't do them any good. Or any harm, either. And here, here's one of the more interesting . . ."

Almeda Sorrells looked up from the screen, glanced toward Jason, back at the screen, and back again to Jason. In a subdued, barely audible whisper, she said: "Jase, you son of a bitch! They made it! *They really made it!*"

Briefly, sharply, uproariously, she laughed, and then, with a still disbelieving shake of her head, she turned back to the pictures and the home-movie commentary that was coming with them across a billion kilometers of space.

And as the alien landscape and the creatures that inhabited it continued to flicker across the screens, the impossible truth drove itself through the surface of Jason's mind, deep into the inner recesses where he lived.

Realization came.

This wasn't a trap.

They *had* made it. Impossibly, they had made it!

Somehow, the FTL-1 had gone to another star system and returned in a little over two years.

Somehow . . .

Then, as his acceptance of the impossible became complete, his mind began the next step. Impossible or not, the journey *had* taken place; therefore there had to be a reason, an explanation.

Ideas from a thousand fantasies he had seen and read, both as child and as adult, darted through his mind. A helping hand from an alien super-race? A practical joke? Folds, shortcuts in space, accidentally broken into by the FTL drive field? Automatic interstellar highways, the rolling roads of space?

Or was it something simple, as simple as his own deceptions had been? The men and women of the crew, forming their own private universe, *knew* they were traveling at several times the speed of light; therefore they actually did travel at several times the speed of light. They thought; therefore they did. Had it been enough to simply deceive a group of special people with special kinds of minds? Minds that could alter not only the biological rhythms of their own bodies, but the greater rhythms of the rest of the universe?

Or could the massed belief of everyone—all the billions who had believed the FTL drive was really working—have done it?

Or had serendipity struck humanity once again? Penicillin had come from moldy bread, and a cancer vaccine had fallen out of an obscure branch of the endless research aimed at curing the common cold, so why shouldn't a true FTL drive be found accidentally buried in the complexities of a phony FTL drive? After all, even Almeda herself had not been able to calculate every single interaction between the continually shifting fields that her generators produced.

But whatever it was, however it had happened, they would eventually find the truth. On FTL-2 there would be a set of *real* monitors. Everything, but *everything,* would be watched and recorded: the crew, the ship, the fields, everything.

As for the rest of the universe—that would have to be watched, too. For instance, Jason suddenly remembered, there had been an unpredicted outburst of solar flares just weeks after the departure of FTL-1. Was there a connection? If something similar happened when FTL-2 was supposed to jump to the other side of the speed of light . . .

Nothing was too farfetched to consider. Nothing.

And they *would* find the answer. Someday, somehow, they would find the answer. Jason knew it in the same way he had known that humanity must, if it was to survive, someday escape the womb of Earth.

As the thoughts and exultations and plans whirled through his mind, an almost familiar vision floated to the surface.

But now the huge, sprawling body, a corpse no longer, was beginning to show signs of life. . . . ☆

An Error In Punctuation

B. Lee Cooper &
Larry S. Haverkos

"Please, gentlemen! This convention must come to order!"

"But we need legislation *now* to prohibit such practices! The International Psychiatric Society must take a stand." Dr. Algis Bagford felt hot, and he knew his face was flushed. His had been one of the most respected voices in the psychiatric world for nearly three decades. He had led the successful battle to outlaw the barbaric pursuit of electroconvulsive therapy. Yet since his retirement from active practice, his authority in professional circles had waned.

"Come out of the Dark Ages, Algie," Will Sargeant pleaded. "All of us have some minor reservations about the computer-counseling process, but we shouldn't be so parochial that we ignore the therapeutic potential of this technological breakthrough. The need is too great today! We just can't keep pace with the demands of our patients. We must proceed—"

"I cannot be still on this issue," Bagford interrupted. "It is ludicrous and denigrating to our profession to accept what these technicians would have us believe. The unique personal problems of an individual cannot be resolved by a computer. I am genuinely horrified that the General Services Division of HEHW would even consider establishing test installations of these magnetic monsters in each of the 10-M residential sectors."

"But, Algie," Sargeant countered, trying to lower the tone of the unexpectedly hostile public exchange, "the pressure of human congestion has forced us to deal with a population that *demands* unprecedented levels of consulting time with analysts. There are just too few psychiatrists to meet this legitimate need. And since the computerized units are programmed for referral as well as for direct advice, the humanistic safety valve which you seem to be demanding is already present. This new system constitutes the only logical way to deal with the day-to-day needs of standard outpatient neurosis patterns."

Scattered applause registered the general approval of Sargeant's remarks.

"It will get out of hand, just like so many other alleged breakthroughs," countered Bagford. His words were also greeted by pockets of applause, but catcalls were mingled with the response.

"Gentlemen," the chairman interjected, "this convention has been debating the issue for too long. Let me recommend that the IPS membership create a five-person task force to examine the operational effectiveness of the new computer-counseling system." All the bustling in the large hall stilled as the chairman continued: "In addition to three delegates to be elected by mail later this month, I propose that Professors William Sargeant and Algis Bagford be charged to draft the Society's official report on the first year's activity of . . ." His arm swept back toward the stage, and his finger pointed directly at the mute subject of the past hour's heated debate. "Dr. Doolittle!" The magnetic tapes of the Malimar-Indexed CST—3400 Functional Interchange Unit that was to be installed in Wichita seemed to glisten as the gavel descended and the chairman left the podium.

Bagford stared glumly at the head-and-shoulders facsimile that protruded from the top of the computerized console. The face was that of a graying, dignified man in his mid-fifties. As the conferees filed from the auditorium, the manikin head tilted slightly, focusing its vacant stare on Bagford's slumped shoulders. It smiled.

He watched her undress. At thirty-five she still had the shape of a twenty-year-old. He folded his hands behind his head, pretending to think deep thoughts. But his mind was locked on her. Combing and teasing her hair, checking her eyes . . . stalling.

Chet Morrow loved his wife. Ann was a devoted mother, a good housekeeper, a talented free-lance writer, and a superb cook. He had admired each of these aspects of his wife for the past six years. But what he liked best about her . . . Damn! This was the only contentious issue in their marriage. Tonight, he knew, would be no different.

"Come on, darling," Chet coaxed. "Take your pill and get into bed."

"All right. Set the alarm."

"Forget it—tomorrow's Saturday," Chet grunted.

Ann swirled back the sheet and slipped into bed. His hand touched her waist and then slid downward. She fidgeted. "Not tonight, dear. I'm not feeling well." His blood began to boil, as it had a hundred times before. But he said nothing. She had other lines: "It's too hot!" "It's too cold!" "The children might hear us." "Is *that* all you ever think about?" "I'm so tired—can't we wait until tomorrow night?" They went on and on. If he wasn't so frustrated by Ann's pleas—and so convinced that she actually believed each and every excuse was legitimate—he would probably have divorced her twelve times over. But when they did make love . . . it was too fantastic to describe. Obviously, Ann needed advice. Psychological help. But what could he do to convince her of it? Last night's paper had suggested a possible answer.

Ann Morrow had eyed the General Services announcement in the *Wichita Sun* with great interest.

Counseling and Psychiatric Assistance
Available at No Charge
Computerized Transmitter
For Private Appointment:
(316) 652-4456
Ask for Dr. Doolittle

She knew that the newsdata page had been folded open to the advertisement by Chet. Maybe he was thinking of contacting a counselor about his problem. Probably not, though, since he didn't actually believe that *he* had any problem. In all their discussions, Chet always insisted that he was not oversexed. In fact, he continued to argue that nonsense about once a week not being enough for a healthy couple. Well, Ann would initiate the necessary action if Chet wouldn't.

She dialed the number. The telecommunicator blinked on, and a pleasant-looking elderly gentleman appeared on the screen. "Good day. I'm Dr. Doolittle. May I be of service to you?"

Ann swallowed hard. "I'd like to make an appointment for computer counseling for my husband and me. Tomorrow afternoon around 1600. But I want to speak to the analyst before we come in together."

"Your appointment time is registered. I'll be your psychiatrist."

"Oh, Doctor, I hope you can help! My husband's sex drive is overwhelming. I'm no prude, but he continually makes unbelievable demands which I think are unhealthy for both of us. If you could just reduce his urge, I know that our marriage would be more stable."

"Well, your problem is not totally unique. I presume that you've been unable to resolve the situation through discussions with your husband?"

"That's correct."

"Let me consider your problem more thoroughly. I'll look forward to seeing you tomorrow."

"But, Doctor, please don't mention this conversation

to my husband. I'm going to tell him that I want to see you to cure *my* fear of flying. He's so proud."

"I'm sure I understand your situation clearly. I will see you tomorrow." The visuscene went black.

". . . and this is the plan, Dr. Doolittle. I'll tell Ann that I'm going to seek your assistance to cure me of my hatred for traveling. I believe you psychiatrists refer to the problem as *mobilephobia,* or something. Anyway, you can suggest that both of us be hypnotized so that we'll be able to mutually reinforce each other's desire to travel. Then, I want you to offer Ann a hypnotic suggestion that sexual relations with her husband every night *is* natural. Since she enjoys the once-a-week activity, I'm certain that your message won't create any strain on her—and it will relieve a hell of a strain on me."

"Mr. Morrow, are you certain that you can't work this problem out directly with your spouse?"

"Yes, Doctor, I'm certain. That's why I'm coming to you. All I'm asking for is a little hypnotic suggestion."

"I believe that I can see you and your wife at 1600 tomorrow afternoon. Have you told her of your plan?"

Chet gritted his teeth. "No, and I don't want you to, either. Just accept my surface story and make the proper suggestion."

Dr. Doolittle appeared to jot down some comment at the end of the conversation. He nodded to Morrow and vanished from the screen.

Ann and Chet Morrow walked into the freshly painted office. A secretary signaled them toward a heavy door bearing the impressive title: "Dr. Doolittle—Director of Computerized Counseling and Psychiatric Services."

"Chet, I'm so glad that both of us will be able to end our fear of traveling long distances. This new government project may be the first one to show immediate, tangible results."

The couple entered the room and glanced around.

The psychiatrist's office was a plush amalgam of leather and wood. Overstuffed reclining chairs flanked an enormous mahogany desk; drawn double-lined draperies provided a cozy atmosphere at the expense of concealing the skyscraper's stunning view of the downtown area. The room was well lighted, but no source of the illumination was visible. Chet noted the variety of tissue dispensers, chewing-gum packages, and throat-lozenge boxes neatly arranged in a row across the front of the large desk. Behind the desk six columns of computer banks began to spin and click at varying rhythms. Ann and Chet were startled as Dr. Doolittle swiveled his head 180 degrees to face them.

"Good afternoon, I'm Dr. Doolittle."

Ann's lips parted as if she was going to speak, but her eyes were transfixed on the psychiatrist's head. The hypnotic capacity of the CST—3400 was unbelievably swift and efficient.

The voice of Dr. Doolittle pierced the quiet darkness of the hypnotic trance. "Mr. Morrow, when you awake you will enjoy every aspect of traveling. You will also be more considerate of your wife's sexual desires. When you hear the word *alarm,* you will make no physical advances toward her for the next twenty-four hours. Do you understand these instructions?"

Chet's voice was hollow, but unwavering. "Yes, I will do as you instruct."

The rotating head then turned to Ann. "Mrs. Morrow, when you awake you will also enjoy every aspect of traveling, particularly air transport. You will also be more considerate of your husband's sexual desires. When he mentions the word *pill,* you will assume the role of a seductive woman and be prepared for an evening of sexual pleasure with the man you love. Do you understand these instructions?"

Ann's response was affirmative.

The Dr. Doolittle head pivoted back to face the blank telecommunicator screen. "You may leave by the door behind you. You will not remember anything about this room other than my face. Good day."

The Morrows left the office, smiled briefly at the secretary, and walked toward the Wichita Metrochute with the feeling of accomplishment.

Chet lay across the king-size bed pretending to read the sports section of the evening paper. Ann had already checked the two children and was slipping out of her robe. She stepped out of her panties, unhitched her bra, and moved into the bathroom. Chet's mind soared.

"Have you seen my comb, darling?" Ann called.

"It's on your dresser," he answered feverishly.

Ann wondered if the visit to the psychiatrist had been of any help to Chet. She hated to have him messing up her curlers by pulling off her nightgown. What would he be like tonight? All hands, probably. Well, as a reward for his willingness to go see Dr. Doolittle, she might even consider . . . No, if the counseling was effective, then she wouldn't need to give in. She tightened the sash of her lavender gown and marched out of the bathroom.

"Did you take your pill?" Chet asked.

"Yes, dear. Set the alarm for 715." She glanced in the mirror again and noticed her husband's handsome body as he lay bare-chested on the bed. She strolled back into the bathroom, removed her curlers, untied the sash and slipped out of her nightgown, and smoothed on a few dabs of Chet's favorite fragrance. She giggled. Then she strolled toward the bed, only to find her lover sound asleep.

"Say, Algie, this Morrow couple is a strange case. They left on a round-the-world tour two days after consultation with the computer and seemed to be completely compatible. Then within four weeks the wife files for a divorce on the grounds of sexual incompatibility. She claims that her old man never touches her anymore. According to the Doolittle tapes, *he* wanted sex, *she* wanted rest, and they *both* desired travel. Guess no one will ever completely figure out the complexity of human motivations."

The five psychiatrists continued to review the client tapes. Finally Algis Bagford rose from his chair, scratching his head and stretching. "I've got to admit it, Will. There's nothing in these tapes to indicate that Doolittle isn't an outstanding counselor."

☆

The Thirteenth Labor

Steven Utley

1

Resurrection was the part he disliked. Dying had never bothered him; it was quick and painless. Oblivion did not terrify him; he had come to welcome it. But oblivion always ended; resurrection always followed. Then, like some waterlogged corpse caught on a barbed metal hook, he was dragged up out of a darkness deeper than space, sweeter than sleep, through layers of purple and blue, green and yellow, orange and red—the stations of the return to life.

Purple was the instant of consciousness rekindled, the moment of awakening, a moment of surprise, physical agony, terror, complete disorientation.

Blue was the level on which confusion yielded to comprehension.

Green was the color of the translucent gelatin that enveloped him.

Yellow was the glare of the lights in the ceiling above his trough as the gelatin was rinsed from his body.

Orange were the three godlike faces hovering over him.

Red was hatred, and his head filled with the thunder of tsunami shattering themselves against cliffsides; mountain ranges trembled and crumbled, winds scoured the land, fissures opened, magma bubbled forth, suns shed their gaseous mantles and collapsed screaming onto themselves.

Needles slid through chinks in his armor, into the soft flesh in the cracks. He opened his mouth and made a sound like that of a handful of dry leaves being crushed to powder. Somebody gently forced a moist plastic tube between his lips. He sucked instinctively, tasted something viscid and salty, spat out the tube. It was replaced immediately. He spat it out a second time and bared his chisellike teeth.

"He's going to make trouble again," one of the faces said in a melodious voice. "This one has always been difficult to get out of the trough."

"We should have re-psyched him while we had the chance," another face replied.

"*I* recommended that after the Boötes VI disaster," said the first face. "*You* vetoed it, Milne."

"We've got no *choice* now," snapped the third face. "Stop arguing. Help me with him."

He concentrated on one of the faces and, after several seconds, identified it as that of Osward. She was as flawlessly beautiful as the two men with her. He thought longingly of cupping her perfect face in one of his enormous hands, of searing away the smooth flesh with acid or electricity from the organs in his unarmored palms, perhaps squeezing just hard enough to crush bones but not cause death. . . .

"Please cooperate with us," one of the men said to him. "Or do you want us to have to pry your mouth open and force-feed you?"

He stared at the feeding tube in the man's hand. It would be so easy, he told himself, to grab that hand, bite off the fingers, one knuckle at a time, then extrude hollow fangs through the skin and watch as the sleek, blemish-free body became gangrenous. . . .

"Come on, now," the man coaxed. "This will cleanse the mucous membrane and convince your stomach that it's alive again."

"*Milne!*" whined the other man. "We haven't got *time* to persuade him to be good. Use the clamp."

He closed his eyes, opened his mouth, and accepted the tube.

"That's much, much better, now," Milne murmured soothingly, as though addressing an infant.

He sucked on the tube, enduring the touch of their hands. They worked quickly, efficiently, saying as little to him or one another as was necessary. Helpless in the trough, he imagined himself rampaging through the ship, seizing people by their ankles, braining them against bulkheads, snapping their necks between his bananalike fingers, tearing off arms, legs, heads, grinding the dismembered bodies to mush between his feet and the deck. . . .

Then, through closed lids, he saw the ghost of Ajax enter the room, gliding through the wall like smoke. Ajax stood behind the three resurrectionists and looked down over the tops of their heads.

Do you haunt them now, Ajax? he asked. Are they beginning to mourn yet? Are they becoming regretful? Do they cry out in their dreams?

Do not hate them, Ajax said, regarding him sorrowfully.

You're dead because of them.

Everything I was and am is their doing. We mustn't question what they ask of us. We owe them something for our strength, for the purpose of our lives.

And they owe nothing for your life?

They gave me my life. It was theirs to reclaim.

"They threw your life away . . ." His voice was a rumbling bass, like thunder from the depths of caverns.

"What did he say?" Osward demanded.

"I didn't hear it," said Milne.

Metal balls were pressed against the palms of his hands. He sadly watched Ajax slip away.

"Pay *attention!*" Osward snapped stridently.

He sighed around the feeding tube, concentrated, and lightning crackled mutedly within his fists.

"Again."

He had to produce six more shocks before Osward grunted, satisfied, and removed the metal balls.

The tube was taken from his mouth and replaced with a hollow plastic wedge. He dutifully extruded his fangs and bit deeply, pretending that the wedge was Osward's shoulder. The wedge was removed and emptied of venom. While Osward was checking its potency, the two men made him hold his breath for eight and a half minutes.

They tested his acid-producing glands, his vision, his hearing, his olfactory powers, his reflexes, his threshold of pain.

Finally, they told him to sit up in the drained trough and then, when they had folded down its sides, to stand.

He rose and looked down at them. He was almost a meter taller than they were, with legs as thick as their bodies and fists as big as their heads. He searched their expressions hungrily for some sign that their attitude toward him had changed, however subtly, now that he was out of the trough, on his feet, invincible, a sullen but helpless hulk no longer. *If only they are afraid of me, if only I see that they know I hold myself in check with effort. . . .*

But Milne began strapping a holster containing a heavy recoilless hand cannon about his thigh, and Osward coolly put away her instruments of resurrection, and the third person, the man whose name he could not remember having ever heard, pushed his trough back into its slot in the wall.

It is not their place to be afraid of you, he heard Ajax mutter.

He shivered within his carapace and looked at his reflection on the mirror-clear wall, pleading with the massive thing with the bullet-shaped head, the mottled gray armor modified from skin and body hair, the smoldering deep-set eyes.

We could come together and crush these gods between us, he told his image, and his image said, after a moment: Yes, we could.

They buckled him into his harness. They attached the power cell, the relay pack, the communicator, the recorder, the radiation detector, the spare clips of ammunition, the thermite grenades, the duralloy crowbar. They checked everything three times.

Then Milne touched the dull metallic disk in the hollow of his elegant throat and said, "Cryogenics to Bridge."

"Bridge." The whispery reply filled the room. "Mohr here."

"Milne speaking. Heavy-Duty Scout Model Herakles has been revived and is standing by for briefing."

"Thank you, Milne." There was a faint, brief buzzing in his ear, and Mohr spoke to him directly. "Herakles."

"Yes, Mohr."

"How do you feel?"

I feel . . . He hesitated, the lids of his eyes sliding shut with an almost audible click, and the words welled up in his mouth and strained against the backs of his teeth. I feel like killing every person aboard, Mohr. On the wall, his image regarded him bleakly.

"I feel excellent, Mohr."

"Excellent," echoed Mohr's quiet, neutral voice. "Report to the shuttlecraft bay immediately. No time to lose. Number Three. The ship will brief you on the way down."

Heavy-Duty Scout Model Herakles muttered assent as, behind him, the wall irised open. He looked at the faces of the three gods standing before him, and his fingers curled up into claws.

Later, his image told him.

Later, he agreed, then turned and stepped through the circular door, onto the ledge of the dropshaft. He stepped off into the air and fell, slowly, guiding himself with a palm pressed gently against the slick warm metal of the cylindrical shaft. Later.

It was a twenty-meter drop to the shuttlecraft bay. He landed lightly, on the thickly padded balls of his knobby new feet, and bent slightly at the knees and waist. Another door irised open. He left the dropshaft and moved along a catwalk to the unlovely deltaic shuttlecraft perched atop its spindly launching rack. The ship opened a hatch to receive him.

"Hello, Herakles," it said.

"Hello, Three."

He heard the hatch close and seal itself as he clanked through the cabin to his berth. The ship automatically strapped him in. It was a two-person vessel, specifically designed to accommodate the Heavy-Duty Scout Model. He de-opaqued the observation ports, then looked across his shoulder at the berth next to his. Ajax's berth.

"Instrument check," said the ship.

Herakles forced himself to concentrate on the routine. On the console before him, a light flashed yellow: BAY DEPRESSURIZING.

"Confirm," he said.

"Control confirms. Bay depressurizing."

The yellow light went out. A red one flashed: BAY DEPRESSURIZED.

"Confirm."

"Control confirms. Bay depressurized."

"Open bay."

"Bay opening."

He looked down through the observation port set in the deck between the berths and saw a widening black line bisect the white floor of the bay.

"Bay opened," said Three.

POSITION FOR LAUNCH. The shuttlecraft's nose began to drop. The ship tilted forward ninety degrees in its rack.

POSITIONED FOR LAUNCH.

RACK LOCKS DISENGAGED.

"Confirm."

"Control confirms. Rack locks disengaged."

ALL SYSTEMS FUNCTIONING.

"All systems checked."

"Ready for launch."

"Control confirms. Ready for launch."

"Launch."

LAUNCH.

With the merest tremor, the shuttlecraft eased forward, out of its rack, out of the bay, into the maw of the universe; and when he saw the stars, he was surprised and angered to feel the faintest flicker of a hunger he had hoped banished by the circumstances of Ajax's death. His was a hunger for the feel of strange soil underfoot, for the warmth of alien suns on his face. It was the hunger they had built into him along with the shock organs, the acid sacs refashioned from perspiration glands, the retractable fangs fed by modified salivary glands. He cursed softly.

He glanced up through an observation port and caught a glimpse of curved silvery hull, a section of the starship's titanic egg-shaped body, just before the shuttlecraft turned slightly on its lateral axis. The point of a crescent of light appeared.

He studied the crescent thoughtfully for several seconds. Then: "Proceed with briefing, Three."

"This isn't going to be your usual survey jaunt, Herakles."

He thought of Ajax dropping to his knees, sinking to his waist in deadly spume. "There is no such thing as a usual survey jaunt. Where are we going this time?"

"Earth," said the ship. "We've come back to Earth. We're home now."

He let his breath hiss through clenched teeth.

"The *Druitt*," Three went on calmly, "is now orbiting Earth at a distance of seven thousand kilometers."

"I don't understand. This isn't right, Three. What happened? Why am I being sent to Earth?"

"Something has happened on Earth during the three hundred and twenty-one years, standard, that the *Druitt*'s been away. Scanners detect almost no functioning technology anywhere on the planet. No one below acknowledges our signals. You are therefore to conduct yourself as if Earth were a completely unknown and potentially hostile planet."

He studied the crescent of the approaching Earth for a minute more, then opaqued the observation ports and relaxed in his berth. Strange, he thought, they said nothing of Earth when they woke me. Golden Earth, Olympus, cradle of Adonis and Aphrodite—yet they said nothing to me about it.

"Find out what has happened," said Three. "Find out

whether the *Cornell* and the *Holtz* ever returned. Find out . . ."

He closed his mind to the shuttlecraft's voice. Ajax seemed to stir in the next berth, but he did not take his eyes from the console before him.

Would it really have made a difference, Ajax said, *if they had told you?*

Herakles considered the question. No, he replied after a long moment, no, Ajax, it wouldn't have made any difference. Earth never really belonged to us, did it?

We belong to it. We were made to serve Earth. To serve them.

And you serve them even in death, Ajax.

Can you do less than I have done, Herakles?

I will do more.

What will you do? What can you do?

I will bring them down out of their heaven. I will raze their temples. I will rub their faces in your blood. I will kill them all. For you, Ajax, and for myself.

My death doesn't matter.

It mattered to me. It should have mattered to them as well.

They are gods, and they cannot be concerned too greatly.

Inside our armor, inside their perfect bodies, we are the same. We are all human beings.

They are gods, Herakles. We are of their flesh yet mortal.

They are wrong to think of us as beasts of burden!

We were made to bear burdens.

They were wrong to make you die. They were wrong not to be affected by your death. Doesn't that make you resent them? Is that not reason enough to hate them?

No. No. There can never be reason enough to hate them. They are everything we are not—beautiful, immortal, omnipotent.

Weak! They are weak. I could kill them easily.

No. They would stop you. They would have ways to

stop you, or they would not be gods. They made themselves gods, and they made us to serve them.

I loved you, Ajax.

Then repent, Herakles.

He closed his eyes. The only sounds were those of the ship muttering to itself, the muted whir of the engines, a brief, biting screech as the shuttlecraft made its first tentative dip into the atmosphere of Earth.

I loved you, Ajax. I loved you. . . .

The ship was skipping through the upper atmosphere now, screaming. He opened his eyes just as a light flashed on the console.

WINGS EXTENDED FIVE DEGREES.

He glanced at the berth next to his and thought, fleetingly: How many times did we do this together, Ajax?

The console light flickered. WINGS EXTENDED TEN DEGREES.

They should have re-psyched you when they had the chance. You heard them talking. Osward wanted to. You're losing control.

Yes. I know.

The shuttlecraft lurched uneasily, yawed, corrected itself. WINGS EXTENDED FIFTEEN DEGREES.

They could make you well, Herakles. They could put you to sleep and cleanse your mind, drain off all of the poison, all the pain, all the hatred. The voice danced around the edges of his consciousness, growing louder with each syllable, growing stronger, shriller, more insistent, sounding less like Ajax, less like any human voice, as it closed in on him, surrounded him, rolled over him in a warm, suffocating tide, compressed him, crushed him, solidified around him like hardening amber. *All the nightmares ghosts psychoses evil things wicked thoughts blasphemies, Herakles, they can redeem you they can save you they can do anything.*

Yes. I know. Yes. I know. Yes.

A light flashed. He stared at the console uncomprehendingly. The shuttlecraft lurched again, startling him into awareness. He peered at the light.

WINGS FULLY EXTENDED.

WINGS LOCKED.

BRAKING JETS.

He de-opaqued the observation ports again. Clouds whipped past. The ocean lay below.

"We'll be setting down," said Three, "in four minutes, fifteen seconds, on the southern coast of the North American continent—the heat readings are highest there."

BRAKING FLAPS EXTENDED. LOCK.

Below, an island whipped past. He tested his straps and said, "Left calf is too loose, Three."

The ship tightened the strap on his leg.

BRAKING JETS flashed again. The shuttlecraft seemed to stagger in the air for a moment, then, as HOVER JETS appeared on the console, it wobbled and rose slightly.

The sea abruptly faded from deep blue to green. Another island crawled past, followed a few seconds later by a strip of grayish beach, a road fringed with nondescript buildings, woodland.

"Welcome home," said Three. The shuttlecraft sounded sincerely moved. "Welcome back to Earth, Herakles—drastically changed though it may be now."

Earth. Herakles rolled the word over in his mind. Earth. A harsh, alien-sounding name for the cradle of the gods. Alien name, alien world. He recalled Three's injunction to conduct his investigation as if Earth were an entirely unknown and potentially hostile planet. Then he nodded to himself. Yes.

2

They stood together, Heavy-Duty Scout Models Ajax and Herakles, in Boötes' midmorning warmth and watched the shuttlecraft of the gods come down the sky.

They stood together, two massive armored men, their wrists almost touching. A strange-smelling breeze moved across the green plain, caressed their broad faces curiously, insistently, as if trying to worm invisible fingers into the seams of their carapaces, to touch the soft flesh underneath and to know what sort of creatures these were.

Their own shuttlecraft squatted before them. Beyond that lay the great plain, covered with a mat of web-rooted vegetation. He could see a few larger growths randomly dotting the flat land. In the distance, the plain yielded slowly to foothills. A hint of mountains separated horizon from sky.

Behind the scouts were the crumbling ruins of structures no human hand had erected. Little was left of the ancient buildings: two debris-filled shells near the rim of a curious circular depression at least a kilometer in diameter and, in the depression itself, half a dozen piles of masonry that might once have been walls, the foundations of houses, pavement.

Of the ancient builders themselves, nothing was left.

There was something unnerving about the depression as far as the two scouts were concerned. Nothing grew there. The ground was badly eroded, slashed by fissures, pocked with mawlike sinkholes.

But Ajax and Herakles, clearers of the way for the gods, had searched the area thoroughly and found nothing. Whatever had blighted the area had vanished as utterly as the unknown beings who had dwelled in the city. After thirty-six hours, the scouts had declared the site safe and signaled the gods to descend from the *Druitt*.

Its wings, brake flaps, and landing gear extended, the shuttlecraft dipped low over the plain and came down gently near the scouts' ship. The whine of the hover jets fell away sharply and died. Hatches opened with reptilian hisses. Ramps slid forth and anchored themselves in the ground. The perfect people, the Adonises and Aphrodites of Golden Earth, descended and stood in the shadow of their vessel.

Ajax and Herakles lumbered over to them.

A woman named Leitch glanced at the two scouts, then said: "Start unloading the ship. I want the huts erected over there by the——"

"Let *one* of them start," a man named Ochs interrupted. He could not take his eyes off the ruins. "I want one of them to show me through the depression."

"You don't need a scout, Ochs. They've already been over the area. It's safe."

"Correction. It isn't dangerous. It *is* hazardous." Ochs looked at Ajax. "Isn't that right?"

"Yes, Ochs," said Ajax. "There are ravines, fissures, and pits all over the depression, and some of them are quite deep. The ground seems to be honeycombed with caverns."

Leitch glared at Ajax, then said to Ochs: "It can *wait*. We have to unload the ship and set up camp first."

"You have no curiosity." Ochs gestured toward the ruins. "Here we have the first irrefutable evidence we've seen of extraterrestrial intelligence, and you insist upon sticking to standard survey procedure. I want to see what they've discovered, Leitch. I have no intention of waiting for you to do your work before I can start doing mine."

Leitch compressed her mouth into a hard line. "Very well," she finally said. "Ajax, start on the ship. Herakles, go with Ochs. See that he doesn't break his neck climbing around on the ruins. Come back and help Ajax as soon as you can."

"Yes, Leitch."

"I'm going with you," Hendrix said, moving to Ochs's side.

"So am I." Travers joined them.

Leitch made an exasperated noise but said nothing. She turned to Ajax and gestured angrily at the ramp leading up into the cargo hold of the shuttlecraft. Ajax gave Herakles a slight, almost imperceptible shrug, then turned and went up the ramp.

"Lead the way, Herakles," said Ochs.

Herakles preceded the three gods to the structures near the rim of the depression. Ochs pressed the palm of his hand against the smooth, weathered stone and pursed his lips thoughtfully.

"Natural stone," he muttered. "Marble. I wonder where they quarried it."

"Certainly not from around here," Hendrix said as she traced a finger along the beveled edges of a seam between two flat stones. "Implying at least a metal-alloy level of technological development. Hard tools to cut the marble. And how do you suppose they transported it across the prairie?"

"And why?" Ochs looked out across the depression. "This doesn't appear to have been a particularly large community, even allowing for the obvious fact that most of the structures have been worn away by the elements. All the ruins seem to be contained within an area no greater than some two hundred square meters." He looked at Herakles questioningly.

"Approximately two hundred and fifty square meters, Ochs."

Ochs nodded, satisfied.

"This might not have been a community per se," said Travers. "Could have been a shrine, a monastery, a—"

"An isolated scientific research laboratory." Hendrix shrugged. "A dumping ground for nuclear wastes. Someone's wilderness retreat."

"Not a dumping ground," Ochs said. "You saw the scouts' report. No untoward radiation of any sort."

Hendrix shrugged again. "Very well, then. It was a fertilizer factory. The people of Boötes VI were technologically fifth-rate tillers of the soil who never discovered fire or the wheel but made the perfect fertilizer."

Travers cocked an eyebrow at Ochs. "Well, maybe they *were* agrarians."

The man snorted derisively. "Primitive farmers would not have built structures out of hard stone not indigenous to the area. They would have been too busy raising their crops to quarry marble and haul it across who knows how great a distance. On the other hand, if they were farmers in a more advanced civilization, we would surely have found signs of that civilization elsewhere on the planet."

"Perhaps these colonists came from a system beyond Boötes," said Travers.

"Perhaps." Ochs nodded to Herakles. "Let's go into the depression now."

Herakles rumbled assent and led them over the rim. Four meters into the sunken area, Travers stooped to crumble the soil between her fingers.

"Most peculiar," she said. "You've noticed how the vegetation blanketing the plain thins out about a meter into the depression and then stops altogether? Well, Ochs, if they were farmers, they sure were appallingly bad ones. This is dead soil. No, it's not even soil. It's almost sand. Sucked dry of organic compounds."

Hendrix knelt beside Travers and detached a stoppered tube from her belt. "I'll get a sample for analysis."

Travers rose, brushed off her hands. "If this is anything less than ninety-nine percent inorganic material, I'll bend over in front of Herakles."

The two women laughed.

Herakles looked away from them. Ochs was standing beside a three-meter-high column, touching it gingerly. He called out to Hendrix and Travers. "This thing is pitted like a meteorite. It looks as if someone had immersed it in acid."

Hendrix held up something small and brown between forefinger and thumb. "Even the pebbles are pitted. This one has a hole eaten through it."

"Yes," said Ochs, "but look at this." He indicated the top of the column.

"It's broken off at an angle. So?"

"No, Hendrix, *look* at it."

"I *am* looking at it."

"The pitting stops about two meters above the ground. The top third is smooth." Ochs circled the column once, then backed away, scowling thoughtfully.

"Ochs," Herakles yelled, "stop!"

The man started and looked at him, astonished.

The scout pointed at something behind Ochs, who

spun and found himself peering down into a sinkhole.

"Oh," said Ochs, blanching slightly. "I didn't notice it. I . . . thank you, Herakles."

"It's advisable to watch where you set your feet."

Ochs stiffened and colored. "Don't be impertinent, Scout!"

Herakles dropped to one knee and bowed his head. "I beg your forgiveness, Ochs."

Ochs grunted. "Get up, you insolent garbage." To the women, he said, "I'm going back for my equipment now."

"Do you think Leitch will let you have it?" asked Travers.

"Leitch can stuff the *Druitt* up her ass! Come on, Herakles."

As the god and the scout ascended the slope, Hendrix called after them, "Tell Allison I want to talk with him. And get Herakles to bring my equipment, too."

Allison was sitting on the ground near the rim of the depression. He had scalped a patch of sod from the plain and was fingering the alien plant's lacelike roots.

Herakles looked back toward the shuttlecraft. Under the unnecessarily watchful eye of Leitch, Ajax had already made one stack of crates, inflated the hemispherical hut mold over it, and sprayed on plastic. While that dried, he lugged more crates from the ship's cargo hold to a spot five meters beyond the hut and stacked them.

"Hendrix wants you," Ochs told Allison. To Herakles, he said: "Separate my equipment, and Hendrix's, and bring them over here. If Leitch tells you to do anything else, tell her that I've given you a direct order."

"Yes, Ochs." Herakles sighed disconsolately as he approached the shuttlecraft. Leitch saw him coming and beckoned impatiently. The scout broke into a lumbering run.

Leitch glared at him when he stopped before her. "Get to work," she snapped.

"Forgive me, Leitch, but Ochs has ordered me to take his and Hendrix's equipment to the depression."

"Get to work, damn you." She strode away in Ochs's

direction without waiting to see whether Herakles complied.

He watched her go and heard her call to Ochs in a belligerent tone. The man and woman began gesticulating at each other wildly. Herakles turned toward the shuttlecraft just as Ajax came down the cargo ramp with an oblong crate cradled in his arms.

"Why the strange expression?" Ajax asked, hefting his burden. "Don't you feel well?"

Herakles shook his head. "It's nothing, Ajax."

A few minutes later, though, as he was manhandling a portable generator out of the cargo hold, he saw Leitch standing near the ship, a triumphant expression on her face. He was surprised to find himself grinding his teeth together.

It took them two hours to finish setting up camp. Herakles and Ajax erected another large hut to house supplies and equipment, two lesser ones for living quarters, and a small shed for the generators. They assembled a two-person land rover, a drill rig and a chassis to support it, a traser barricade around the perimeter marked by Leitch, enclosing the ships and the plastic domes.

Ochs showed up at almost the precise moment they had finished. "Now," he demanded hotly of Leitch, "can I get one of them to carry my equipment?"

"Of course," Leitch said with poisonous sweetness. "They live but to serve you, Ochs. Ajax, Herakles, where did we put Ochs's equipment?"

"In Hut Two, Leitch," said Ajax.

"Where in Hut Two?"

"Under the crates containing Mitchell's equipment, Leitch."

Ochs exploded. "Damn you, Leitch! Why didn't you set it aside?"

Leitch shrugged and turned her back on him. "Standard survey procedure, Ochs. Scouts, take Hendrix's equipment to the depression, then his." She jerked a thumb over her shoulder. "In that order, precisely."

"Leitch, I'll kill you one of these days!"

"Probably when my back is turned," Leitch snapped, walking away.

Herakles watched Ochs's mouth open and close, soundlessly, like a fish gasping in air. Then the man lashed out and struck him on the sternum with the edge of his fist. It was a light blow, but the scout grunted in surprise.

"I hate that woman!" Ochs snarled, staring after her. "I *hate* her!"

The two scouts stood very, very still.

"Damn it!" Herakles took another ineffectual blow on his carapace. Ochs unballed his fists and said, "All right, get my things. And Hendrix's. Bring them over to the sunken area. I want everything there in five minutes, you understand?"

"Yes, Ochs."

The scouts glumly removed the crates containing Ochs's and Hendrix's equipment and lugged them to the rim of the depression. They unpacked scanning and recording instruments, digging mechanisms, data processors, and a radiocarbon-dater.

Ochs's fury appeared to have passed by the time the last of his boxes had been emptied. Clipping a communicator to his belt, he nodded at a surveyor's tripod and said, "Bring that, Herakles. We're going to get some work done. Finally."

Herakles folded the tripod legs together, shouldered the instrument, and fell into step behind the god. They picked their way down the slope carefully, past Raymond the geologist, past a still perplexed-looking Travers, skirting fissures, gullies, and sinkholes, the ancient pockmarked masonry. Well ahead of them, Herakles spotted Allison making his way across the rough ground toward the silt- and rubble-clogged cavity at the center of the depression.

Ochs and Herakles stopped by two piles of stones about sixty meters from the rim of the depression. "Set that up over there," the man said, and the scout unfolded the tripod legs and placed the instrument at the spot indicated. Ochs rubbed his hands together and looked around. "Now I want you—"

They felt a tremor, followed at once by a muted gurgling sound like that of water being sucked down a drain.

"What was that?" Ochs demanded. "What—"

The second tremor was much more violent than the first. Herakles felt the ground sag beneath his feet, heard a whimpering cry from the perfect man at his side, saw rough stones slide, clattering, down the mounds of rubble nearby. He looked about anxiously. Up the slope, Travers was scrambling to her feet. The geologist was looking at his instruments and waving his arms frantically. The gurgling noise was repeated.

"I thought you said it was *safe!*" Ochs screeched.

Herakles opened his mouth to say something, then a scream punctured his mounting irritation. It was a scream so high, so shrill, that it took him a second to recognize the sound as human.

Ochs stared toward the center of the depression. "Allison . . ."

Herakles glanced toward the rim and saw people gathering there, saw Ajax lurching down the slope, then turned and headed toward the bottom of the basin, moving as quickly as he could, skidding past chasms, hurdling holes. The erosion of the land grew markedly worse the farther he went. Ravines deepened and widened. The sinkholes became more numerous. The angle of descent increased steeply.

He headed down the side of a gully on his armor-plated backside. The gully was almost four meters deep and it curved sharply to the right. He was half walking, half sliding around the curve, bellowing Allison's name, when he saw the man. Allison was on his belly, his face a mask of shock commingled with pain, his fingers clawing at the ground.

Herakles took another step forward, the coarse soil crunching underfoot like insect husks, and stopped dead and gaped, not at the man's open mouth and glazed eyes, not even at the stumps of his legs, but at the glistening frothy stuff welling up behind him, bubbling up the walls of the gully, licking at the bloody trail of its victim.

The disk at Allison's throat was beeping angrily. It was that small sound which made the scout shake off his paralysis. He hurried to the man and picked him up. The froth massed and seemed to lunge at him as he backed away.

When he had put a dozen meters between it and himself, Herakles laid Allison against the side of the gully and examined him. His feet and ankles were gone, dissolved. Two decayed nubs of bone protruded from the gory stump of each calf. Herakles quickly removed two narrow straps from his harness and bound them tightly about Allison's legs. Then he shouldered him gently and scrambled out of the gully.

He activated his communicator and reported: "Ajax, I've got Allison. There's something deadly down here. I can't get close enough to see, but the stuff is probably coming up out of the central pit. Get everyone out of the depression immediately."

Another tremor. Herakles sat down hard. Allison whimpered against his breast. About three meters up the slope, a sinkhole gurgled; spume overflowed and cascaded down the walls of the gulley, rolled toward the scout.

Herakles got to his feet and skirted the moving mat of bubbles.

"Herakles!" Ajax called. "It's starting to come up here, too!"

Herakles topped a mound and looked toward the rim of the basin. Spume geysered from several pits and spread across the ground. He saw Ajax and lesser figures struggling up the slope, stones tilting out of place, falling, tumbling into chasms.

Ahead and to the left, a hole belched thunderously and spat, and a rain of bubbles fell on him. The stuff did not adhere to what it touched, but what it touched, it consumed. Allison's body disintegrated. Herakles plunged out of the iridescent spray and dropped to one knee, scattering his burden's limbs and torso. The froth closed over the bloody meat, and bubbles sparkled pinkly.

"Come *on!*" he heard Ajax screech.

Herakles pushed himself to his feet. Along the length of the calf that had been immersed in the spume, the armor was rough and pitted, a lighter gray than he was used to seeing. The soles of his feet began to feel uncomfortably warm. He clamped his jaws shut and plodded onward, past Ochs's tripod, past fountains of froth and toward Ajax and the gods and safety beyond the basin. He was less than twenty-five meters from the rim when the armor sloughed off below the ankle. His feet literally disintegrated under him, and pain, a worse pain than any he had previously known or imagined possible, lanced up his legs. He screamed and went down on his knees. He would have fallen forward upon his face had Ajax not reached him two seconds later.

Ajax put his hands under Herakles' arms and, somehow, pulled him to the top of the slope. Herakles lay on his back, feeling the ground quiver beneath him, listening to the excited voices of the beautiful men and women without understanding a word they said. There was a hiss as Ajax sprayed something cool on the stumps of his legs. He found himself staring up into Travers' lovely, thoughtful eyes.

"Herakles," she said, "what is that stuff? Where did it come—"

Ochs's scream cut her short. "My *equipment!*"

Travers glared over her shoulder at him. "What?"

"Ajax!" Herakles caught a glimpse of Ochs's livid face and flailing fists. "You forgot to bring back my equipment, damn you! It'll be *ruined!*"

"You should complain," said Hendrix, somewhere out of Herakles' field of vision. "What am *I* going to do without Allison?"

"Get my equipment!" Ochs shrieked at Ajax. "Before it's too late!"

Herakles heard Ajax's slow, resigned reply. "Yes, Ochs."

He heard himself murmur: "No, Ajax."

He rolled onto his side and pushed himself up on his elbow and looked up at Ajax's face, into his deep, dark eyes. In that single instant of locked gazes, the precepts by which they had lived and by which one of them was about to die came to him like a prayer.

We live but to serve the gods.

We go where the gods will.

We are born to hazard.

We honor and obey.

We are of their flesh yet mortal.

The words came as a prayer, but it was not enough.

Ajax turned and ran back down into the basin, through the froth. He had almost reached Ochs's tripod when the ground heaved violently. Ajax stumbled and fell, sinking waist-deep in bubbles. Fresh gouts of the stuff rose.

"Get my equipment, damn you!"

Ajax fell forward, and the tripod toppled. Then the spume closed over both.

"Damn it!" said Ochs. "What am I going to do without equipment?"

"What are *we* going to do," demanded Leitch, "with one scout dead and the other crippled?"

On the ground between the gods, Herakles dug his fingers into the soil and opened his mouth in a scream too loud, too full of anguish, to be uttered—a scream that was the sound of the firmament turning brittle and shattering into a billion razor-edged shards; the sound that rolled back seas, leveled mountain ranges, split the earth, blasted planets from their orbits, caved in stars; the sound that signaled the end of time and the edge of space; the sound of all the little angers at once.

Whatever the nature of the thing that had lain dormant in the caverns below the depression, however it had come to be there, however it had aerated itself and forced itself to the surface—the stuff did not cease to bubble out of the ground until it had filled the basin almost to the rim. A single column poked through the glistening surface. Then—again, for whatever reasons—

the stuff began to settle, sucking itself back down into the ground, leaving the depression almost imperceptibly wider, almost imperceptibly deeper, considerably freer of organic matter and certain elements.

By that time, Herakles had been returned to the *Druitt.* Milne, Osward, and the man whose name he did not know put him on a gleaming metal table and let him mutter to himself while they grafted raw tissue to the stumps of his legs. Milne gave him the feeding tube at one point, and he bit through it. They put a clamp on his face, pried his jaws apart, and forced salty mush down his throat.

He regenerated his feet and the armor that had been eaten away by spattering foam, and then he was returned to his gelatin-filled trough in Cryogenics. As he sank through the variegated levels to his latest death, his hatred of the gods, the perfect men and women of Golden Earth, was as certain as the promise of resurrection.

3

Moving through the city of the gods, Herakles felt awe in spite of himself. He had never before visited the habitats of the gods, had only seen their elegant buildings from afar, and the deeper he penetrated this enclave of Olympus, the more like a trespasser he felt. Adonis and Aphrodite had divided the world into cities for themselves and crèches for those who served them.

As he walked along the deserted boulevards, past empty houses, stopping every few minutes to make unnecessary adjustments of the instruments attached to his harness, his childhood lessons recited themselves, unbidden, in his mind:

In their great cities, the gods look down upon us, their creations, and see every deed, know every innermost thought.

In their great cities, the gods look out across the world and know it is theirs, and they look up at the stars and know those can be theirs, too.

In their great cities . . .

But the great city was empty. Creepers twined about towers and spires. Drifts of powdery dust had begun to accumulate in the plazas. The trees lining the avenues were wild-looking and had not been tended in a long time. There were no signs of actual decay—the materials the gods had used to construct their city endured—but neither were there signs of life.

Herakles struggled with his terrors, calling to mind the sight of Ajax foundering in deadly froth, fanning the embers of his rage. The memory was not enough to completely dispel his uneasiness. Fear of the gods went back to childhood and the crèche. Like the threat of the ravenous *something* that, long before the age of Golden Earth, had lurked in the darkness, slavering for the tender flesh of disobedient children, like the ancient Christians' threats of hellfire and torment forevermore—fear of the gods could not be exorcised with age, reason, or familiarity. Repulsed by anger, routed by hatred, fear of the gods lived deep in Herakles, but it lived nonetheless.

There was a sound of beating wings in the air above his head. Herakles looked up, one hand curled around the stout plastic butt of the recoilless hand cannon holstered on his thigh, and saw a batlike shape dip and pass at a height of about ten meters. Small of skull and body, with a deep, narrow keel of a breastbone and filmy pink membranes stretched across enormously elongated fingers, it was barely recognizable as anything whose ancestors had been human.

The bat-person wheeled gracefully in the air and dropped to earth a short distance from the scout. Folding its wings over its back, it waddled forward on calloused thumb stumps and the padded balls of virtually toeless feet. It stopped about three meters away from him and regarded him happily.

Herakles caressed the smooth handle of his weapon and said, "I am Heavy-Duty Scout Model Herakles, *S. V. Druitt.*"

"You are a pilgrim to this holy place." The bat-person's voice was shrill and parrotlike. "We welcome you."

"Where are the gods?"

"We welcome you. You are a pilgrim to this holy place."

Herakles frowned. "Where have the gods gone?" he persisted. "What has happened to them?"

"We welcome you. You are a pilgrim to this holy place." The bat-person opened its wings with a sharp snap and started to rise laboriously.

"Stop." Herakles drew the cannon and chambered a round. "Answer me!"

The creature rose, circled once, then flew away, toward the heart of the city.

The scout stared after it, contemplated the weapon in his hand, and, with a perplexed sigh, returned it, safety on, to its holster. It would have been useless, he realized, to capture the bat-person and attempt to interrogate it. Obviously the thing had greeted him without real comprehension of what it was saying to him. Herakles trudged along in the direction the creature had taken, and as he passed a dark alcove, he glimpsed a shadowy gray hulk from the corner of his eye.

Ajax seemed to step forth and pace at his side. *You are starting to repent,* he said. *It shows in your expression.*

I have started to repent nothing. I have nothing to repent.

Ajax made a reproachful sound. *You blaspheme in the city of the gods. Yet you are afraid. You are becoming such a mystery to me, Herakles.*

Herakles stopped. There was a lump of raw agony in his throat. He clenched his fists and glared at the ghost. Why, he demanded, why, Ajax, do you haunt me and not those who sent you to your death?

Because I love you. Because I fear for you. Because you and I have grown apart somehow.

You are dead. I am alive. That makes a good deal of difference between us.

No. I speak of a worse separation than death. You

have come to hate the gods, where once you loved them. You have come to dream of killing them, though you used to serve them gladly. Why? How? We were two and the same, you and I. How have you become afflicted with such unnatural passions? How have you become what you are, a blasphemer, a harborer of treachery? How have you managed to harden your heart against them?

Herakles felt a great and terrible sadness settle upon him. He could think of nothing to say.

They had been born within minutes of each other, Ajax and Herakles, two large but outwardly normal baby boys, in a crèche where large but outwardly normal baby boys and girls soon became thick-skinned and lumpy. They had taken their training together. They had learned the same lessons. They had grown up together, seeing little and knowing less of the world beyond the crèche, the world of the gods, knowing only that they were special mortals designed to perform heroic tasks in the service of Golden Earth. They had become lovers, and the gods, whether by chance or through a rare sense of compassion for lesser beings, had deigned to assign the two of them, Ajax and Herakles, the inseparables, the indissolubles, to duty aboard the same starship.

Herakles could think of nothing to say except: I loved you, Ajax. I grieve because you are dead. I loved you dearly.

And I loved you. The gods love you. They—

Herakles snarled. Lightning crackled from his hands. They can't love anything! They love no one, Ajax!

Herakles!

They're all crazy, Ajax! Crazy and childish and full of hate! They hate us, and they hate one another!

Herakles. Herakles . . .

There was a hollow clopping sound behind him. Herakles wheeled, drawing his weapon in the same smooth motion. He saw two large creatures step out of the shadows beneath a massive arch, into the sunlight. Their androgynous human faces and torsos glittered with beadlets of perspiration. Crouched upon the broad equine back of one was the bat-person.

The scout lowered the muzzle of the hand cannon slightly and studied the creatures as they approached. After men and women had learned how to reshape themselves, after they had attained physical perfection and immortality, thereby raising themselves to godhood, they had taken a portion of their flesh and fashioned it into lesser beings to serve them: seal-people to tend the ocean farms on the continental shelves, gill-breathers to mine the bottoms of the seas, people who could endure hardships in deserts and polar wildernesses, giants who could face danger on other worlds, cybernetic people . . . and people whose sole function in the scheme of Golden Earth was purely decorative. Fairy-tale people. Centaurs.

The bat-person chirped idiotically as the centaurs came to a stop before Herakles. "You are a pilgrim to this holy place," it screeched. "We welcome you."

The scout looked into the centaurs' large, liquid brown eyes and said hopefully: "I am Heavy-Duty Scout Model Herakles, *S. V. Druitt.*"

One of the creatures tossed its tawny mane and gave him a dazzling smile. "We welcome you. You are a pilgrim to this holy place."

Herakles groaned inwardly. "Where are the gods? What has become of them?"

The centaurs turned and calmly walked away.

"Where are the *gods?*" he shouted after them, and there was a strange quality to his voice, a note of something that was very like despair. One of the centaurs paused and looked over its shoulder curiously. It gave him another smile, then trotted to catch up with its companion.

Yes, Ajax murmured at Herakles' side, *you are beginning to repent.*

Away, phantom! Herakles set out after the centaurs. Go back to your gods.

Ajax sighed, a quiet, sorrowful sound, and said, *I truly do not understand you, Herakles.*

But I understand you, Ajax! I have been you. Docile, faithful, obedient Ajax . . . Ajax, my beloved, don't you see? Both of us were precisely the kind of creature they intended us to be. . . .

Several bat-people passed overhead noisily, bound for the heart of the city. The thing riding upon the centaur's back made a sound like laughter, unfurled its wings, stretched lazily, refolded the membranes.

With Ajax hovering at the extreme edge of his field of vision, Herakles let the centaurs precede him in silence disturbed only by the clack of their hooves on pavement, through more deserted streets and plazas, past more empty houses, dry fountains, dusty works of sculpture, under arches, over ornately decorated bridges.

At the heart of the city, ringed by towers, protected by a bell of energy indicated by the play of scintillae in the air, was an amphitheater so immense that it was almost a valley. The centaurs led Herakles to the edge of the bowl, past the bat-people he had seen previously, and he gazed down across the terraces, thoroughly awed.

Something as white, as brilliantly white, as clean crusted snow blanketed the slopes before him.

Herakles blinked, closed his eyes tightly for several seconds, then peered up at the sparkling lights on the invisible surface of the energy dome. Then, stunned, unable to stand, he dropped to his knees.

He heard one of the centaurs standing behind him shift its hard feet, heard the leathery rustle of membranous wings, heard a mewling whimper from the back of his own throat.

He stared down across the amphitheater, and that shadow, that fusion of lost mate and engrained faith, that ghost whom he called Ajax, cried out in disbelief, in horror, in agony, in misery.

He stared down across the amphitheater, and he knew, without having to make any closer examination, without even having to really think about what he was seeing, that the thousands upon thousands upon *thou-*

sands of bones covering the terraced slopes were the bones of immortals.

Far, far below, rising out of the mounds of skulls and femurs and shoulder blades, thick black pylons shimmered suddenly, and the scintillae in the sky above the amphitheater coalesced into a blindingly bright cloud the color of molten silver. A tentacle of something cool and slippery tickled the inner surface of Herakles' cranium.

> You are a pilgrim to this holy place. We welcome you.
>
> Though trembling and afraid, you have come, because you are one of the faithful, and we hear your prayers.
>
> Your loyalty and devotion move us deeply.
>
> We see into your heart, we know your innermost thoughts, and we forgive you your mortal limitations, for you are of our flesh.
>
> But there is still much evil in the world.
>
> We still know anger, for we have been renounced by those whom we authored: they grew apart from us, and we could not hold them to us; they formed godless societies in the wilderness and under the seas, and they abandoned us.
>
> We still know sorrow: our world has been hurled from its natural state by the wickedness of our creatures.
>
> Hear us, pilgrim, and know that, when all have repented, then shall we return and clothe ourselves in flesh again.
>
> Abide in this holy place and receive those who will surely follow.
>
> Do not surrender your faith to despair or doubt.
>
> Do not lose heart.
>
> Do not falter.
>
> Endure.

The pylons stopped shimmering. Herakles sat back on his calves and, after a long moment, turned his head to stare at the exalted faces of the centaurs. The bat-people beat their wings and babbled among themselves wordlessly. Then, a minute or two later, the centaurs turned and cantered away into the city. The winged things took to the air in a flurry of beating membranes and cacophonous cries. The scout watched them until they had disappeared beyond the tops of the buildings encircling the amphitheater.

They are the last, Ajax. The last of the faithful. The final believers. Mindless descendants of useless creatures. Fit and proper worshipers for false gods.

They made themselves immortal. They authored us. They changed the world and foolishly expected it to change no more. Despite their immortality, or because of it, they settled into senility, into a second childhood that would have lasted an eternity but for us.

We who kept Golden Earth moving in the orbit they had prescribed for it . . . we who live but to serve, who go where the gods will, who are mortal yet of their flesh, who are born to hazard, who honor and obey . . . we outgrew them. We tired of them. We didn't need them any longer. We abandoned them. They came here, and they died, and there was nothing noble, nothing dignified . . . nothing godlike about their passing. They died insane. They did this out of sheer childish petulance.

They took themselves away, Ajax, and they truly believed that we would be sorry.

They are gone, all save a handful, circling helplessly above Golden Earth, waiting for a report they cannot accept. We are well rid of them.

We are free of immortal children.

He listened for the shadow's reply. There was no sound at the heart of the city.

And I am free of ghosts.

Herakles got to his feet and activated his communicator. "Three," he said.

"Yes, Herakles," replied the shuttlecraft, kilometers away.

"Stand by to relay my report to the *Druitt.*"

"Yes, Herakles." There was a brief, static-filled pause. Then: "Standing by. Proceed with your report."

He gazed into the amphitheater. On the terrace immediately below the lip of the bowl, skulls leered up at him.

"Go ahead," said Three, and waited.

The scout said nothing.

"Herakles?"

Herakles tore the communicator off its cord. He pulled the relay pack and the power cell from his harness and tossed them away contemptuously. He grinned down at the skulls.

Then he turned and moved away. Somewhere the ones who had abandoned their gods were living their own lives.

He would find them. ✫

The People Who Could Not Kill

Bill Starr

A conscience can be a terrible thing, especially if it works.

That was the kind Grimes had. So I wasn't too surprised when he told me he had decided to stay on Paradise IV when we had completed our survey and were ready to lift off.

Not that anyone, except he himself, blamed him for killing the native. As the ship's security officer, it was his job to protect the crew. How could he have known that the primitive humanoids were culturally incapable of hostile action? What he had taken for a violent attack was just their traditional welcoming ceremony.

The simple-hearted natives quickly forgot the incident and entertained us with their carefree hospitality, which happily included sharing their women. Only Grimes refrained from the festivities, brooding guiltily alone in his cabin. Finally he told me of his decision: He hoped to pay for his crime by spending the rest of his life serving the natives in any way he could.

I hated to lose him, and of course I could have ordered him to stay aboard. But I owed him too many favors, and besides, he was due for retirement soon anyway. I did try to talk him out of it, pointing out that he would be hopelessly isolated from his own kind out there at the edge of the galaxy, where even our Exploration Corps ships rarely called.

But Grimes was determined, and I suspected an ulterior motive in his plan. Throughout his long career as a space soldier, he had lived under the constant threat of deadly violence that had often and unexpectedly become reality. Now he was tired of fighting, and he had found the kind of gentle, peaceful society that all of us dream of at least once in our turbulent lives. I couldn't blame him—in fact I envied him—for wanting to stay.

So I gave him his discharge and wished him luck. The last I saw of him—on one of my viewscreens as we lifted—he was waving farewell, with a lovely native girl on his arm and a look of deep contentment in his weary eyes.

I thought about Grimes often in the following years, wondering how he had made out in his adopted homeland. But nearly a half-century passed before duty again took me to Paradise IV. He had been dead many years by then, but several elderly natives revered his memory and told of his great works.

The tribal elders had quickly found a job suitable to his special talents. I was shocked by their choice, but on reflection I saw the inescapable logic of it. After all, what position could he have been offered by a people strongly conditioned against homicide but still plagued by the hatreds, jealousies, frustrations, and other violence-breeding emotions common to all intelligent beings—except that of Executioner?

And of course his conscience wouldn't let him refuse the duty. They say he hardly ever had an idle moment all during his stay on Paradise IV.   ✬

We Hold These Rights . . .

Henry Melton

"And I'm telling *you* that I won't have a coward on my ship!"

I tried to reason with the maniac: "Come on, Quail! It's my ship, too. We *have* to have an engineer."

"We'll get another one!" His voice echoed off the walls of the control room. I hadn't seen him like this before, and Quail Gren and I had been shoving rocks for six years. It was frightening.

"Where, Quail? Where will we get another engineer? After today, there won't be an unemployed beam controller anywhere in the Asteroid Belt—and if there were, he'd be somebody worse than Willis Fario."

"What's the matter with you, Clement Ster? Why are you sticking up for him? Are you wanting to sell us out to the Terrans, too?"

That was too much. My fist caught him clumsily in the chest. He was bigger than me, but he rocked back a little. "You shut up!" I yelled. "The Belt is my home, just like it is yours. I know you're worried about Marine and the kids, but don't be *crazy*. I'm not about to let some Earthside commission steal the Belt out from beneath me. You make another crack like that, and I'll deck you!"

Quail looked away toward his control console. My punch couldn't have hurt, but I think my trying it shocked him. I didn't often lose my temper. I stalked over to my seat at the geologist's station and automatically stabbed the keys on the geotyping files. It would be another three days before I would be needing to search them in earnest, but it was something to do until the air cleared.

He spoke, finally, in a lowered voice. "Okay, Clement. You're my friend. I know you're loyal to the Belt. But why'd you defend that *neon?*"

I sighed. It had been a very long and exhausting day, and I had no hope it would get any better. I reviewed my arguments again. "Two reasons. Like I said before, we're not going to be able to find a beam controller who can handle our beam projector the way we have it jury-wired, with no computer controls. You can plot your courses all you want up here, but unless we have someone down in the engine room who can make the beam move the ship like it's supposed to, then the *Monarch* isn't a ship—it's just a funny-shaped asteroid. And, secondly, I'm not so sure that he said anything wrong."

"Nothing wrong! Are you deaf? Didn't he, just a few minutes ago, tell us that it is perfectly all right for the Earth Assembly to move right in and order us off our own rocks? Now, didn't he?" Quail's face started getting red again.

I tried to keep my voice calm, but my impatience stuck out with every word I said. "Quail, I really don't know *what* he said. Now, leave me alone for a while!"

It was the truth. I didn't know what Willis had said. He had a funny way of talking and I was never exactly sure. But I promised myself right then that I was going to find out what he had meant by his crack—but after I got some sleep. We were at war with Earth, only hours into it, and my nerves needed rest.

When I woke, Quail was still up in the control room. I didn't think he had gotten any sleep, and that worried me. I hoped he could take the strain.

It took a war to make me glad, for the first time, that I hadn't married. I remembered when the Terrans took over Mars in their insane desire to make over the entire solar system into a pattern of habitable planets. For their own safety—so they said—three generations of colonists were uprooted and shipped back to Earth. Many couldn't adjust to the crowded, smelly home planet. I didn't imagine we would fare much better under Terran control. They surely had some plan to use even Quail's home rock, Greenstone, as raw material for their terraforming engineers. I hated to think that such a thing might happen.

I marveled that Quail could resist the impulse to boost straight home. We were only a six-day trip from there. I wouldn't have argued. Ceres had no authority over us. If they had ordered us on the mission, rather than asking, I doubt we would have done it. No Belt miner would have. But Quail thought it would be best to act with the others.

The volunteer navy at Ceres had formed about thirty seconds after the bad news from the Terran Assembly arrived. As usual, we didn't find out about it until two hours later, when we turned the radio on to get an orbit allotment from Ceres Port Control. We grabbed the first slot we could get, and Quail and I took the scooter straight to Coro's place. In the excitement, we both forgot about Willis.

It had been a good bet. Jake Coro—that is, *Admiral* Jake Coro, T.P.N., Ret.—had been blowing the independence trumpet for years, not that anyone had paid much serious attention to him. The Belt, or so everybody thought, already *was* independent. But when the Terrans tried their move, he had been ready. We landed the scooter near his place, almost setting down on a couple of people who were scurrying about the place. A couple of dozen scooters were about, as Jake's Restaurant and Club had become general headquarters for the Ceres Defense Brigade. Jake had been retired from the Terran Navy for ten years, but those ten years had made him every bit a Belt man. As Quail and I walked into his place, I saw that he was still every bit an admiral. The Defense Brigade was his show, and he had the right. Seven years worth of contingency plans worked out for this very day were spread out in a couple of hundred sealed envelopes on the pool table. When he saw us come in, he took several minutes to talk to us and to ask our help. We left with one of those envelopes and a hope that we just *might* be able to hold the rocks we called home.

I really had no home other than the *Monarch,* but that hope of victory meant a lot to me—because Quail *did* have a home, and he had shared it with me. Every few months, when we had a bit more cash than bills, the *Monarch* would dock at Greenstone and Quail would take up being a family man where he had left off last time. For the first day or so he and Marine would disappear somewhere down in the rock and I would babysit the kids.

Baby Stephen was barely human the last time we were there, but then, Emme had looked like that not too many trips ago, and she was a little angel. She may have had a crush on me, hanging around wherever I was. I could visualize her, hovering over my shoulder in zero-g as I reset the house tractor field back up to normal after the baby had come. Toby and I were good friends. He had been around before I started visiting. We'd played a lot together over the years. I taught him how to use the rifle last trip. I'd hoped he would never have to use it.

Willis hadn't come up from the engine room for the night, but that was nothing unusual. We had hired him to monitor and control the machines down there when we limped into Vesta Village a month or so before with a fried computer. He slipped into the computer's place as if he were a repair module. He did the jobs well, executing orders Quail called down over the intercom. But he *acted* like a machine, too. He was quiet, impassive, and he stayed in his place. He ate and slept down there. It was always a shock when he *did* come up into people country.

Crawling down the cramped tube connecting the engine room with the rest of the ship, I felt maybe it *wasn't* so odd he rarely came up. The tube was narrow and too long. It was slanted downward and had an uncomfortable bend in the middle. It was dark at the bottom. The tube had come out next to the massive chamber that held tractor-pressor beams in a dynamic equilibrium, the accumulator that held all of our power.

"Willis? Are you asleep?" In the dim light shed by the indicators, I could make out his sleeping bag, strung, hammock-wise, between two supports. He said nothing, but the bag started moving and he began to crawl out. He was brown-skinned, hairy, and massive. He looked like a brown bear awakened from its winter nap, blinking his eyes as the light came on.

"What do you want?" he mumbled.

"I just wanted to talk. A lot has happened."

Willis gestured to a place where I could sit, as he slumped into the control seat we had moved down for his use. "Is there anything to say?"

I thought of Toby and Emme and that Terran fleet probably already on its way, and bit back the cutting answer that came to mind. I wanted to find out what *he* felt, in spite of his cynical manner. He looked at home, sitting there before the uprooted mass detector and among the various emergency-wired hand controls. But he was a big unknown to me. How he looked was about the limit of what I knew about him.

I took a stab at opening communications. "Quail got upset by some of the things you said yesterday. I hope we can clear the misunderstanding."

Willis grunted and nodded. "I could tell Mr. Gren didn't know what I was talking about. But I didn't figure you comprehended any more than he did."

"I can't say that I did. I just don't want a bunch of bad feelings to keep the *Monarch* from doing its best. Too much is at stake."

He just shrugged, and, inside, I sympathized with Quail's dislike of the man. I could tell he couldn't care less about what I was ready to fight and die for. We had been free men in the Belt far too long to take annexation with only a shrug. It didn't sit right.

"Don't you care?" I asked. I suddenly had a moment of doubt—Quail and I *hadn't* explained to him what was up when we left Ceres City at full speed, and we hadn't really discussed it when he was up in the control room. "You *are* aware of what is going on, aren't you?"

He shrugged again. "Mr. Ster, I really don't know how to answer you. All I've heard is a bunch of nonsense. And I can't get upset about nonsense."

"What kind of nonsense?"

"A bunch of gibberish on the radio as we left Ceres—in violation of port ordinances, by the way. I hope you've got a good reason for that; I've got *enough* marks against my record at Ceres Port. Anyway, the radio was full of it. On the Voice, instead of news, I was getting a *horrible* mishmash of *vile* treachery, *sacred* rights, *loyal* miners, and of *all* things, the defense of our *home* spaces. There was a lot more of the stuff, all variations on the same rabble-rousing theme. A lot of nonsense!"

"You said that in the control room. What do you mean? Are you saying it's nonsense that we want to defend our right to live our own lives? Do you think we don't have the *right* to defend our rocks from being stolen out from beneath us?"

Willis visibly sagged, as if disappointed in the conversation. "I've given up trying to make people understand. You won't understand—but yes, that *is* what I think. You don't have any rights."

I stopped listening right there and got to my feet. *What kind of man,* I thought, *wouldn't blink an eye at Terran goons forcing Toby and Emme down into their rat-hive cities in that high-gravity and fouled air? No right to resist!* I clamped my jaws. I wasn't about to lose my temper in front of him. I mumbled an excuse to leave and turned to go. *Quail is right. Even I won't be able to stomach working with him. We'll have to replace him. And this is the worst possible time!*

"Mr. Ster?" he asked calmly, stopping me. "Where are we going? You haven't said."

"Maybe it's best if I don't!" I snapped, hating myself for letting my feelings show. But I wanted to get out of that dark little room, fast. He turned my stomach. A man couldn't ignore what the Terrans had planned for ten million innocent people. Only a machine.

"Sir," he said, but I wasn't listening to what he said, only to the metal in his voice. "You don't understand what I said. *(Click)* But don't let that bother you. *(Click)* I do my job. *(Whirr-click)*!"

I didn't reply. The hatch on the entrance tube was open and I left. Up in the control room, Quail brought up the subject of Willis again, but I couldn't argue about it anymore. After this mission, Willis had to go.

Forty hours out from Ceres, we had to change the beam. We had been pulling ourselves along smoothly toward Jupiter with the *Monarch*'s tractor beam, but we needed a few hours of pull toward the sun to shift our vector. Quail spoke his directions down the intercom in as emotionless a voice as he could manage, but the contempt was still there. He had no use for anyone who would not help him fight. I had gotten him to take sleeping tablets, but he never stopped worrying about Marine. Willis kept his replies to a minimum. He did his job like a machine. The final piloting change was switching the propulsion beam from tractor to pressor and realigning it on Jupiter for another forty hours of deceleration.

When we finally cut that beam, the *eta* navigation beacon was strong in the nav receiver. Quail and I were at our duty stations. He wanted a short course to get us a little closer to the beacon, and I was hunting rocks. Willis walked into the room. We both looked up in surprise.

Quail growled, "What are you doing up here?"

He shrugged. "I thought it might be a good idea to find out what you were doing."

"Well, you can just crawl back into your hole and . . ."

"No, Quail," I interrupted. It looked as if I was to be the one to keep personal friction to the minimum until our job was done, in spite of how I felt. "Let him stay. He'll find out soon enough. I don't think we can destroy the beacon without his help."

A ripple of concern passed over Willis's face. "Destroy the beacon?"

I nodded. "Yes. We *live* in the rocks. Quail could navigate the Great Circle by instinct alone. But if we can break up the nav-beacon system, the Terran ships won't be able to use their fancy automated nav systems. They will have to shoot the stars, and it's a safe bet that not many will know how to do that. At worst, this operation will slow them down."

Willis thought a moment, then: "That beacon is Terran property. Destroying it would be a felony, with possible civil suits caused by the lack of its services. Have you thought about that?"

Quail exploded. "Of all the ridiculous . . . This is *war*, man!"

"Has there been a declaration of hostilities?" Willis displayed a machinelike calm. His face was undecipherable.

I tried to explain, before his manner drove Quail to blows. "Look, Willis, the Belt has never had a formal government, other than an occasional commission the Terran Assembly has tried to palm off on us. The closest we have are city governments such as Ceres Port. This *is* more a civil uprising than a formal war, but it is no less real. The *Monarch* isn't the only ship out taking action. Almost every ship in the Belt is doing something. When the Terran fleet arrives, the real fighting will start. Nobody will ever consider this a criminal action. Quail is right: This is war."

Willis said nothing, but he frowned as he turned and left. I threw a questioning look at Quail, but he shrugged in puzzlement. Neither of us could make him out. Right then, neither of us cared.

Our problem was to destroy the beacon. Thirty years before, the Terran engineers who had set them up built well. In all, there were better than a score of the monsters scattered through the Belt and in orbits around the nearer planets. Each was four times as massive as our ship and equipped with an impressive automated pressor-beam system to deflect the rocks that happened to wander too close. Inside their computers were supposedly a hundred strategies to handle everything from pebbles to Ceres itself. I had never heard of any of them being damaged in any way. It would have been easier if we had packed a laser with us, but we were a mining/survey ship, not a battlewagon.

Quail griped about that. "Jake Coro should've sent an armed ship, or at least a couple more like us, so we'd have a chance to overload the beacon's defenses. As it is, even if we throw a *bunch* of rocks at it, *our* power will run out before its will."

"You know he would have if he could've spared the ships. Face it, Quail—our job is important, but it is merely an afterthought compared to his job of drumming up enough ships to put together a defense around Ceres that isn't a joke. He wouldn't have sent an armed ship out here for anything."

Quail nodded at my words, but he was right about the problem we faced. No matter what we threw at it, the *eta* beacon could repel it with ease. And with Jupiter so close, it could recharge its power accumulator as easily as we could. There was no doubt that its capacity was greater. But, somehow, we had to find a way . . .

The intercom clicked on. Quail's head swung around as quickly as mine. *Willis? He never calls us first.*

"Mr. Ster? Are there any rocks in the close vicinity?"

I had my screen covered with the geotyping files of every rock that was likely to be near, looking for a good one to throw. "No. Nothing over a kilogram in a hundred kilometers. Why?"

"Well, my mass readings down here show a ship-sized mass hanging just off the beacon. You may have your war sooner than you thought."

I glanced instinctively at the gaping hole in the console where the mass detector had been mounted before we moved it down to the engine room. I wished I had it back. I swiveled back to my screen and punched up radar and visual. Nothing. *If there is a ship there,* I thought, *it is very well hidden.* I didn't want it to be there.

Quail said something vile across the room. I looked at him bending over the radar. He looked at me. "He's right! There's a double doppler. Terrans, just waiting there, watching us."

"They have to be painted black, then; there's nothing on the visual."

"That clinches it." He hit his fist on the console. "It's a warship."

I put the visual on the big center screen. The image showed the bright sunlight reflecting off the beacon, with the tiny disk of Jupiter behind it. Other than a scattering of stars, nothing else showed in the dark. "What do we do now?" The Terrans had planned better than I had given them credit. Anything we could try now had even less chance of success. They could even attack us.

"We've got to do something!" Quail paced, glaring up at the screen. *He* wasn't scared. The sight made me feel better, although I could see no hope.

"But what can we do, Quail? They've got lasers and sucker bombs as sure as anything. They can blast us to vapor in seconds. And you can be sure they'll act if we try anything. They aren't dead out there!"

"I don't know, but we have to do something! If this beacon is protected, then so are the others. This shows the Terrans need the beacons, so that makes it all the more important that we take this one out. The rest of the Belt is counting on us to do our job. We have to do it. I'm not going to have my wife and kids sent back to Earth as prisoners."

Not if I can help it, either, I said to myself. Quail and I had always backed each other up. I was not going to stop then. Breathing in his determination was like pure oxygen.

The intercom clicked. "Mr. Gren, plot a course back the way we came. Hurry, before they come at us."

What? I thought. *No!*

Quail's face darkened. "I will do no such thing, you coward! We've got a job to do and we'll do it if it kills us!"

"Mr. Gren," he said in his naggingly calm voice, "you will do as I say, or I will try to plot the course myself from down here with the mass detector."

I could have strangled him! It was a critical time. It could be disastrous to give up.

Quail yelled, "Over my dead body! We've got to stay and fight!"

"I must remind you I have control down here. Your controls of the engine and the accumulator all route through me. I have secured the latches on my hatch down here. You'd be wasting your time to fight about it. I repeat, plot a reverse course, immediately. That is the only thing that will save us."

I was thinking dark thoughts of the welding rig stowed in the hallway storage bin and what I would do to him. It would be difficult to sneak it down the engine-room connecting tube, but it could be done. I would not have a mutineer on the *Monarch*. No way. She was mine, mine and Quail's.

Quail was yelling abuse at the intercom, but he was weakening. Willis, for a little while, did have control of the ship. I fingered the silent keys on my console, spelling out a message to Quail on the screen.

LET WILLIS MOVE US OUT OF RANGE OF THE TERRAN SHIP, FOR NOW. COOPERATE. WE WON'T BE GOING FAR!

Quail got my meaning. He reluctantly got down to the business of plotting the line toward Jupiter that the pressor beam would follow. It was too risky a maneuver to let Willis plot his own; the mass detector didn't have enough resolution to bull's-eye a planet at that distance. For a change, Willis was on top of everything we did. The course was a simple one, but he questioned everything, down to the exact location of the beacon and the Terran ship. The suspicion was overpowering that he was some kind of Terran spy. I don't know what Quail was thinking. I saw him hesitate. He looked at me and I shook my head. We could easily feed him inaccurate data, but that wouldn't help us. Quail frowned deeply and gave him the last of the data.

I waved his attention to my screen again.

HE MAY HAVE ENGINE CONTROL, BUT WE . . .

Willis's voice on the intercom interrupted, "Are you ready to activate?"

Quail's answer was short and profane. I stepped into the following silence. I had to give him one last chance. "Willis? Why don't you help us? We can do more than run away. I'm sure that I can talk Quail into taking you on as a partner after the war." I frantically had to wave down Quail's anger before he said something to alienate Willis even more. "Come on, Willis. You are a Belt man like us. Help us fight for our rights . . ."

Willis replied in a voice as flat as any machine's: "Mr. Ster, we don't have time for that now. Just tell me if the board is clear, so I can activate the beam."

Quail spat out, "Yes, the board's clear, you traitor!"

"Thank you." His voice clicked off.

I swiveled back to my screen. Quail watched.

BUT WE HAVE CONTROL OF HIS AIR. FADE DOWN HIS OXYGEN AND THEN USE THE WELDER ON HIS HATCH.

Quail nodded. Doing so would be dangerous for Willis, but I was ready for him to take his chances. He was a mutineer at wartime.

A flicker of the indicators caught my eye. Willis had triggered the beam, sending its influence toward Jupiter at the speed of light. In twice the time it took the beam to get there, we would be moving. I glanced at the visual on the screen and noticed the beacon partially eclipsing Jupiter. Our beam had to be passing through it as well, although we were showing no acceleration yet. More of Willis's machinelike control over the beam. I had heard that there were beam controllers who could make their projectors play such tricks.

I got up and watched over Quail's shoulder as he carefully reset the air flow so that Willis would not notice the change until too late. It would take a while for it to act. I nodded my approval, and we sat down to await the beginning of the acceleration. My head was full of thoughts about Willis and the Terran ship and the beacon. I had an inspiration about how to attack the beacon and turned to my files to see how difficult doing so would be. I wanted to arrange a *compressed* bombardment, taking several days and many recharges to set dozens of rocks into high-speed collision courses, timed to arrive almost together, overloading the beacon's defenses. Not even the Terran ship could help in such a hailstorm.

I glanced up at the beam indicators. Then I looked again, because what I saw the first time didn't make any sense. I needed a second to get my mental bearings—suddenly everything looked wrong. Then everything focused. Three indicators were entirely off scale! As I watched, a fourth climbed to its danger point, and then past. I heard blood rushing in my ears. *What is happening?*

"Quail! Look!"

I knew nothing of the workings of the beam projector, but I could read Quail's face. It went from puzzled to dead white!

He spun around and yelled at the intercom: "Willis! What are you doing? That's a high-tension beam! Are you trying to blow us up? Stop it!"

There was no reply. Quail was out of his seat, heading for the welder's storage bin. In seconds, the scorching tide of power Willis had evoked from Jupiter's orbital motion was due to arrive. We would be nothing but vapor. I could only think stupidly that the oxygen shortage couldn't have worked so quickly!

I was too confused to do anything but follow after Quail, although time had run out.

There was a flash of light. I saw my shadow on the wall before me. I turned.

On the big screen was a new sun. The image was saturated white with a growing ball of superheated gas where the beacon had been. I glanced at the radiation meter, just a tiny bit above normal. The explosion hadn't been nuclear. Quail walked to his station and touched a control.

"That was the beacon," he said. "And our beam is gone."

I looked, startled, and the indicators that had scared me senseless were sitting calmly at their neutral positions. *Willis! What did he do?* I turned to the hatchway. There he was, watching the screen with that same undecipherable expression on his face.

He looked at me and asked, "Have you checked on our friend?"

It took me a second to think of what he meant, then I reached for the radar. I found it after a minute, red hot and tumbling sunward. The Terran ship must have been sitting right on top of the beacon when it exploded.

"But how?" I asked.

"It was the beam," Quail answered.

Willis nodded. "I set the inflection voltage as high as the projector would go and kept the beam thin for maximum blacklash. When the beam hit Jupiter, the energy of a head-on collision started back at us. At the last minute, I opened the beam and cut our accumulator out of the circuit. The only convenient place for the energy to go was into the beacon's accumulator."

"And it couldn't take it," I finished.

"It took quite a bit, before it blew." Quail smiled. "That ship won't bother us again." He faced Willis and held out his hand. "I see I was wrong about you. Will you accept my apology?"

Willis backed off, suddenly sullen. "None of you will ever understand." And he walked out the door.

Quail looked hurt and confused. I had to do something. I dashed after him.

"Willis, I want to talk to you!" I stopped him at the head of the tube.

"Can you?" he asked. "At times I thought we talked, but it turned out we were just making noises at each other."

"Willis, we both want to apologize for not understanding you. It was inexcusable for us to think that you would be any less loyal to the Belt than—"

"Oh, stop all this mishmash! Don't bother to apologize. I haven't changed and neither have you. You'll think I'm a traitor again as soon as I say something you don't understand."

"No." I didn't want to lose him now. Not since he had shown what he could do. And what he would do. "We've seen what you did. We understand, now, that just because you talk differently about things, it doesn't mean you are any different in what is inside you."

"No! *I'm not the same as you!*" he screamed at me. I stepped back instinctively; Willis never screamed. But he suddenly blazed: "I *can't* believe the lies you live by!" His voice abruptly dropped to a fatigued whisper. "Oh, how I wish I could." He straightened and looked back at me with demon eyes. "Listen to me, Clement Ster. I'll say this only once. I said *before* that you had no right to fight the Terrans. You condemned me for it. I say it *again! You have no right.*"

"But the beacon—the Terran ship?"

He grabbed my shoulder tight in his huge hand and shook me. "*Listen,* Ster! I had no *right* to destroy them. Neither do the Terrans have the *right* to take over the Belt. *Rights* don't exist! There is only *power* and *action.* Your imaginary rights are only good for keeping people like you and Gren happy and righteous while slaughtering your enemies, if you can call *that* good."

I opened my mouth to reply, but he shook me silent like a misbehaving child. "Understand me, Ster. I murdered the crew of that Terran ship, and I destroyed someone else's beacon worth more than I could make all of my life. I did it because I had the power, and a fair chance of getting away with it. I did it purely for the *selfish* reason that I don't want the Terrans controlling the Belt and running my life! Just the same as you would have—if you had been the one with the power.

"Don't tell me about defending our sacred rights, and wars against the oppressor. As long as there are people, there will be men killing each other for property, for power, whatever. The winner will always have been just defending his rights. The losers are the criminals. It's all *fiction*, Ster! If you have to kill somebody, then kill him. But don't talk nonsense about rights!"

He stopped and I twisted out of his iron grip. He didn't look as if he noticed, away in some place inside his head. I didn't know what to do or say. I wished Quail were with me. I glanced back toward the control room, but there was no sign of him. I was alone.

"Clement," Willis said, in an easy conversational tone, so unlike him, "those men in that ship. They lived all their lives under a government that promised them the right to life. And that government lied, 'cause I just killed them! I wonder how big a slice of their souls their government charged for that politicians' promise. *Rights!* Moral excuses and politicians' lies." He shook his head in amusement, then abruptly looked me directly in the eyes, pinning me in place. "Clement Ster, if you have to lie, steal, destroy, and murder, then *do* it! But then have the strength to take responsibility for what you do. Do you understand?"

I couldn't move. I couldn't talk. He was like an elemental force. His words flared out at me. His eyes searched my face.

Then it was as if he clouded over. I was released. He seemed to be talking to himself, as if I were no longer there. "No. I can see that you don't." He reached for the hatch and started back down to his solitary room. "You will never understand. You will always believe in your rights—your wars—your holy causes. I wish I could." His voice was pained as he whispered, "Oh, how I wish *I* could!"   ✰

Chasing Shadows

Jeffrey M. Wallmann

The imbedder dropped again.

Primate Kinella gripped the rim of his pulpit as reverberations trembled his meager congregation. The imbedder was sinking new pylons in single blows, one every ten minutes four hundred feet above them on the surface of Zenobia. Its drilling force was sufficient to rattle the Saints in the niches and to baptize those in attendance in Plastile dust from the ceiling. Swallowing a blasphemy, Kinella picked up the thread of his service and surged on.

In itself, that was easy. The Fane of Universal Theosophy was rigid with liturgy, petrified by tradition. As Primate of Zenobia, Kinella knew all its forms: the Aspirations, the Predications, the Ordinations. He was halfway through the Invocation, reaffirming that intelligent species are brethren whatever their form and that humanity's mission is to end anarchy and barbarism in the galaxies, when the imbedder dropped again.

Feet stirred uneasily. Hands brushed shoulders of clothing with increased annoyance. Primate Kinella observed the shuffling and raised his voice in defense, but the restlessness continued. He whittled the rest of the service, editing the Invocation as he spoke and quickening the pace of the Function of Seventy-Two Steps with Chorale. The imbedder struck during the Function, unfortunately, and Brooks with his game leg stumbled, almost falling. The Day had become a shambles.

At the latch, Primate Kinella stood murmuring words, braving a beatific smile he was sure looked as hem-stitched as it felt. Nice to see you, Mrs. Pearson; and Mrs. Pearson heaved the prow of her magnificent old bosom and said he had invigorated her, just as she always did. You're looking well, Mr. Asoka, and Mr. Asoka coughed as he said he felt fine. See you next Day, Mr. Verhoeven, and Mr. Verhoeven said yes in a voice like Kinella's smile. Some natures, like the Fane, never varied no matter the time or distance.

His flock scattered along the well-lit corridors connecting the underground human colony of Ville. Alone, Primate Kinella walked slowly back through the empty nave. The air seemed cloying and heavy to him, as if the congregation had forgotten to take their salvations with them. He stepped into the vestry to change his robes, sighing, and the imbedder dropped again.

The balding, corpulent priest wrapped on his tunis and loons, wiping them closed while glowering heavenward with righteousness. Verhoeven would be here next Day, or what passed for Day in the Zenobian rotation of things. That is, he would if he didn't land an overtime spot on the construction project up there instead. That's where most of the congregation had been during services, building the new landing grid instead of praying. And worse, not only had the virile lifeblood of the Fane been seduced by triple wages, but not a solitary native Zebe had been to service. Kinella knew what the Zebes were up to, and it was definitely not construction. That galled him still further. Paganism! And just when he had hoped he'd stamped it all out and converted the natives of this impossible planet.

Hurrying now to miss the next imbedding, Primate Kinella left the Fane and walked down the Ruc de Ganges. He reached the Falls Square by the time he heard the imbedder again, mercifully in the background and not overhead. Then left on Amazonstrasse, with its peculiarly whistling oxygen ducts, heading automatically along a few other tunnels named after Earthly rivers, nodding as he brushed past passersby. Ah, blessed be the Day when the tunnels are widened; they should have been named after Earthly trickles, not great rivers. Yet in a tiny frontier settlement two hundred twenty light-years from Earth, there had to be priorities, which was why the tunnels weren't the size of self-respecting sewers and an imbedder was used instead of a gadget that could melt rock like margarine. And yes, why he had transferred to the Zenobian Fane at Ville in the first place. Evangelicalism was his burden, his right and his sword.

At MOSA—Ministry of Special Affairs—on Niger Terrace, he briskly entered Lieutenant Quince's office, hardly pausing to tap on the latch. The lieutenant was a lean, black-haired man in his thirties, his face exceptionally round and bland looking. Kinella didn't feel the respect toward Quince he might have toward an older man, and moreover, with the government growing more secular, Quince wasn't even ordained the way an older man would have been. Still, the contrast of Quince's features of his cozy manner always reminded Primate Kinella of one of the more inscrutable Asian gods, now Sainted and with its own icon and niche in the Fane, plastic leg raised and fingers outstretched just so.

"Hello, Primate," Lieutenant Quince said from behind his desk. If he was surprised by the sudden entrance, he didn't show it; but then, he never would. "Slip the latch and sit down. I haven't had the pleasure of seeing you in a long time, have I?"

"Perhaps because you haven't been to service recently."

"Well, yes. Very busy, I'm afraid." On turned the smile, unctuous as lard. "But you're not here about just me, are you?"

Primate Kinella clasped his hands behind him, standing rather than sitting, and hoping his countenance was properly stern. "Lieutenant, this new extension on the landing grid. It simply can't be allowed to continue on Days."

"You mean stop work?"

"Precisely."

Quince cocked an eyebrow toward a section map on the wall. "Ah, I think I see. It's being installed directly over the Fane now, isn't it? I wouldn't worry about it if I were you. By this time next week, the work will be all finished there and—"

"Blast the imbedder," Kinella said too quickly. "No, it's not that. It's the nonattendance, and I don't mean just yours."

"Others?"

"The men working on the grid. They're there instead of at Fane, working overtime on Days. That's wrong, Lieutenant."

"Perhaps." The lieutenant folded his hands, leaning on the desk. "But you must realize their absence is a necessity, a sacrifice for the good of our small community. The ships will be coming soon, larger ships with more supplies, and we must be ready."

"Ready with what? Ready with new shops and servibars, open even during Days? Your permitting work is bad enough, but your policy of allowing trade and sales on Days is just too much to accept."

"I'm sorry, Primate, but the rules will have to remain in effect. After all, a ship arrives when it arrives, and you can't expect hundreds of crewmen to have nothing to do for a Day, can you?"

"There is the Fane."

"Yes, there's the Fane." Quince closed his eyes as he rose from the chair, then opened them and was smiling again. "I'm sure we can work out something, Primate. However, you can see I'm a bit backlogged with work today, and if we could discuss this some other time . . . ?"

"You can't throw me out," Kinella wanted to shout. But doing so would have merely resulted in a greater flow from the lieutenant, more syrup to soothe the cantankerous child. Then he would have been swept right through the latch, sticky and silent. He felt himself shivering, and attempted to pull himself together. "Next week, then. But before I go, there's one other matter that can't wait."

"Oh?"

"The Zebes. They're ascending this afternoon."

"They're doing what?"

"As close a word as we can find to describe their mensual rites. Hasn't been performed in years, long before your time. I saw to that, of course, but incredibly, one's being planned for this afternoon. My sources are unimpeachable."

"I'm sure. Is the ceremony dangerous?"

"If you mean do they sacrifice virgins, no. But it *is* a ritual that's part of their heathen superstitions, and it *is* being held on a Day."

"They're hardly meaning it as an insult to the Fane."

"Don't be too positive. The whole thing is being led by Srbija."

"The old . . . ?"

"That's right, ancient even by Zebe standards. Srbija is the last of . . . well, I suppose we'd call them hereditary tribal chieftains, or sorcerers. It would be just like him to stage this comeback."

"Strange way to refer to a bunch of birds."

"They're brethren, Lieutenant. They're intelligent enough to be aware of the inevitability of death, and that means they're capable of being saved for eternal life. I take strong offense to—"

"I'm sorry." Quince looked as if he were, a rarity for him. "This ascending of theirs. They know it's against the Day?"

"They know because I've told them so," Kinella replied stubbornly. "Besides, to hold such a ritual on *any* Day is a slur. Don't tell me you weren't aware of their doings."

"Naturally I had reports of a flight, but I had no idea . . . Primate, what do you propose to do about it?"

"Why, to stop them. They're not that far from the grid. Some of the Guards, even the nearby workers, could move in and disband them."

"Strong measures," Quince said, pursing his lips. "Don't know where it might lead. Settlement policy is not to interfere with the natives, you realize. Disrupts trade with them, and the whole basis for being on Zenobia is to earn as much for Earth as cheaply as possible."

"But this is different! This is serious!"

"For the Fane."

"Yes, for the Fane, and that means everybody."

"Forgive me, Primate, but does it?"

"You question? For how many centuries have the Fane and the government worked concertedly to carry civilization and peace and above all, the knowledge of the Truth, to the uttermost ends of the universe?"

"Noble objectives, not always harmonious." Quince tented his fingers, settling back in his chair again. "I recall in the Text about the rendering of different items. The construction and the shops, they're my problems to deal with and I have as I've felt best. But the Zebes and their superstitions are . . . different."

"Nothing?" Kinella could hear himself choke. "You'll do nothing?"

"The Zebes are peaceful. So little harm a ritual can do, and . . . Tomorrow you'll see that . . . But yet and so forth and slide oneself out of it, words without end . . ."

Primate Kinella left the lieutenant drowning in his own honey. He couldn't stand it, not today, not after the imbedder. He wasn't sure he ever could stand it again. He left with dignity and bearing, but it was difficult to keep from slipping, like false teeth in the mouth of an old man. He left not knowing what to do next, but the Fane was a doer, not a whiner. He had to do something—*anything*—but what?

Stop that sacrilegious ascension, that's what.

Then with the momentum of one victory, he could tackle Quince and his construction and the shops open on Days. Yes, but first the Zebes' ceremony. The lieutenant was right. "Render unto God what is God's . . ."

Primate Kinella hurried to the Falls Square with renewed vigor. Riding up in the Surfashaft, he flexed his muscles, becoming pleased by the turn of events. Complacency had set in, but by heavens, no longer. His joints were being shaken loose of their rust, and his ligaments oiled for battle, his mind sharpening with anticipation. Like the old days, decades past, when he had first arrived with zeal and precious little else; he was a copy of ancient missionaries. He'd show them; he vowed to show them all.

The workmen at ground zero were surprised to see him, and more so when he told them he wished to go outside. He prevailed, as he knew he must. They bundled him in Insuwrap till he resembled a plump Cassock, and strapped on a Scubedu system so he could breathe while in the preponderantly hydrogen atmosphere. Going through the latch-lock, Kinella thought Scubedu was a foolish name. It was connected somehow with the barbarian swimmers of old Earth, of mistily romantic eras when men were Men. A foolish name indeed, but highly commercial. Wasn't everything, he asked himself wearily and set a Sofshu down on Zenobia's stone surface. Wasn't he fighting that along with everything else?

He fought the planet now, trudging across flinty tiers toward the bluff where the Zebes nested. Above was a late, yellowing sun, and the monstrous plum of a close-orbiting moon. Zenobia, being young, hadn't sufficient free oxygen yet to form an ozone layer. The result was a planet hostile to man: too much ultraviolet light, an oppressive eclipsing by the moon, and monstrous tides that swept continents at will. Only the upper reaches of what eventually would become mountain peaks were habitable at all, and on these were perched the rookeries of the Zebes.

The Zebes were young as well, but as a species, fit the requisites of the Fane. They were intelligent, not merely alive, and were capable of technology; these in turn produced a culture, albeit primitive. And as the Fane had learned over the centuries, where there were the disciplines of society, there were its rationalizations by religion. The forceful tides being the greatest impact

upon the Zebes, it was logical that their superstitions
were cyclical in concept. They believed in reincarna-
tion; a Zebe was able to return as long as his descendants revered him. They believed absolute death to be
failure—the failure of reverence, not of body.

Or rather, Kinella thought grimly, they *had* believed
thus. The coming of man had changed their culture, and
it was up to him to keep it changed, even to overriding
the tides themselves. The Zebe perspired his water; his
waste had the consistency of rabbit pellets, and the pellets were important to Earth—being concentrates of
magnesium, bromine, and iodine, plus other metals and
alloys now in scarcity. The Zebe was an incredibly efficient miner of the oceans, and as always, man was an
efficient milker of the product. More commercialism.
Kinella wondered what fancy name had been dreamed
up for the waste of an alien race. Zetonion, or Natro-
zebe, or perhaps Zenobian Wonders Balls. He must be
getting delirious from the oxygen. Better underground
in Ville, where conditions could be controlled. But
where they weren't any longer, not where they were important. . . .

He trekked higher doggedly, through coarse grasses,
over gritty, shifting gravel, and among sharp boulders.
The tank hurt his back, the sound of his breathing a pul-
sation through his mind. Behind him, the port took shape
by perspective: squat ugly buildings of ochre, prickly
with tendrils of electronic equipment; a square-mile net
of steel rods set on pylons to sieve the ships from their
exhausts; a reflecting stalk of a ship that wasn't a ship,
but only the metal column of the imbedder set against
the horizon. Its poundings were brittle in the air, chasing Kinella over the rocks.

He neared the Zebes' rookery, a haphazard complex
of nests chiseled in the sides of cliffs and spires. It all
seemed to converge on a wide, scrubby plateau overlooking the lucent brown ocean, and there too the Primate headed. He could see now that almost every native
old enough to waddle had collected on this, their holy
field. Zebes had thin spearing beaks of fish-eaters, their

torsos longer than man's and streamlined for diving Their skin was leathery, wings formed of webbing with hands at the tips, like bats', each having six tapering fingers. They walked uncomfortably as do most birds, but managed to keep their elongated heads graceful and elegant even so.

The most elegant among them was Srbija. Primate Kinella picked out the withered Zebe immediately, astonished to find that he somehow, someway stood above the others, intense and triumphal. This was the occasion of Srbija's return from ostracism, his day of reckoning over Kinella and man in general. Kinella recalled how some Zebes, particularly the older ones, feared and resented the port's expansion, and it infuriated him to know that Srbija had used this fear to do some encroaching of his own. He sensed intuitively that his presence was felt, even as far away as he was—that indeed, he had been anticipated, the ceremony waiting for him before starting.

A contest. So be it. Kinella lurched forward, filled by the ecstasy of spiritual duty. Yet the ruffle of Zebian wings was oddly disquieting, and their guttural, rudimentary talk seemed antagonistic to him, his own voice a harsh whip of his emotions.

"Stop! Stop, I demand it!"

His words were muffled behind the mask and mostly swallowed.

As if in repudiation, Srbija began his ascent. His membranous wings stroked the air, lifting him. He was a slim climbing dart, his lean bill piercing ahead, the plateau falling behind and beneath. Out across the water, soaring now, calling to his flock. *Arise* . . . His command flowed sonorous from his chest, an inner living song. *Arise* . . . The call spread among the Zebes and echoed off their towers, a single pure note summoning them in line behind him. *Arise* . . .

"Stop!" Primate Kinella charged on, staggering, flailing his arms even as the Zebes beat and throbbed high with answering cries. Kinella halted, panting, realizing the basic futility. He could only watch with craning an-

guish while the air grew dark with swirling Zebes. They
swept the water and spiraled into the wispy sky, blos-
soming on cue into an intricate lattice of symbol and
myth. The once-discarded Srbija circled with blending
currents, slitted eyes kindled momentarily by a spill of
sunlight. Or had it been a reflection from within? Kinella didn't know. Nothing had substance enough for
him to identify, the rite like a dream provoking only the
depths of his subconscious. When it started frightening
him, he shook himself free, growing horns of righteous
indignation. By God, it was time, time right now, to put
an end to—

Ah, but he was here and they were there. He was
impotent, forced to stare, shrunken. And while study-
ing, perversely trying to follow the ancient maze, he saw
a young Zebe break formation and pluck a few seeds
from some floating grass. Srbija weaved impatiently,
continuing with renewed perseverance. Then three more
drifted from the tiresome routine, snapping at a swarm
of insects. Distress cried out from Srbija, softly pleading, intimate and tormented. The ritual faltered, others
splashing the water now in pursuit of fish, dodging still
others' playful attacks. Those remaining attempted
completion, but it was an outward compulsion un-
matched by inner dedication.

The ascent crumbled as swiftly as it had been
formed.

The flock dissipated like ripples; the show was over
and not a very good one at that. It was time to return to
normal activities, which were more fun anyway. Ig-
nored, Srbija glided ashore, body stiff with remaining
pride, angling toward Kinella, who stood rooted,
stunned by the collapse. The Zebe landed, approaching
broken and afumble, throat arched, head downcast,
glazed eyes averted.

After some moments, Srbija said, "It's over." His
Terranian was a turgid rasp. "Reverence has been lost
and cannot return."

"Yes," Kinella murmured, thinking in terms of his
own religion.

"I'm sorry for using your Day, Primate, but I'd hoped . . ."

"Never mind." His anger was gone, but Kinella wasn't sure what, if anything, had replaced it. "It doesn't matter, not really."

"Ah . . ." Srbija lapsed silent, and together they listened to the natives and the evening wind. Then in the distance came the sound of the imbedder falling once again. It had a clear ring to it, like the tolling of a bell. Srbija canted his head in its direction, straining to catch the dim outline.

Gently he asked: "Your God has failed too?"

Metafusion

Charles W. Runyon

The engineer gazed down the long passenger cabin with a total absence of emotion. The port side held a thirty-foot-long gash with metal curling inside; pink stains bordered the gap. The passengers hadn't known what hit them, Max thought with a hint of envy. Just suddenly *whoosh!* sucked into space with unbelievable force. Now they were a cloud of free atoms in the stellar drift. A million years from now they would join with other atoms to become suns, planets, rocks, trees—maybe even people.

You never knew.

The meteorite had ended its savage life in the engine room, breaking into a thousand ricocheting fragments that smashed and melted the instruments into striated globs of glass and metal. I'd be dead, Max reflected, if I hadn't gotten into that debate with Jon and Eda over whether to visit the botanical gardens on Skypt or to blow a month's pay in the narco pads.

A debate which had become moot, as they say.

Max opened the door of the pilot's cabin. Jon turned from the bank of dials and lifted his arching black brows into a still higher arch. The gold rockets on his collar flashed red, reflecting the *blink-blink-blink* of a dozen warning lights. Beside Jon, Eda turned and looked at Max with blankness in her blue eyes.

175

"The rods are fused." Max was laying it down cold like a poker hand. "The engine's building up for a jump. I can't shut it off from back there, and the circuits are out between here and the drive chamber."

Jon nodded silently. His eyes held their usual cool watchfulness, warmed by a hint of humor.

"Can't you rig up a connection?" Eda asked.

"In a few hours I could. But we jump in ten minutes."

"The lifeboat—"

"It was on the port side."

"Our suits—"

"We'd never get clear in time."

Eda drew a deep breath, then sighed. "What will happen?"

"There's no way to cut it off, with the rods fused. The fusion reaction will just eat up the ship. Us with it."

Eda's face turned pale as a marble sculpture. Jon put his hand on her shoulder. "Like a chicken eats a grain of corn." He snapped his fingers. "You won't feel a thing."

For a moment all three were silent, each waiting for one of the others to speak. Then Eda rose and pressed her palms to her stomach, wiping the wrinkles from her metallic-blue skirt. She disappeared into her private alcove, and Max heard the clatter of plastic. He looked in and saw her standing at the counter with her back to him. Her long legs, bared to the hips by her uniform skirt, were as trim as when he had first shipped with her and Jon. He thought of the nights he'd spent with her, and the nights never to be. He felt a hot lump rise in his throat.

"What are you doing?"

"Making coffee," she said.

"Are you that calm?"

"Is there anything we can do to save ourselves?"

"No."

"Then let's have coffee."

He watched her arrange the tray. Two spoons. Cream for Jon. Max's black. Loads of sugar in Eda's. Twenty years. How many cups of coffee had he drunk with these two?

Max sat down opposite Jon as Eda set the tray between them, then drew up a stool for herself. He thought they should be doing something besides drinking coffee. Saying last words or something. Wasn't your whole life supposed to pass in front of you?

He saw Jon watching him with a sardonic half-smile. Max felt a sudden urge to dash his coffee into the captain's handsome face. For twenty years he had envied the tall man's self-assurance, easy wit, calm control. Who gave *him* that, and left me short, stocky, with uneven teeth and an agonizing sense of inadequacy among people? Strange they should die together. The only thing they agreed on was Eda.

Max looked at her, loving the way she held her cup in both hands, hanging her upper lip over the edge. He recalled the touch of her lips, heated by her breath, perfumed by its presence within her body. Tinkle of spoon as she aroused the sugar from the bottom of the cup. Heard it a million times. Never again. *Oh, Eda!*

He found himself listening for the approaching jump, but he knew there would be no warning. He wished he could relax like Jon.

"Why should I feel glad I never had children?" asked Eda.

"You're leaving nothing behind," Jon said.

"She's leaving her parents, her brothers," said Max.

"She left them long ago. Her first jump."

Max thought, Of course it's true. They had spent most of their lives cut off by time and space from the rest of humanity. Passengers were merely seat-sitters whose faces changed from time to time. Maybe that was how they had fallen into this strange three-way marriage—even though he didn't think of Eda as his wife while they were in space. During planetfall, yes, he usually bought her a gift. Sometimes he forgot, and Jon bought her one for both of them. When he had been a young engineer and Jon a young pilot and Eda a young stewardess, the situation had seemed impossible. Max had been about to transfer to another ship, find another girl. But Eda had said there was no need to sacrifice anything except his urge for possession.

"Max, are you sorry you didn't?"

Take another wife. He knew what she meant; he was used to her snaking thoughts out of his head. "No, but if you hadn't known about that planet in the Cabul cluster where group marriages were legal—"

"We'd be dying in sin," said Jon. "All of which matters as much as yesterday's coffee grounds."

Max felt a sudden burst of tenderness for his companions. He wanted to take their hands, but the idea of touching flesh soon to disintegrate—or whatever flesh did when it was consumed by runaway fusion—was repugnant to him. He rose and went to the port to look at the stars. On and on and on, beyond his vision, beyond his understanding. Soon his body would become energy, and so would theirs; together they would flow through endless space . . .

He felt Eda's soft handclasp. "It's happening," she said.

Jon took his other hand, and Max turned to look into the eyes that had always seemed to mock him, but now seemed aglitter with friendly teasing, like that of a father, or an older brother. Eda's eyes were soft; they made him think of his mother's long ago, when she was very young . . .

He felt his body-sense being distorted, pulled apart. He set his teeth to keep from screaming, saw the other two faces being warped beyond recognition into something . . . else.

I-ness was a thread stretching into infinity. It broke, and Max became a word in search of a referent. There was nothing, anywhere. There was no . . . *where.* He felt the essence of Eda, let it merge and blend into the idea of Max. He perceived another ego, rejected it.

Max, you can't keep him out. Don't you understand? It takes three.

No. Coalescing little hub of spirit. *I want you to myself.*

But it can't be that way. He's part of it.

Existence in any form was . . . better? No, preferable to no existence at all. He let the blue idea come closer, touching the red-yellow swirl of himself and Eda. The three merged into a single cloud which spiraled into a pinpoint of white light which exploded into . . .

Maedon.

He was an energy unit composed of 350,000,000,000 orbits which to the materialistic eye could be described as a pulsating radiance. He dissolved himself into a mini-vortex and emerged in the control section of the vessel, which was a tight magnetic field enclosing a clot of latency. The clot was cargo. In the control cabin, a second energy form took on a coloration that signified awareness of his proximity.

"Maedon," vibrated the other. "Sleep well?"

"Fine," Maedon responded, assuming the color variation that implied a mild affirmative acceptance of his friend's tentative hypothesis. "Funny dreams, though. I had this feeling of living in another universe . . ."

"Like what?"

"Like . . . some other plane of existence, where energy is invisible."

Kamafr projected a mild, scornful amusement. "Dreams, little brother. This is all there is." He detached himself from the drive pattern. "Keep a straight course as we go through that vortex ahead. I'll send Fanina in with your breakfast."

Maedon fit himself into the drive pattern, and the sense of blueness which was Kamafr faded. He was the cool one; he had an air of maturity that made him seem . . . not older, for their configurations had emerged simultaneously from the Great Vortex . . . but as if he were the leader.

Maedon could detect shifting hues, crackles of energy, and the white starburst of the vortex ahead. He tried to contact other vessels on their way to other destinations, but they were too far away. Space was so big, and he so small.

Fanina's presence impinged. "Good morning, darling."

Maedon felt his color shift from an irritable, nervous mustard hue to a quiet crimson. He absorbed the artfully arranged tidbits of latent energy she presented, and then, replete, persuaded her to meld with him. Gently she phased her vibrations with his until their orbits meshed. Maedon felt imbued with great strength and purpose, increasing the frequency of his vibration until the radiation from their interlocked structure rose into the infrared. He lost self-awareness for one ecstatic moment, and when it returned, Fanina had separated herself and was pulsating her own lemon-yellow hue.

"I have to go," she said. "Kamafr is waiting."

Maedon pictured the interlocked configurations of Fanina and Kamfr and felt a stab of jealousy. He was about to ask her to stay with him when he noticed that the entire vessel was becoming attenuated along its directional axis. He tried to reduce output, but the giant white vortex was pulling them in, faster and faster . . .

Kamafr appeared, vibrating disgust and anger. "What were you doing, *daydreaming?*"

"Negative. Fanina and I were . . ."

"On duty? You fool! We're going in too fast and we can't maintain configuration. This is the end!"

Fanina came between them; Maedon felt her orbit bisecting his in warm reassurance. Her vibrations were deep and slow.

"There is no end," she said. "Let's meld together."

Maedon felt himself drawn to her. She accepted him, though they had just finished. Then he perceived that the orange glow which was himself and Fanina was merging with the green aura of Kamafr-Fanina. It had never happened like this before. The strain of the all-consuming vortex ahead had elongated Fanina's orbit so that she could absorb them both at the same time. He couldn't tell where she left off or, for that matter, where anyone left off. There was only a red-blue-yellow swirl of energy which was neither Maedon nor Fanina nor Kamafr, but all three at once, whirling and merging with the ship and cargo until it became a blinding whiteness.

Richard took an apple from the picnic basket and bit into it. "I just got an idea, Mary," he said around the foamy fragments. "Why don't we get married?"

She accepted, and out of this union was born a girl-child named Eda.   ☆

Auk House

Clifford D. Simak

David Latimer was lost when he found the house. He had set out for Wyalusing, a town he had only heard of but had never visited, and apparently had taken the wrong road. He had passed through two small villages, Excelsior and Navarre, and if the roadside signs were right, in another few miles he would be coming into Montfort. He hoped that someone in Montfort could set him right again.

The road was a county highway, crooked and narrow and bearing little traffic. It twisted through the rugged headlands that ran down to the coast, flanked by birch and evergreens and rarely out of reach of the muted thunder of surf pounding on giant boulders that lay tumbled on the shore.

The car was climbing a long, steep hill when he first saw the house, between the coast and road. It was a sprawling pile of brick and stone, flaunting massive twin chimneys at either end of it, sited in front of a grove of ancient birch and set so high upon the land that it seemed to float against the sky. He slowed the car, pulled over to the roadside, and stopped to have a better look at it.

A semicircular brick-paved driveway curved up to the entrance of the house. A few huge oak trees grew on

182

the well-kept lawn, and in their shade stood graceful stone benches that had the look of never being used.

There was, it seemed to Latimer, a pleasantly haunted look to the place—a sense of privacy, of olden dignity, a withdrawal from the world. On the front lawn, marring it, desecrating it, stood a large planted sign:

FOR RENT OR SALE
See Campbell's Realty—Half Mile Down the Road

And an arrow pointing to show which way down the road.

Latimer made no move to continue down the road. He sat quietly in the car, looking at the house. The sea, he thought, was just beyond; from a second-story window at the back, one could probably see it.

It had been word of a similar retreat that had sent him seeking out Wyalusing—a place where he could spend a quiet few months at painting. A more modest place, perhaps, than this, although the description he had been given of it had been rather sketchy.

Too expensive, he thought, looking at the house; most likely more than he could afford, although with the last couple of sales he had made, he was momentarily flush. However, it might not be as expensive as he thought, he told himself; a place like this would have small attraction for most people. Too big, but for himself that would make no difference; he could camp out in a couple of rooms for the few months he would be there.

Strange, he reflected, the built-in attraction the house had for him, the instinctive, spontaneous attraction, the instant knowing that this was the sort of place he had had in mind. Not knowing until now that it was the sort of place he had in mind. Old, he told himself—a century, two centuries, more than likely. Built by some now forgotten lumber baron. Not lived in, perhaps, for a number of years. There would be bats and mice.

He put the car in gear and moved slowly out into the

road, glancing back over his shoulder at the house. A half mile down the road, at the edge of what probably was Montfort, although there was no sign to say it was, on the right-hand side, a lopsided, sagging sign on an old, lopsided shack, announced Campbell's Realty. Hardly intending to do it, his mind not made up as yet, he pulled the car off the road and parked in front of the shack.

Inside, a middle-aged man dressed in slacks and turtleneck sat with his feet propped on a littered desk.

"I dropped in," said Latimer, "to inquire about the house down the road. The one with the brick drive."

"Oh, that one," said the man. "Well, I tell you, stranger, I can't show it to you now. I'm waiting for someone who wants to look at the Ferguson place. Tell you what, though. I could give you the key."

"Could you give me some idea of what the rent would be?"

"Why don't you look at it first. See what you think of it. Get the feel of it. See if you'd fit into it. If you like it, we can talk. Hard place to move. Doesn't fit the needs of many people. Too big, for one thing, too old. I could get you a deal on it."

The man took his feet off the desk, plopped them on the floor. Rummaging in a desk drawer, he came up with a key with a tag attached to it and threw it on the desk top.

"Have a look at it and then come back," he said. "This Ferguson business shouldn't take more than an hour or two."

"Thank you," said Latimer, picking up the key.

He parked the car in front of the house and went up the steps. The key worked easily in the lock and the door swung open on well-oiled hinges. He came into a hall that ran from front to back, with a staircase ascending to the second floor and doors opening on either side into ground-floor rooms.

The hall was dim and cool, a place of graciousness. When he moved along the hall, the floorboards did not creak beneath his feet as in a house this old he would have thought they might. There was no shut-up odor, no smell of damp or mildew, no sign of bats or mice.

The door to his right was open, as were all the doors that ran along the hall. He glanced into the room—a large room, with light from the westering sun flooding through the windows that stood on either side of a marble fireplace. Across the hall was a smaller room, with a fireplace in one corner. A library or a study, he thought. The larger room, undoubtedly, had been thought of, when the house was built, as a drawing room. Beyond the larger room, on the right-hand side, he found what might have been a kitchen with a large brick fireplace that had a utilitarian look to it—used, perhaps, in the olden days for cooking, and across from it a much larger room, with another marble fireplace, windows on either side of it and oblong mirrors set into the wall, an ornate chandelier hanging from the ceiling. This, he knew, had to be the dining room, the proper setting for leisurely formal dinners.

He shook his head at what he saw. It was much too grand for him, much larger, much more elegant than he had thought. If someone wanted to live as a place like this should be lived in, it would cost a fortune in furniture alone. He had told himself that during a summer's residence he could camp out in a couple of rooms, but to camp out in a place like this would be sacrilege; the house deserved a better occupant than that.

Yet, it still held its attraction. There was about it a sense of openness, of airiness, of ease. Here a man would not be cramped; he'd have room to move about. It conveyed a feeling of well-being. It was, in essence, not a living place, but a place for living.

The man had said that it had been hard to move, that to most people it had slight appeal—too large, too old—and that he could make an attractive deal on it. But, with a sinking feeling, Latimer knew that what the man had said was true. Despite its attractiveness, it was far too large. It would take too much furniture even for a summer of camping out. And yet, despite all this, the pull—almost a physical pull—toward it still hung on.

He went out the back door of the hall, emerging on a wide veranda that ran the full length of the house. Below him lay the slope of ancient birch, running down a smooth green lawn to the seashore studded by tumbled boulders that flung up white clouds of spume as the racing waves broke against them. Flocks of mewling birds hung above the surging surf like white phantoms, and beyond this, the gray-blue stretch of ocean ran to the far horizon.

This was the place, he knew, that he had hunted for—a place of freedom that would free his brush from the conventions that any painter, at times, felt crowding in upon him. Here lay that remoteness from all other things, a barrier set up against a crowding world. Not objects to paint, but a place in which to put upon his canvases that desperate crying for expression he felt within himself.

He walked down across the long stretch of lawn, among the age-striped birch, and came upon the shore. He found a boulder and sat upon it, feeling the wild exhilaration of wind and water, sky and loneliness.

The sun had set and quiet shadows crept across the land. It was time to go, he told himself, but he kept on sitting, fascinated by the delicate deepening of the dusk, the subtle color changes that came upon the water.

When he finally roused himself and started walking up the lawn, the great birch trees had assumed a ghostliness that glimmered in the twilight. He did not go back into the house, but walked around it to come out on the front. He reached the brick driveway and started walking, remembering that he'd have to go back into the house to lock the back door off the hall.

It was not until he had almost reached the front entrance that he realized his car was gone. Confused, he stopped dead in his tracks. He had parked it there; he was sure he had. Was it possible he had parked it off the road and had walked up the drive, now forgetting that he had?

He turned and started down the driveway, his shoes clicking on the bricks. No, dammit, he told himself, I did drive up the driveway—I remember doing it. He looked back and there wasn't any car, either in front of the house or along the curve of driveway. He broke into a run, racing down the driveway toward the road. Some kids had come along and pushed it to the road—that must be the answer. A juvenile prank, the pranksters hiding somewhere, tittering to themselves as they watched him run to find it. Although that was wrong, he thought—he had left it set on "Park" and locked. Unless they broke a window, there was no way they could have pushed it.

The brick driveway came to an end and there wasn't any road. The lawn and driveway came down to where they ended, and at that point a forest rose up to block the way. A wild and tangled forest that was very dark and dense, great trees standing up where the road had been. To his nostrils came the damp scent of forest mold, and somewhere in the darkness of the trees, an owl began to hoot.

He swung around, to face back toward the house, and saw the lighted windows. It couldn't be, he told himself quite reasonably. There was no one in the house, no one to turn on the lights. In all likelihood, the electricity was shut off.

But the lighted windows persisted. There could be no question there were lights. Behind him, he could hear the strange rustlings of the trees and now there were two owls, answering one another.

Reluctantly, unbelievingly, he started up the driveway. There must be some sort of explanation. Perhaps, once he had the explanation, it would all seem quite simple. He might have gotten turned around somehow, as he had somehow gotten turned around earlier in the day, taking the wrong road. He might have suffered a lapse of memory, for some unknown and frightening reason have experienced a blackout. This might not be the house he had gone to look at, although, he insisted to himself, it certainly looked the same.

He came up the brick driveway and mounted the steps that ran up to the door, and while he was still on the steps, the door came open and a man in livery stepped aside to let him in.

"You are a little late, sir," said the man. "We had expected you some time ago. The others waited for you, but just now went in to dinner, thinking you had been unavoidably detained. Your place is waiting for you."

Latimer hesitated.

"It is quite all right, sir," said the man. "Except on special occasions, we do not dress for dinner. You're all right as you are."

The hall was lit by short candles set in sconces on the wall. Paintings also hung there, and small sofas and a few chairs were lined along the wall. From the dining room came the sound of conversation.

The butler closed the door and started down the hall. "If you would follow me, sir."

It was all insane, of course. It could not be happening. It was something he imagined. He was standing out there, on the bricks of the driveway, with the forest and the hooting owls behind him, imagining that he was here, in this dimly lighted hallway with the talk and laughter coming from the dining room.

"Sir," said the butler, "if you please."

"But, I don't understand. This place, an hour ago . . ."

"The others are all waiting for you. They have been looking forward to you. You must not keep them waiting."

"All right, then," said Latimer. "I shall not keep them waiting."

At the entrance to the dining room, the butler stood aside so that he could enter.

The others were seated at a long, elegantly appointed table. The chandelier blazed with burning tapers. Uniformed serving maids stood against one wall. A sideboard gleamed with china and cut glass. There were bouquets of flowers upon the table.

A man dressed in a green sports shirt and a corduroy jacket rose from the table and motioned to him.

"Latimer, over here," he said. "You are Latimer, are you not?"

"Yes, I'm Latimer."

"Your place is over here, between Enid and myself. We'll not bother with introductions now. We can do that later on."

Scarcely feeling his feet making contact with the floor, moving in a mental haze, Latimer went down the table. The man who stood had remained standing, thrusting out a beefy hand. Latimer took it and the other's handshake was warm and solid.

"I'm Underwood," he said. "Here, sit down. Don't stand on formality. We've just started on the soup. If yours is cold, we can have another brought to you."

"Thank you," said Latimer. "I'm sure it's all right."

On the other side of him, Enid said, "We waited for you. We knew that you were coming, but you took so long."

"Some," said Underwood, "take longer than others. It's just the way it goes."

"But I don't understand," said Latimer. "I don't know what's going on."

"You will," said Underwood. "There's really nothing to it."

"Eat your soup," Enid urged. "It is really good. We get such splendid chowder here."

She was small and dark of hair and eyes, a strange intensity in her.

Latimer lifted the spoon and dipped it in the soup. Enid was right; it was a splendid chowder.

The man across the table said, "I'm Charlie. We'll talk later on. We'll answer any questions."

The woman sitting beside Charlie said, "You see, we don't understand it, either. But it's all right. I'm Alice."

The maids were removing some of the soup bowls and bringing on the salads. On the sideboard the china and cut glass sparkled in the candlelight. The flowers on the table were peonies. There were, with himself, eight people seated at the table.

"You see," said Latimer, "I only came to look at the house."

"That's the way," said Underwood, "that it happened to the rest of us. Not just recently. Years apart. Although I don't know how many years. Jonathon, down there at the table's end, that old fellow with a beard, was the first of us. The others straggled in."

"The house," said Enid, "is a trap, very neatly baited. We are mice caught in a trap."

From across the table, Alice said, "She makes it sound so dreadful. It's not that way at all. We are taken care of meticulously. There is a staff that cooks our food and serves it, that makes our beds, that keeps all clean and neat . . ."

"But who would want to trap us?"

"That," said Underwood, "is the question we all try to solve—except for one or two of us, who have become resigned. But, although there are several theories, there is no solution. I sometimes ask myself what difference it makes. Would we feel any better if we knew our trappers?"

A trap neatly baited, Latimer thought, and indeed it had been. There had been that instantaneous, instinctive attraction that the house had held for him—even only driving past it, the attraction had reached out for him.

The salad was excellent, and so were the steak and baked potato. The rice pudding was the best Latimer had ever eaten. In spite of himself, he found that he was enjoying the meal, the bright and witty chatter that flowed all around the table.

In the drawing room, once dinner was done, they sat in front of a fire in the great marble fireplace.

"Even in the summer," said Enid, "when night comes on, it gets chilly here. I'm glad it does, because I love a fire. We have a fire almost every night."

"We?" said Latimer. "You speak as if you were a tribe."

"A band," she said. "A gang, perhaps. Fellow conspirators, although there's no conspiracy. We get along together. That's one thing that is so nice about it. We get along so well."

The man with the beard came over to Latimer. "My name is Jonathon," he said. "We were too far apart at dinner to become acquainted."

"I am told," said Latimer, "that you are the one who has been here the longest."

"I am now," said Jonathon. "Up until a couple of years ago, it was Peter. Old Pete, we used to call him."

"Used to?"

"He died," said Enid. "That's how come there was room for you. There is only so much room in this house, you see."

"You mean it took two years to find someone to replace him?"

"I have a feeling," said Jonathon, "that we belong to a select company. I would think that you might have to possess rather rigid qualifications before you were considered."

"That's what puzzles me," said Latimer. "There must be some common factor in the group. The kind of work we're in, perhaps."

"I am sure of it," said Jonathon. "You are a painter, are you not?"

Latimer nodded. "Enid is a poet," said Jonathon, "and a very good one. I aspire to philosophy, although I'm not too good at it. Dorothy is a novelist and Alice a musician—a pianist. Not only does she play, but she can compose as well. You haven't met Dorothy or Jane as yet."

"No. I think I know who they are, but I haven't met them."

"You will," said Enid, "before the evening's over. Our group is so small we get to know one another well."

"Could I get a drink for you?" asked Jonathon.

"I would appreciate it. Could it be Scotch, by any chance?"

"It could be," said Jonathon, "anything you want. Ice or water?"

"Ice, if you would. But I feel I am imposing."

"No one imposes here," said Jonathon. "We take care of one another."

"And, if you don't mind," said Enid, "one for me as well. You know what I want."

As Jonathon walked away to get the drinks, Latimer said to Enid, "I must say that you've all been kind to me. You took me in, a stranger . . ."

"Oh, not a stranger, really. You'll never be a stranger. Don't you understand? You are one of us. There was an empty place and you've filled it. And you'll be here forever. You'll never go away."

"You mean that no one ever leaves?"

"We try. All of us have tried. More than once for some of us. But we've never made it. Where is there to go?"

"Surely there must be someplace else. Some way to get back."

"You don't understand," she said. "There is no place but here. All the rest is wilderness. You could get lost if you weren't careful. There have been times when we've had to go out and hunt down the lost ones."

Underwood came across the room and sat down on the sofa on the other side of Enid.

"How are you two getting on?" he asked.

"Very well," said Enid. "I was just telling David there's no way to get away from here."

"That is fine," said Underwood, "but it will make no difference. There'll come a day he'll try."

"I suppose he will," said Enid, "but if he understands beforehand, it will be easier."

"The thing that rankles me," said Latimer, "is why. You said at the dinner table everyone tries for a solution, but no one ever finds one."

"Not exactly that," said Underwood. "I said there are some theories. But the point is that there is no way for us to know which one of them is right. We may have already guessed the reason for it all, but the chances are we'll never know. Enid has the most romantic notion. She thinks we are being held by some super-race from some far point in the galaxy who want to study us. We are specimens, you understand. They cage us in what amounts to a laboratory, but do not intrude upon us. They want to observe us under natural conditions and see what makes us tick. And under these conditions, she thinks we should act as civilized as we can manage."

"I don't know if I really think that," said Enid, "but it's a nice idea. It's no crazier than some of the other explanations. Some of us have theorized that we are being given a chance to do the best work we can. Someone is taking all economic pressure off us, placing us in a pleasant environment, and giving us all the time we need to develop whatever talents we may have. We're being subsidized."

"But what good would that do?" asked Latimer. "I gather we are out of touch with the world we knew. No matter what we did, who is there to know?"

"Not necessarily," said Underwood. "Things disappear. One of Alice's compositions and one of Dorothy's novels and a few of Enid's poems."

"You think someone is reaching in and taking them? Being quite selective?"

"It's just a thought," said Underwood. "Some of the things we create do disappear. We hunt for them and we never find them."

Jonathon came back with the drinks. "We'll have to settle down now," he said, "and quit all this chatter. Alice is about to play. Chopin, I believe she said."

It was late when Latimer was shown to his room by Underwood, up on the third floor. "We shifted around a bit to give this one to you," said Underwood. "It's the only one that has a skylight. You haven't got a straight ceiling—it's broken by the roofline—but I think you'll find it comfortable."

"You knew that I was coming, then, apparently some time before I arrived."

"Oh, yes, several days ago. Rumors from the staff; the staff seems to know everything. But not until late yesterday did we definitely know when you would arrive."

After Underwood said good night, Latimer stood for

a time in the center of the room. There was a skylight, as Underwood had said, positioned to supply a north light. Standing underneath it was an easel, and stacked against the wall were blank canvases. There would be paint and brushes, he knew, and everything else that he might need. Whoever or whatever had sucked him into this place would do everything up brown; nothing would be overlooked.

It was unthinkable, he told himself, that it could have happened. Standing now, in the center of the room, he still could not believe it. He tried to work out the sequence of events that had led him to this house, the steps by which he had been lured into the trap, if trap it was—and on the face of the evidence, it had to be a trap. There had been the realtor in Boston who had told him of the house in Wyalusing. "It's the kind of place you are looking for," he had said. "No near neighbors, isolated. The little village a couple of miles down the road. If you need a woman to come in a couple of times a week to keep the place in order, just ask in the village. There's bound to be someone you could hire. The place is surrounded by old fields that haven't been farmed in years and are going back to brush and thickets. The coast is only half a mile distant. If you like to do some shooting, come fall there'll be quail and grouse. Fishing, too, if you want to do it."

"I might drive up and have a look at it," he had told the agent, who had then proceeded to give him the wrong directions, putting him on the road that would take him past this place. Or had he? Had it, perhaps, been his own muddleheadedness that had put him on the wrong road? Thinking about it, Latimer could not be absolutely certain. The agent had given him directions, but had they been the wrong directions? In the present situation, he knew that he had the tendency to view all prior circumstances with suspicion. Yet, certainly, there had been some psychological pressure brought, some misdirection employed to bring him to this house. It could not have been simple happenstance that had brought him here, to a house that trapped practitioners of the arts. A poet, a musician, a novelist, and a philosopher—although, come to think of it, a philosopher did not seem to exactly fit the pattern. Maybe the pattern was more apparent, he told himself, than it actually was. He still did not know the professions of Underwood, Charlie, and Jane. Maybe, once he did know, the pattern would be broken.

A bed stood in one corner of the room, a bedside table and a lamp beside it. In another corner three comfortable chairs were grouped, and along a short section of the wall stood shelves that were filled with books. On the wall beside the shelves hung a painting. It was only after staring at it for several minutes that he recognized it. It was one of his own, done several years ago.

He moved across the carpeted floor to confront the painting. It was one of those to which he had taken a special liking—one that, in fact, he had been somewhat reluctant to let go, would not have sold it if he had not stood so much in need of money.

The subject sat on the back stoop of a tumbledown house. Beside him, where he had dropped it, was a newspaper folded to the "Help Wanted" ads. From the breast pocket of his painfully clean, but worn, work shirt an envelope stuck out, the gray envelope in which welfare checks were issued. The man's work-scarred hands lay listlessly in his lap, the forearms resting on the thighs, which were clad in ragged denims. He had not shaved for several days and the graying whiskers lent a deathly gray cast to his face. His hair, in need of barbering, was a tangled rat's nest, and his eyes, deep-set beneath heavy, scraggly brows, held a sense of helplessness. A scrawny cat sat at one corner of the house, a broken bicycle leaned against the basement wall. The man was looking out over a backyard filled with various kinds of litter, and beyond it the open countryside, a dingy gray and brown, seared by drought and lack of care, while on the horizon was the hint of industrial chimneys, gaunt and stark, with faint wisps of smoke trailing from them.

The painting was framed in heavy gilt—not the best

choice, he thought, for such a piece. The bronze title tag was there, but he did not bend to look at it. He knew what it would say:

UNEMPLOYED
David Lloyd Latimer

How long ago? he wondered. Five years, or was it six? A man by the name of Johnny Brown, he remembered, had been the model. Johnny was a good man and he had used him several times. Later on, when he had tried to find him, he had been unable to locate him. He had not been seen for months in his old haunts along the waterfront and no one seemed to know where he had gone.

Five years ago, six years ago—sold to put bread into his belly, although that was silly, for when did he ever paint other than for bread? And here it was. He tried to recall the purchaser, but was unable to.

There was a closet, and when he opened it, he found a row of brand-new clothes, boots and shoes lined up on the floor, hats ranged neatly on the shelf. And all of them would fit—he was sure they would. The setters and the baiters of this trap would have seen to that. In the highboy next to the bed would be underwear, shirts, socks, sweaters—the kind that he would buy.

"We are taken care of," Enid had told him, sitting on the sofa with him before the flaring fire. There could be, he told himself, no doubt of that. No harm was intended them. They, in fact, were coddled.

And the question: Why? Why a few hand-picked people selected from many millions?

He walked to a window and stood looking out of it. The room was in the back of the house so that he looked down across the grove of ghostly birch. The moon had risen and hung like a milk-glass globe above the dark blur of the ocean. High as he stood, he could see the whiteness of the spray breaking on the boulders.

He had to have time to think, he told himself, time to sort it out, to get straight in his mind all the things that had happened in the last few hours. There was no sense in going to bed; tense as he was, he'd never get to sleep. He could not think in this room, nor, perhaps, in the house. He had to go some place that was uncluttered. Perhaps if he went outside and walked for an hour or so, if no more than up and down the driveway, he could get himself straightened out.

The blaze in the fireplace in the drawing room was little more than a glimmer in the coals when he went past the door.

A voice called to him: "David, is that you?"

He spun around and went back to the door. A dark figure was huddled on the sofa in front of the fireplace.

"Jonathon?" Latimer asked.

"Yes, it is. Why don't you keep me company. I'm an old night owl and, in consequence, spend many lonely hours. There's coffee on the table if you want it."

Latimer walked to the sofa and sat down. Cups and a carafe of coffee were on the table. He poured himself a cup.

"You want a refill?" he asked Jonathon.

"If you please." The older man held out his cup and Latimer filled it. "I drink a sinful amount of this stuff," said Jonathon. "There's liquor in the cabinet. A dash of brandy in the coffee, perhaps."

"That sounds fine," said Latimer. He crossed the room and found the brandy, brought it back, pouring a dollop into both cups.

They settled down and looked at one another. A nearly burned log in the fireplace collapsed into a mound of coals. In the flare of its collapse, Latimer saw the face of the other man—beard beginning to turn gray, an angular yet refined face, eyebrows that were sharp exclamation points.

"You're a confused young man," said Jonathon.

"Extremely so," Latimer confessed. "I keep asking all the time why and who."

Jonathon nodded. "Most of us still do, I suppose. It's worst when you first come here, but you never quit. You keep on asking questions. You're frustrated and depressed when there are no answers. As time goes on, you come more and more to accept the situation and do less fretting about it. After all, life is pleasant here. All our needs are supplied, nothing is expected of us. We do much as we please. You, no doubt, have heard of Enid's theory that we are under observation by an alien race that has penned us here in order to study us."

"Enid told me," said Latimer, "that she did not necessarily believe the theory, but regarded it as a nice idea, a neat and dramatic explanation of what is going on."

"It is that, of course," said Jonathon, "but it doesn't stand up. How would aliens be able to employ the staff that takes such good care of us?"

"The staff worries me," said Latimer. "Are its members trapped here along with us?"

"No, they're not trapped," said Jonathon. "I'm certain they are employed, perhaps at very handsome salaries. The staff changes from time to time, one member leaving to be replaced by someone else. How this is accomplished we do not know. We've kept a sharp watch in the hope that we might learn and thus obtain a clue as to how we could get out of here, but it all comes to nothing. We try on occasions, not too obviously, to talk with the staff, but beyond normal civility, they will not talk with us. I have a sneaking suspicion, too, that there are some of us, perhaps including myself, who no longer try too hard. Once one has been here long enough to make peace with himself, the ease of our life grows upon us. It would be something we would be reluctant to part with. I can't imagine, personally, what I would do if I were turned out of here, back into the world that I have virtually forgotten. That is the vicious part of it—that our captivity is so attractive, we are inclined to fall in love with it."

"But certainly in some cases there were people left behind—wives, husbands, children, friends. In my own case, no wife and only a few friends."

"Strangely enough," said Jonathon, "where such ties existed, they were not too strong."

"You mean only people without strong ties were picked?"

"No, I doubt that would have been the case. Perhaps among the kind of people who are here, there is no tendency to develop such strong ties."

"Tell me what kind of people. You told me you are a philosopher and I know some of the others. What about Underwood?"

"A playwright. And a rather successful one before he came here."

"Charlie? Jane?"

"Charlie is a cartoonist, Jane an essayist."

"Essayist?"

"Yes, high social consciousness. She wrote rather telling articles for some of the so-called little magazines, even a few for more prestigious publications. Charlie was big in the Middle West. Worked for a small daily, but his cartoons were widely reprinted. He was building a reputation and probably would have been moving on to more important fields."

"Then we're not all from around here. Not all from New England."

"No. Some of us, of course. Myself and you. The others are from other parts of the country."

"All of us from what can be roughly called the arts. And from a wide area. How in the world would they— whoever they may be—have managed to lure all these people to this house? Because I gather we had to come ourselves, that none of us was seized and brought here."

"I think you are right. I can't imagine how it was managed. Psychological management of some sort, I would assume, but I have no idea how it might be done."

"You say you are a philosopher. Does that mean you taught philosophy?"

"I did at one time. But it was not a satisfactory job. Teaching those old dead philosophies to a group of youngsters who paid but slight attention was no bargain, I can tell you. Although, I shouldn't blame them, I suppose. Philosophy today is largely dead. It's primitive, outdated, the most of it. What we need is a new philosophy that will enable us to cope with the present world."

"And you are writing such a philosophy?"

"Writing at it. I find that as time goes on, I get less and less done. I haven't the drive any longer. This life of ease, I suppose. Something's gone out of me. The anger, maybe. Maybe the loss of contact with the world I knew. No longer exposed to that world's conditions, I have lost the feel for it. I don't feel the need of protest, I've lost my sense of outrage, and the need for a new philosophy has become remote."

"This business about the staff. You say that from time to time it changes."

"It may be fairly simple to explain. I told you that we watch, but we can't have a watcher posted all the time. The staff, on the other hand, can keep track of us. Old staff members leave, others come in when we are somewhere else."

"And supplies. They have to bring in supplies. That would not be as simple."

Jonathon chuckled. "You've really got your teeth in this."

"I'm interested, dammit. There are questions about how the operation works and I want to know. How about the basement? Tunnels, maybe. Could they bring in staff and supplies through tunnels in the basement? I know that sounds cloak-and-dagger, but . . ."

"I suppose they could. If they did, we'd never know. The basement is used to store supplies and we're not welcome there. One of the staff, a burly brute who is a deaf-mute, or pretends to be, has charge of the basement. He lives down there, eats and sleeps down there, takes care of supplies."

"It could be possible, then."

"Yes," said Jonathon. "It could be possible."

The fire had died down; only a few coals still blinked in the ash. In the silence that came upon them, Latimer heard the wind in the trees outside.

"One thing you don't know," said Jonathon. "You will find great auks down on the beach."

"Great auks? That's impossible. They've been . . ."

"Yes, I know. Extinct for more than a hundred years. Also whales. Sometimes you can sight a dozen a day. Occasionally a polar bear."

"Then that must mean . . ."

Jonathon nodded. "We are somewhere in prehistoric North America. I would guess several thousand years into the past. We hear and, occasionally, see moose. There are a number of deer, once in a while woodland caribou. The bird life, especially the wildfowl, are here in incredible numbers. Good shooting if you ever have the urge. We have guns and ammunition."

Dawn was beginning to break when Latimer went back to his room. He was bone-tired and now he could sleep. But before going to bed he stood for a time in front of the window overlooking the birch grove and the shore. A thin fog had moved off the water and everything had a faery, unrealistic cast.

Prehistoric North America, the philosopher had said, and if that was the case, there was little possibility of escape back to the world he knew. Unless one had the secret—or the technology—one did not move in time. Who, he wondered, could have cracked the technique of time transferral? And who, having cracked it, would use it for the ridiculous purpose of caging people in it?

There had been a man at M.I.T., he recalled, who had spent twenty years or more in an attempt to define time and gain some understanding of it. But that had been some years ago and he had dropped out of sight, or at least out of the news. From time to time there had been news stories (written for the most part with tongue firmly in cheek) about the study. Although, Latimer told himself, it need not have been the M.I.T. man; there might have been other people engaged in similar studies who had escaped, quite happily, the attention of the press.

Thinking of it, he felt an excitement rising in him at the prospect of being in primitive North America, of being able to see the land as it had existed before white explorers had come—before the Norsemen or the Cabots or Cartier or any of the others. Although there must be Indians about—it was funny that Jonathon had not mentioned Indians.

Without realizing that he had been doing so, he found that he had been staring at a certain birch clump. Two of the birch trees grew opposite one another, slightly behind but on opposite sides of a large boulder that he estimated at standing five feet high or so. And beyond the boulder, positioned slightly down the slope, but between the other two birch trees, was a third. It was not an unusual situation, he knew; birch trees often grew in clumps of three. There must have been some feature of the clump that had riveted his attention on it, but if that had been the case, he no longer was aware of it and it was not apparent now. Nevertheless, he remained staring at it, puzzled at what he had seen, if he had seen anything at all.

As he watched, a bird flew down from somewhere to light on the boulder. A songbird, but too far away for identification. Idly he watched the bird until it flew off the rock and disappeared.

Without bothering to undress, simply kicking off his shoes, he crossed the room to the bed and fell upon it, asleep almost before he came to rest upon it.

It was almost noon before he woke. He washed his face and combed his hair, not bothering to shave, and went stumbling down the stairs, still groggy from the befuddlement of having slept so soundly. No one else was in the house, but in the dining room a place was set and covered dishes remained upon the sideboard. He chose kidneys and scrambled eggs, poured a cup of coffee, and went back to the table. The smell of food triggered hunger, and after gobbling the plate of food, he went back for seconds and another cup of coffee.

When he went out through the rear door, there was no one in sight. The slope of birch stretched toward the coast. Off to his left, he heard two reports that sounded like shotguns. Perhaps someone out shooting duck or quail. Jonathon had said there was good hunting here.

He had to wend his way carefully through a confused

tangle of boulders to reach the shore, with pebbles grating underneath his feet. A hundred yards away the inrolling breakers shattered themselves upon randomly scattered rocks, and even where he stood he felt the thin mist of spray upon his face.

Among the pebbles he saw a faint gleam and bent to see what it was. Closer to it, he saw that it was an agate—tennis-ball size, its fractured edge, wet with spray, giving off a waxy, translucent glint. He picked it up and polished it, rubbing off the clinging bits of sand, remembering how as a boy he had hunted agates in abandoned gravel pits. Just beyond the one he had picked up lay another one, and a bit to one side of it, a third. Crouched, he hunched forward and picked up both of them. One was bigger than the first, the second slightly smaller. Crouched there, he looked at them, admiring the texture of them, feeling once again, after many years, the thrill he had felt as a boy at finding agates. When he had left home to go to college, he remembered, there had been a bag full of them still cached away in one corner of the garage. He wondered what might have become of them.

A few yards down the beach, something waddled out from behind a cluster of boulders, heading for the water. A bird, it stood some thirty inches tall and had a fleeting resemblance to a penguin. The upper plumage was black, white below, a large white spot encircled its eye. Its small wings shifted as it waddled. The bill was sharp and heavy, a vicious striking weapon.

He was looking at, he knew, a great auk, a bird that up in his world had been extinct but which, a few centuries before, had been common from Cape Cod to far north in Canada. Cartier's seamen, ravenous for fresh meat as a relief from sea rations, had clubbed hundreds to death, eating some of them at once, putting what remained down in kegs with salt.

Behind the first great auk came another and then two more. Paying no attention to him, they waddled down across the pebbles to the water, into which they dived, swimming away.

Latimer remained in his crouch, staring at the birds in fascination. Jonathon had said he would find them on the beach, but knowing he would find them and actually seeing them, were two different things. Now he was convinced, as he had not been before, of exactly where he was.

Off to his left, the guns banged occasionally, but otherwise there were no signs of the others in the house. Far out across the water, a string of ducks went scudding close above the waves. The pebbled beach held a sense of peace—the kind of peace, he thought, that men might have known long years ago when the earth was still largely empty of humankind, when there was still room for such peace to settle in and stay.

Squatting there upon the beach, he remembered the clump of birch and now, suddenly and without thinking of it, he knew what had attracted his attention to it—an aberration of perspective that his painter's eye had caught. Knitting his brow, he tried to remember exactly what it was that had made the perspective wrong, but whatever it had been quite escaped him now.

He glimpsed another agate and went to pick it up, and a little farther down the beach he found yet another one. This, he told himself, was an unworked, unpicked rock-hunter's paradise. He put the agates in his pocket and continued down the beach. Spotting other agates, he did not pick them up. Later, at some other time, if need be, he could find hours of amusement hunting them.

When he climbed the beach and started up the slope, he saw that Jonathon was sitting in a chair on the veranda that ran across the back of the house. He climbed up to where he sat and settled down in another chair.

"Did you see an auk?" asked Jonathon.

"I saw four of them," said Latimer.

"There are times," said Jonathon, "that the beach is crowded with them. Other times, you won't see one for days. Underwood and Charlie are off hunting woodcock. I suppose you heard them shooting. If they get back in time, we'll have woodcock for dinner. Have you ever eaten woodcock?"

"Only once. Some years ago. A friend and I went up to Nova Scotia to catch the early flight."

"I guess that is right. Nova Scotia and a few other places now. Here I imagine you can find hunting of them wherever you can find alder swamps."

"Where was everyone?" asked Latimer. "When I got out of the sack and had something to eat, there was no one around."

"The girls went out blackberrying," said Jonathon. "They do that often. Gives them something to do. It's getting a little late for blackberries, but there are some around. They got back in time to have blackberry pie tonight." He smacked his lips. "Woodcock and blackberry pie. I hope you are hungry."

"Don't you ever think of anything but eating?"

"Lots of other things," said Jonathon. "Thing is, here you grab onto anything you can to think about. It keeps you occupied. And I might ask you, are you feeling easier than you were last night? Got all the immediate questions answered?"

"One thing still bothers me," said Latimer. "I left my car parked outside the house. Someone is going to find it parked there and will wonder what has happened."

"I think that's something you don't need to worry over," said Jonathon. "Whoever is engineering this business would have seen to it. I don't know, mind you, but I would guess that before morning your car was out of there and will be found, abandoned, some other place, perhaps a hundred miles away. The people we are dealing with would automatically take care of such small details. It wouldn't do to have too many incidents clustered about this house or in any other place. Your car will be found and you'll be missing and a hunt will be made for you. When you aren't found, you'll become just another one of the dozens of people who turn up missing every year."

"Which leaves me to wonder," said Latimer, "how many of these missing people wind up in places such as this. It is probable this is not the only place where some of them are being trapped."

"There is no way to know," said Jonathon. "People drop out for very many reasons."

They sat silent for a time, looking out across the sweep of lawn. A squirrel went scampering down the slope. Far off, birds were calling. The distant surf was a hollow booming.

Finally, Latimer spoke. "Last night, you told me we needed a new philosophy, that the old ones were no longer valid."

"That I did," said Jonathon. "We are faced today with a managed society. We live by restrictive rules, we have been reduced to numbers—our Social Security numbers, our Internal Revenue Service numbers, the numbers on our credit cards, on our checking and savings accounts, on any number of other things. We are being dehumanized and, in most cases, willingly, because this numbers game may seem to make life easier, but most often because no one wants to bother to make a fuss about it. We have come to believe that a man who makes a fuss is antisocial. We are a flock of senseless chickens, fluttering and scurrying, cackling and squawking, but being shooed along in the way that others want us to go. The advertising agencies tell us what to buy, the public relations people tell us what to think, and even knowing this, we do not resent it. We sometimes damn the government when we work up the courage to damn anyone at all. But I am certain it is not the government we should be damning, but, rather, the world's business managers. We have seen the rise of multinational complexes that owe no loyalty to any government, that think and plan in global terms, that view the human populations as a joint labor corps–consumer group, some of which also may have investment potential. This is a threat, as I see it, against human free will and human dignity, and we need a philosophical approach that will enable us to deal with it."

"And if you should write this philosophy," said Latimer, "it would pose a potential threat against the managers."

"Not at first," said Jonathon. "Perhaps never. But it might have some influence over the years. It might start a trend of thinking. To break the grip the managers now hold would require something like a social revolution . . ."

"These men, these managers you are talking about— they would be cautious men, would they not, farseeing men? They would take no chances. They'd have too much at stake to take any chance at all."

"You aren't saying . . ."

"Yes, I think I am. It is, at least, a thought."

Jonathon said, "I have thought of it myself but rejected it because I couldn't trust myself. It follows my bias too closely. And it doesn't make sense. If there were people they wanted to get out of the way, there'd be other ways to do it."

"Not as safely," said Latimer. "Here there is no way we could be found. Dead, we would be found . . ."

"I wasn't thinking of killing."

"Oh, well," said Latimer, "it was only a thought. Another guess."

"There's one theory no one has told you, or I don't think they have. An experiment in sociology. Putting various groups of people together in unusual situations and measuring their reactions. Isolating them so there is no present-world influence to modify the impact of the situation."

Latimer shook his head. "It sounds like a lot of trouble and expense. More than the experiment would be worth."

"I think so, too," said Jonathon.

He rose from his chair. "I wonder if you'd excuse me. I have the habit of stretching out for an hour or so before dinner. Sometimes I doze, other times I sleep, often I just lie there. But it is relaxing."

"Go ahead," said Latimer. "We'll have plenty of time later on to talk."

For half an hour or more after Jonathon had left, he

remained sitting in the chair, staring down across the lawn, but scarcely seeing it.

That idea about the managers being responsible for the situation, he told himself, made a ragged sort of sense. Managers, he thought with a smile—how easy it is to pick up someone else's lingo.

For one thing, the idea, if it worked, would be foolproof. Pick up the people you wanted out of the way and pop them into time, and after you popped them into time still keep track of them to be sure there were no slipups. And, at the same time, do them no real injustice, harm them as little as possible, keep a light load on your conscience, still be civilized.

There were two flaws, he told himself. The staff changed from time to time. That meant they must be rotated from here back to present time and they could be a threat. Some way would have had to be worked out to be sure they never talked, and given human nature, that would be a problem. The second flaw lay in the people who were here. The philosopher, if he had remained in present time, could have been a threat. But the rest of them? What threat could a poet pose? A cartoonist, maybe, perhaps a novelist, but a musician-composer—what threat could lie in music?

On the surface of it, however, it was not as insane as it sounded if you happened not to be on the receiving end of it. The world could have been spared a lot of grief in the last few hundred years if such a plan had been operative, spotting potential troublemakers well ahead of the time they became a threat and isolating them. The hard part of such a plan—from where he sat, an apparently impossible part of it—would lie in accurately spotting the potential troublemakers before they began making trouble. Although that, he supposed, might be possible. Given the state of the art in psychology, it might be possible.

With a start, he realized that during all this time, without consciously being aware of it, he had been staring at the birch clump. And now he remembered another thing. Just before he had stumbled off to bed, he had seen a bird light on the boulder, sit there for a time, then lift itself into the air and disappear—not fly away, but disappear. He must have known this when he saw it, but been so fogged by need of sleep that the significance of it had not made an impression. Thinking back on it, he felt sure he was not mistaken. The bird had disappeared.

He reared out of the chair and strode down the slope until he stood opposite the boulder with the two trees flanking it and the other growing close behind it. He took one of the agates out of his pocket and tossed it carefully over the boulder, aimed so that it would strike the tree behind the rock. It did not strike the tree; he could not hear it fall to the ground. One by one, he tossed all the other agates as he had tossed the first. None of them hit the tree, none fell to the ground. To make sure, he went around the tree to the right and, crouching down, crawled behind the boulder. He carefully went over the ground. There were no agates there.

Shaken, his mind a seething turmoil of mingled doubt and wonder, he went back up the hill and sat in the chair again. Thinking the situation over as calmly as he could, there seemed to be no doubt that he had found a rift of some sort in—what would you call it?—the time continuum, perhaps. And if you wriggled through the rift or threw yourself through the rift, you'd not be here. He had thrown the agates and they were no longer here; they had gone elsewhere. But where would you go? Into some other time, most likely, and the best guess would seem to be back into the time from which he had been snatched. He had come from there to here, and if there were a rift in the time continuum, it would seem to be reasonable to believe the rift would lead back into present time again. There was a chance it wouldn't, but the chance seemed small, for only two times had been involved in the interchange.

And if he did go back, what could he do? Maybe not a lot, but he damn well could try. His first move would be to disappear, to get away from the locality and lose himself. Whoever was involved in this trapping scheme would try to find him, but he would make it his business to be extremely hard to find. Then, once he had done that, he would start digging, to ferret out the managers Jonathon had mentioned, or if not them, then whoever might be behind all this.

He could not tell the others here what he suspected. Inadvertently, one of them might tip off a staff member, or worse, might try to prevent him from doing what he meant to do, having no wish to change the even tenor of the life they enjoyed here.

When Underwood and Charlie came up the hill with their guns, their hunting coats bulging with the woodcock they had bagged, he went inside with them, where the others had gathered in the drawing room for a round of before-dinner drinks.

At dinner, there was, as Jonathon had said there would be, broiled woodcock and blackberry pie, both of which were exceptionally tasty, although the pie was very full of seeds.

After dinner, they collected once again before the fire and talked of inconsequential things. Later on, Alice played and again it was Chopin.

In his room, he pulled a chair over to the window and sat there, looking out at the birch clump. He waited until he could hear no one stirring about, and then two more hours after that, to make sure all were safely in their beds, if not asleep. Then he went softly down the stairs and out the back door. A half-moon lighted the lawn so that he had little trouble locating the birch clump. Now that he was there, he was assailed by doubt. It was ridiculous to think, he told himself, what he had been thinking. He would climb up on the boulder and throw himself out toward the third tree that stood behind the boulder and he would tumble to the ground between the tree and boulder and nothing would have happened. He would trudge sheepishly up the slope again and go to bed, and after a time he would manage to forget what he had done and it would be as if he had never done it. And yet, he remembered, he had thrown the agates, and when he had looked, there had not been any agates.

He scrambled up the face of the boulder and perched cautiously on its rounded top. He put out his hands to grasp the third birch and save himself from falling. Then he launched himself toward the tree.

He fell only a short distance, but landed hard upon the ground. There had not been any birch to catch to break his fall.

A hot sun blazed down upon him. The ground beneath him was not a grassy lawn, but a sandy loam with no grass at all. There were some trees, but not any birches.

He scrambled to his feet and turned to look at the house. The hilltop stood bare; there was no house. Behind him, he could hear the booming of the surf as it battered itself to spray against the rocky coastline.

Thirty feet away, to his left, stood a massive poplar, its leaves whispering in the wind that blew off the sea. Beyond it grew a scraggly pine tree and just down the slope, a cluster of trees that he thought were willows. The ground was covered—not too thickly covered, for rain-runneled soil showed through—by a growth of small ferns and other low-growing plants he could not identify.

He felt the perspiration starting from his body, running in rivulets from his armpits down his ribs—but whether from fear or sun, he did not know. For he was afraid, stiff and aching with the fear.

In addition to the poplar and the pine, low-growing shrubs were rooted in the ground among the ferns and other ground cover. Birds flew low, from one clump of shrubbery to another, chirping as they flew. From below him, their cries muted by the pounding of the surf, other birds were squalling. Gulls, he thought, or birds like gulls.

Slowly the first impact of the fear drained from him and he was able to move. He took a cautious step and then another and then was running toward the hilltop where the house should be, but wasn't.

Ahead of him, something moved and he skidded to a halt, poised to go around whatever had moved in the patch of shrubbery. A head poked out of the patch and stared at him with unblinking eyes. The nose was blunt and scaly and farther back the scales gave way to plates of armor. The thing mumbled at him disapprovingly and lurched forward a step or two, then halted.

It stood there, staring at him with its unblinking eyes. Its back was covered by overlapping plates. Its front legs were bowed. It stood four feet at the shoulder. It did not seem to be threatening; rather, it was curious.

His breath caught in his throat. Once, long ago, he had seen a drawing, an artist's conception, of this thing—not exactly like it, but very much the same. An anky, he thought—what was it?—an ankylosaurus, that was what it was, he realized, amazed that he should remember, an ankylosaurus. A creature that should have been dead for millions of years. But the caption had said six feet at the shoulder and fifteen feet long, and this one was nowhere near that big. A small one, he thought, maybe a young one, maybe a different species, perhaps a baby anky-whatever-the-hell-it-was.

Cautiously, almost on tiptoe, he walked around it, while it kept turning its head to watch him. It made no move toward him. He kept looking over his shoulder to be sure it hadn't moved. Herbivorous, he assured himself, an eater of plants—posing no danger to anything at all, equipped with armor plate to discourage the meat eaters that might slaver for its flesh. He tried hard to remember whether the caption had said it was herbivorous, but his mind, on that particular point, was blank.

Although, if it were here, there would be carnivores as well—and, for the love of God, what had he fallen into? Why hadn't he given more thought to the possibility that something like this might happen, that he would not, necessarily, automatically go back to present time, but might be shunted off into another time? And why, just as a matter of precaution, hadn't he armed himself before he left? There were high-caliber guns in the library and he could have taken one of them and a few boxes of ammunition if he had just thought about it.

He had failed to recognize the possibility of being dumped into a place like this, he admitted, because he had been thinking about what he wanted to happen, to the exclusion of all else, using shaky logic to convince himself that he was right. His wishful thinking, he now knew, had landed him in a place no sane man would choose.

He was back in the age of dinosaurs and there wasn't any house. He probably was the only human on the planet, and if his luck held out, he might last a day or two, but probably not much more than that. He knew he was going off the deep end again, thinking as illogically as he had been when he launched himself into the time rift. There might not be that many carnivores about, and if a man was observant and cautious and gave himself a chance to learn, he might be able to survive. Although the chances were that he was stuck here. There could be little hope that he could find another rift in time, and even if he did, there would be no assurance that it would take him to anything better than this. Perhaps, if he could find the point where he had emerged into this world, he might have a chance to locate the rift again, although there was no guarantee that the rift was a two-way rift. He stopped and looked around, but there was no way to know where he had first come upon this place. The landscape all looked very much the same.

The ankylosaurus, he saw, had come a little out of the shrub thicket and was nibbling quite contentedly at the ground cover. Turning his back upon it, he went trudging up the hill.

Before he reached the crest, he turned around again to have a look. The ankylosaurus was no longer around, or perhaps he did not know where to look for it. Down in the swale that had been the alder swamp where Underwood and Charlie had bagged the woodcock, a herd of small reptiles were feeding, browsing off low-growing shrubs and ground cover.

Along the skyline of the hill beyond which the herd was feeding, a larger creature lurched along on its hind legs, its body slanted upight at an angle, the shriveled forearms dangling at its side, its massive, brutal head jerking as it walked. The herd in the swale stopped their feeding, heads swiveling to look at the lurching horror. Then they ran, racing jerkily on skinny hind legs, like a flock of outsize, featherless chickens racing for their lives.

Latimer turned again and walked toward the top of the hill. The last slope was steep, steeper than he remembered it had been on that other, safer world. He was panting when he reached the crest, and he stopped a moment to regain his breath. Then, when he was breathing more easily, he turned to look toward the south.

Half turned, he halted, amazed at what he saw—the last thing in the world that he had expected to see. Sited in the valley that lay between the hill on which he stood and the next headland to the south, was a building. Not a house, but a building. It stood at least thirty stories high and looked like an office building, its windows gleaming in the sun.

He sobbed in surprise and thankfulness, but even so, he did not begin to run toward it, but stood for a moment looking at it, as if he must look at it for a time to believe that it was there. Around it lay a park of grass and tastefully planted trees. Around the park ran a high wire fence and in the fence at the foot of the hill closest to him was a gate, beside which was a sentry box. Outside the sentry box stood two men who carried guns.

Then he was running, racing recklessly down the hill, running with great leaps, ducking thickets of shrubs. He stubbed his toe and fell, pinwheeling down the slope. He brought up against a tree and, the breath half knocked out of him, got to his feet, gasping and wheezing. The men at the gate had not moved, but he knew that they had seen him; they were gazing up the hill toward him.

Moving at a careful, slower pace, he went on down

the hill. The slope leveled off and he found a faint path that he followed toward the gate.

He came up to the two guards and stopped.

"You damn fool," one of them said to him. "What do you think you're doing, going out without a gun? Trying to get yourself killed?"

"There's been an old Tyranno messing around here for the last several days," said the other guard. "He was seen by several people. An old bastard like that could go on the prod at the sight of you and you wouldn't have a chance."

The first guard jerked his rifle toward the gate. "Get in there," he said. "Be thankful you're alive. If I ever catch you going out again without a gun, I'll turn you in, so help me."

"Thank you, sir," said Latimer.

He walked through the gate, following a path of crushed shells toward the front entrance of the office building. But now that he was there, safe behind the fence, the reaction began setting in. His knees were wobbly and he staggered when he walked. He sat down on a bench beneath a tree. He found that his hands were shaking and he held them hard against his thighs to stop the trembling.

How lucky could one get? he asked himself. And what did it mean? A house in the more recent past, an office building in this place that must be millions of years into the past. There had not been dinosaurs upon the earth for at least sixty million years. And the rift? How had the rift come about? Was it something that could occur naturally, or had it come about because someone was manipulating time? Would such rifts come when someone, working deliberately, using techniques of which there was no public knowledge, was putting stress upon the web of time? Was it right to call time a web? He decided that it made no difference, that the terminology was not of great importance.

An office building, he thought. What did an office building mean? Was it possible that he had stumbled on the headquarters of the project/conspiracy/program that was engaged in the trapping of selected people in the past? Thinking of it, the guess made sense. A cautious group of men could not take the chance of operating such an enterprise in present time, where it might be nosed out by an eager-beaver newsman or a governmental investigation or by some other means. Here, buried in millions of years of time, there would be little chance of someone unmasking it.

Footsteps crunched on the path and Latimer looked up. A man in sports shirt and flannels stood in front of him.

"Good morning, sir," said Latimer.

The man asked, "Could you be David Latimer, by any chance?"

"I could be," said Latimer.

"I thought so. I don't remember seeing you before. I was sure I knew everyone. And the guards reported . . ."

"I arrived only an hour or so ago."

"Mr. Gale wanted to see you as soon as you arrived."

"You mean you were expecting me?"

"Well, we couldn't be absolutely sure," said the other. "We are glad you made it."

Latimer got off the bench and the two of them walked together to the front entrance, climbed the steps, and went through the door. They walked through a deserted lounge, then into a hallway flanked by numbered doors with no names upon them. Halfway down the hall, the man with Latimer knocked at one of the doors.

"Come in," a voice said.

The man opened the door and stuck his head in. "Mr. Latimer is here," he said. "He made it."

"That is fine," said the voice. "I am glad he did. Please show him in."

The man stepped aside to allow Latimer to enter, then stepped back into the hall and closed the door. Latimer stood alone, facing the man across the room.

"I'm Donovan Gale," said the man, rising from his desk and coming across the room. He held out his hand and Latimer took it. Gale's grasp was a friendly corporate handshake.

"Let's sit over here," he said, indicating a davenport. "It seems to me we may have a lot to talk about."

"I'm interested in hearing what you have to say," said Latimer.

"I guess both of us are," said Gale. "Interested in what the other has to say, I mean."

They sat down on opposite ends of the davenport, turning to face one another.

"So you are David Latimer," said Gale. "The famous painter."

"Not famous," said Latimer. "Not yet. And it appears now that I may never be. But what I don't understand is how you were expecting me."

"We knew you'd left Auk House."

"So that is what you call it. Auk House."

"And we suspected you would show up here. We didn't know exactly where, although we hoped that it would be nearby. Otherwise you never would have made it. There are monsters in those hills. Although, of course, we could not be really sure that you would wind up here. Would you mind telling us how you did it?"

Latimer shook his head. "I don't believe I will. Not right now, at least. Maybe later on when I know more about your operation. And now a question for you. Why me? Why an inoffensive painter who was doing no more than trying to make a living and a reputation that might enable him to make a better living?"

"I see," said Gale, "that you have it figured out."

"Not all of it," said Latimer. "And, perhaps, not all of it correctly. But I resent being treated as a bad guy, as a potential threat of some sort. I haven't got the guts or the motive to be a bad guy. And Enid, for Christ's sake. Enid is a poet. And Alice. All Alice does is play a good piano."

"You're talking to the wrong men," Gale told him. "Breen could tell you that, if you can get him to tell you. I'm only personnel."

"Who is Breen?"

"He's head of the evaluation team."

"Those are the ones who figure out who is going to be picked up and tossed into time."

"Yes, that is the idea, crudely. There's a lot more to it than that. There is a lot of work done here. Thousands of newspapers and other periodicals to be read to spot potential subjects. Preliminary psychological determinations. Then it's necessary to do further study back in prime world. Further investigation of potential subjects. But no one back there really knows what is going on. They're just hired to do jobs now and then. The real work goes on here."

"Prime world is present time? Your old world and mine?"

"Yes. If you think, however, of prime world as present time, that's wrong. That's not the way it is. We're not dealing with time, but with alternate worlds. The one you just came from is a world where everything else took place exactly as it did in prime world, with one exception—man never evolved. There are no men there and never will be. Here, where we are now, something more drastic occurred. Here the reptiles did not become extinct. The Cretaceous never came to an end, the Cenozoic never got started. The reptiles are still the dominant species and the mammals still are secondary."

"You're taking a chance, aren't you, in telling me all this."

"I don't think so," said Gale. "You're not going anywhere. There are none of us going anywhere. Once we sign up for this post, we know there's not any going back. We're stuck here. Unless you have a system . . ."

"No system. I was just lucky."

"You're something of an embarrassment to us," said Gale. "In the years since the program has been in operation, nothing like this has happened at any of the stations. We don't know what to make of it and we don't quite know what to do with you. For the moment, you'll stay on as a guest. Later on, if it is your wish, we could find a place for you. You could become a member of the team."

"Right at the moment," said Latimer, "that holds no great attraction for me."

"That's because you aren't aware of the facts, nor of the dangers. Under the economic and social systems that have been developed in prime world, the great mass of mankind has never had it so good. There are ideological differences, of course, but there is some hope that they eventually can be ironed out. There are underprivileged areas; this cannot be denied. But one must also concede that their only hope lies in their development by free-world business interests. So-called big-business interests are the world's one hope. With the present economic structure gone, the entire world would go down into another Dark Age, from which it would require a thousand years or more to recover, if recovery, in fact, were possible at all."

"So to protect your precious economic structure, you place a painter, a poet, a musician into limbo."

Gale made a despairing gesture with his hands. "I have told you I can't supply the rationale on that. You'll have to see Breen if he has the time to see you. He's a very busy man."

"I would imagine that he might be."

"He might even dig out the files and tell you," said Gale. "As I say, you're not going anywhere. You can pose no problem now. You are stuck with us and we with you. I suppose that we could send you back to Auk House, but that would be undesirable, I think. It would only upset the people who are there. As it is, they'll probably figure that you simply wandered off and got killed by a bear or bitten by a rattlesnake, or drowned in a swamp. They'll look for you and when they don't find you, that will be it. You only got lost; they'll never consider for a moment that you escaped. I think we had better leave it at that. Since you are here and, given time, would nose out the greater part of our operation, we have no choice but to be frank with you. Understandably, however, we'd prefer that no one outside this headquarters knew."

"Back at Auk House, there was a painting of mine hanging in my room."

"We thought it was a nice touch," said Gale. "A sort of friendly thing to do. We could bring it here."

"That wasn't why I asked," said Latimer. "I was wondering—did the painting's subject have something to do with what you did to me? Were you afraid that I would go on painting pictures pointing up the failures of your precious economic structure?"

Gale was uncomfortable. "I couldn't say," he said.

"I was about to say that if such is the case, you stand on very flimsy ground and carry a deep guilt complex."

"Such things are beyond me," said Gale. "I can't even make a comment."

"And this is all you want of me? To stand in place? To simply be a guest of all these big-hearted corporations?"

"Unless you want to tell us how you got here."

"I have told you that I won't do that. Not now. I suppose if you put me to the torture . . ."

"We wouldn't torture you," said Gale. "We are civilized. We regret some of the things that we must do, but we do not flinch from duty. And not the duty to what you call big-hearted corporations, but to all humankind. Man has a good thing going; we can't allow it to be undermined. We're not taking any chances. And now, perhaps I should call someone to show you to your room. I take it you got little sleep last night."

Latimer's room was on one of the topmost floors and was larger and somewhat more tastefully furnished than the room at Auk House. From a window, he saw that the conformation of the coastline was much the same as it had been at Auk House. The dirty gray of the ocean stretched off to the east and the surf still came rolling in to break upon the boulders. Some distance off shore, a school of long-necked creatures were cavorting in the water. Watching them more closely, Latimer made out that they were catching fish. Scattered reptilian monstrosities moved about in the hills that ran back from the sea, some of them in small herds, some of them alone. Dwarfed by distance, none of them seemed unusually large. The trees, he saw, were not a great deal different from the ones he had known. The one thing that was wrong was the lack of grass.

He had been a victim of simplistic thinking in believing, he told himself, that when he threw himself into the rift he would be carried to present time or prime world or whatever one might call it. In the back of his mind, as well, although he had not really dared to think it, had been the idea that if he could get back to the real world, he could track down the people who were involved and put a stop to it.

There was no chance of that now, he knew, and there never had been. Back on prime world, there would be no evidence that would stand up, only highly paid lackeys who performed necessary chores. Private investigators, shady operators like the Boston realtor and the Campbell who had listed Auk House for sale or rent. Undoubtedly, the sign announcing the house was available was posted only when a potential so-called customer would be driving past. Campbell would have been paid well, perhaps in funds that could not be traced, for the part he played, offering the house and then, perhaps, driving off the car left behind by the customer. He took some risks, certainly, but they were minimal. Even should he have been apprehended, there would be no way in which he could be tied into the project. He, himself, would have had no inkling of the project. A few men in prime world would have to know, of course, for some sort of communications had to be maintained between this operations center and prime world. But the prime-world men, undoubtedly, would be solid citizens, not too well known, all beyond suspicion or reproach. They would be very careful against the least suspicion, and the communications between them and this place must be of a kind that could not be traced and would have no record.

Those few upright men, perhaps a number of hired hands who had no idea of what was being done, would be the only ones in prime world who would play any part in the project. The heart of the operation was in this building. Here the operations were safe. There was no way to get at them. Gale had not even bothered to deny what was being done, had merely referred him to Breen for any further explanation. And Breen, should he talk with him, probably would make no denial, either.

And here he stood, David Latimer, artist, the one man outside the organization who, while perhaps not realizing the full scope of the project, still knew what was happening. Knew and could do nothing about it. He ran the facts he had so far acquired back and forth across his mind, seeking some chink of weakness, and there seemed to be none.

Silly, he thought, one man pitting himself against a group that held the resources of the earth within its grasp, a group at once ruthless and fanatical, that commanded as its managers the best brains of the planet, arrogant in its belief that what was good for the group was good for everyone, brooking no interference, alert to even the slightest threat, even to imagined threat.

Silly, perhaps absurdly quixotic—and, yet, what could he do? To save his own self-respect, to pay even lip service to the dignity of humanity, he must make at least a token effort, even knowing that the possibility of his accomplishing anything was very close to zero.

Say this much for them, he thought, they were not cruel men. In many ways, they were compassionate. Their imagined enemies were neither killed nor confined in noisome prisons, as had been the case with historic tyrants. They were held under the best of circumstances, all their needs were supplied, they were not humiliated. Everything was done to keep them comfortable and happy. The one thing that had been taken from them was their freedom of choice.

But man, he thought, had fought for bitter centuries for that very freedom. It was not something that should be lightly held or easily relinquished.

All this, at the moment, he thought, was pointless. If he should be able to do anything at all, it might not be until after months of observation and learning. He could remain in the room for hours, wallowing in his doubt and incompetency, and gain not a thing by it. It was time to begin to get acquainted with his new surroundings.

The parklike grounds surrounding the building were ringed by the fence, twelve feet high or more, with a four-foot fence inside it. There were trees and shrubs and beds of flowers and grass—the only grass he had seen since coming here, a well-tended greensward.

Paths of crushed shell ran among the trees and underneath them was a coolness and a quiet. A few gardeners worked in flower beds and guards stood at the distant gates, but otherwise there were few people about. Probably it was still office hours; later on, there might be many people.

He came upon the man sitting on the bench when the walk curved sharply around a group of head-high shrubbery. Latimer stopped, and for a moment they regarded one another as if each was surprised at the appearance of the other.

Then the man on the bench said, with a twinkle in his eye, "It seems that the two of us are the only ones who have no tasks on this beautiful afternoon. Could you be, possibly, the refugee from Auk House?"

"As a matter of fact, I am," said Latimer. "My name is David Latimer, as if you didn't know."

"Upon my word," said the other, "I didn't know your name. I had only heard that someone had escaped from Auk House and had ended up with us. News travels swiftly here. The place is a rumor mill. There is so little of consequence that happens that once some notable event does occur, it is chewed to tiny shreds.

"My name, by the way, is Horace Sutton and I'm a paleontologist. Can you imagine a better place for a paleontologist to be?"

"No, I can't," said Latimer.

"Please share this bench with me," invited Sutton. "I take it there is nothing of immediate urgency that requires your attention."

"Not a thing," said Latimer. "Nothing whatsoever."

"Well, that is fine," said Sutton. "We can sit and talk a while or stroll around a bit, however you may wish. Then, as soon as the sun gets over the yardarm, if by that time you're not totally disenchanted with me, we can indulge ourselves in some fancy drinking."

Sutton's hair was graying and his face was lined, but there was something youthful about him that offset the graying hair and lines.

Latimer sat down and Sutton said to him, "What do you think of this layout? A charming place, indeed. The tall fence, as you may have guessed, is electrified, and the lower fence keeps stupid people such as you and I from blundering into it. Although, there have been times I have been glad the fence is there. Comes a time when a carnivore or two scents the meat in here and is intent upon a feast, you are rather glad it's there."

"Do they gather often? The carnivores, I mean."

"Not as much as they did at one time. After a while, the knowledge of what to keep away from sinks into even a reptilian brain."

"As a paleontologist you study the wildlife here."

"For the last ten years," said Sutton. "I guess a bit less time than that. It was strange at first; it still seems a little strange. A paleontologist, you understand, ordinarily works with bones and fossil footprints and other infuriating evidence that almost tells you what you want to know, but always falls short.

"Here there is another problem. From the viewpoint of prime world, many of the reptiles, including the dinosaurs, died out sixty-three million years ago. Here they did not die out. As a result, we are looking at them not as they were millions of years ago, but as they are after millions of additional years of evolutionary development. Some of the old species have disappeared, others have evolved into something else in which you can see the traces of their lineage, and some entirely new forms have arisen."

"You sound as if your study of them is very dedicated," said Latimer. "Under other circumstances, you would probably be writing a book . . ."

"But I am writing a book," said Sutton. "I am hard at work on it. There is a man here who is very clever at drawing and he is making diagrams for me and there will be photographs . . ."

"But what's the point?" asked Latimer. "Who will publish it? When will it be published? Gale told me that no one ever leaves here, that there is no going back to prime world."

"That is right," said Sutton. "We are exiled from prime world. I often think of us as a Roman garrison stationed, say, on Britain's northern border or in the wilds of Dacia, with the understanding that we'll not be going back to Rome."

"But that means your book won't be published. I suppose it could be transmitted back to prime world and be printed there, but the publishing of it would destroy the secrecy of the project."

"Exactly how much do you know about the project?" Sutton asked.

"Not much, perhaps. Simply the purpose of it—the trapping of people in time—no, not time, I guess. Alternate worlds, rather."

"Then you don't know the whole of it?"

"Perhaps I don't," said Latimer.

"The matter of removing potentially dangerous personnel from prime world," said Sutton, "is only part of it. Surely if you have thought of it at all, you could see other possibilities."

"I haven't had time to think too deeply on it," said Latimer. "No time at all, in fact. You don't mean the exploitation of these other worlds?"

"It's exactly what I mean," said Sutton. "It is so obvious, so logical. Prime world is running out of resources. In these worlds, they lie untouched. The exploitation of the alternate worlds not only would open new resources, but would provide employment, new lands for colonization, new space for expansion. It is definitely a better idea than this silly talk you hear about going off into outer space to find new worlds that could be colonized."

"Then why all the mummery of using it to get rid of potential enemies?"

"You sound as if you do not approve of this part of the project."

"I'm not sure I approve of any of it and certainly not of picking up people and stashing them away. You seem to ignore the fact that I was one of those who was picked up and stashed away. The whole thing smells of paranoia. For the love of God, the big business interests of prime world have so solid a grip on the institutions of the Earth and, in large part, on the people of the Earth, that there is no reason for the belief that there is any threat against them."

"But they do take into account," said Sutton, "the possibility of such threats rising in the years to come, probably based upon events that could be happening right now. They have corps of psychologists who are pursuing studies aimed against such possibilities, corps of economists and political scientists who are looking at possible future trends that might give rise to antibusiness reactions. And, as you know, they are pinpointing certain specific areas and peoples who could contribute, perhaps unwittingly, either now or in the future, to undesirable reactions. But, as I understand it, they are hopeful that if they can forestall the trends that would bring about such reactions for a few centuries, then the political, the economic, and the social climates will be so solidly committed in their favor, that they can go ahead with the exploitation of some of the alternate worlds. They want to be sure before they embark on it, however, that they won't have to keep looking over their shoulders."

"But hundreds of years! All the people who are engaged in this project will have been long dead by then."

"You forget that a corporation can live for many centuries. The corporations are the driving force here. And, in the meantime, those who work in the project gain many advantages. It is worth their while."

"But they can't go back to Earth—back to prime world, that is."

"You are hung up on prime world," said Sutton. "By working in the project, you are showered with advantages that prime world could never give you. Work in the project for twenty years, for example, and at the age of fifty—in some cases, even earlier—you can have a wide choice of retirements—an estate somewhere on Auk world, a villa on a paradise world, a hunting lodge in another world where there is a variety of game that is unbelievable. With your family, if you have one, with servants, with your every wish fulfilled. Tell me, Mr. Latimer, could you do as well if you stayed on prime world? I've listed only a few possibilities; there are many others."

"Gale told me it would be possible to send me back to Auk House. So people can move around these alternate worlds, but not back to prime world?"

"That is right. Supplies for all the worlds are transported to this world and from here sent out to other stations."

"But how? How is this done?"

"I have no idea. There is an entire new technology involved. Once I had thought it would be matter transmitters, but I understand it's not. Certain doors exist. Doors with quote marks around them. I suppose there is a corps of elite engineers who know, but would suspect that no one else does."

"You spoke of families."

"There are families here."

"But I didn't see . . ."

"The kids are in school. There aren't many people about right now. They'll begin showing up at the cocktail hour. A sort of country-club routine here. That's why I like to get up early. Not many are about. I have this park to myself."

"Sutton, you sound as if you like this setup."

"I don't mind it," Sutton said. "It's far preferable to what I had in prime world. There my reputation had been ruined by a silly dispute I fell into with several of my colleagues. My wife died. My university let me stay on in sufferance. So when I was offered a decent job . . ."

"Not telling you what kind of job?"

"Well, no, not really. But the conditions of employment sounded good and I would be in sole charge of the investigation that was in prospect. To be frank with you, I jumped at it."

"You must have been surprised."

"In fact, I was. It took a while to reconcile myself to the situation."

"But why would they want a paleontologist?"

"You mean, why would money-grabbing, cynical corporations want a paleontologist."

"I guess that's what I mean."

"Look, Latimer—the men who make up the corporations are not monsters. They saw here the need for a study of a truly unique world—a continuation of the Cretaceous, which has been, for years, an intriguing part of the planet's history. They saw it as a contribution to human knowledge. My book, when it is published, will show this world at a time before the impact of human exploitation fell upon it."

"When your book is published?"

"When it is safe to make the announcement that alternate worlds have been discovered and are being opened for colonization. I'll never see the book, of course, but nevertheless, I take some pride in it. Here I have found confirmation for my stand that brought about condemnation by my colleagues. Fuzzy thinking, they said, but they were the fuzzy thinkers. This book will vindicate me."

"And that's important? Even after you are dead?"

"Of course it is important. Even after I am dead."

Sutton looked at his watch. "I think," he said, "it may be time now. It just occurred to me. Have you had anything to eat?"

"No," said Latimer. "I hadn't thought of it before. But I am hungry."

"There'll be snacks in the bar," said Sutton. "Enough to hold you until dinner."

"One more question before we leave," said Latimer. "You said the reptiles showed some evolutionary trends. In what direction? How have they changed?"

"In many ways," said Sutton. "Bodily changes, of course. Perhaps ecological changes as well—behavioral changes, although I can't be sure of that. I can't know what their behavior was before. Some of the bigger carnivores haven't changed at all. Perhaps a bit more ability in a number of cases. Their prey may have become faster, more alert, and the carnivores had to develop a greater agility or starve. But the most astonishing change is in intelligence. There is one species, a brand-new species so far as I know, that seems to have developed a pronounced intelligence. If it is intelligence, it is taking a strange direction. It's hard to judge correctly. You must remember that of all the stupid things that ever walked the earth, some of the dinosaurs ranked second to none. They didn't have a lick of sense."

"You said intelligence in a strange direction."

"Let me try to tell you. I've watched these jokers for hours on end. I'm almost positive that they handle herds of herbivores—herbivorous reptiles, that is. They don't run around them like sheepdogs manage sheep, but I am sure they do control them. There are always a few of them watching the herds, and while they're watching them, the herds do no straying—they stay together like a flock of sheep tended by dogs. They move off in orderly fashion when there is need to move to a new pasture. And every once in a while, a few members of the herd will detach themselves and go ambling off to a place where others of my so-called intelligent dinosaurs are hanging out, and there they are killed. They walk in to be slaughtered. I can't get over the feeling that the herbivores are meat herds, the livestock of the intelligence species. And another thing. When carnivores roam in, these intelligent jokers shag them out of there. Not by chasing them or threatening them. Just by moving out where they can be seen. Then they sit down, and after the carnivores have looked them over, the carnivores seem to get a little jittery, and after a short time they move off."

"Hypnotism? Some sort of mental power?"

"Possibly."

"That wouldn't have to be intelligence. It could be no more than an acquired survival trait."

"Somehow I don't think so. Other than watching herds and warning off carnivores—if that is what they're doing—they sit around a lot among themselves. Like a bunch of people talking. That's the impression I get, that they are talking. None of the social mannerisms that are seen among primates—no grooming, horseplay, things like that. There seems to be little personal contact—no touching, no patting, no stroking. As if none of this were needed. But they dance. Ritualistic dancing of some sort. Without music. Nothing to make music with. They have no artifacts. They haven't got the hands that could fashion artifacts. Maybe they don't need tools or weapons or musical instruments. Apparently they have certain sacred spots. Places where they go, either singly or in small groups, to meditate or worship. I know of one such place; there may be others. No idols, nothing physical to worship. A secluded spot. Seemingly a special place. They have been using it for years. They have worn a path to it, a path trod out through the centuries. They seem to have no form of worship, no rituals that must be observed. They simply go and sit there. At no special time. There are no Sundays in this world. I suspect they go only when they feel the need of going."

"It is a chilling thought," said Latimer.

"Yes, I suppose it is."

He looked at his watch again. "I am beginning to feel the need of that drink," he said. "How about you?"

"Yes," said Latimer, "I could do with one."

And now, he told himself, he had a few more of the answers. He knew how the staff at Auk House was changed, where the supplies came from. Everything and everyone, apparently, was channeled and routed from this operations center. Prime world, from time to time, furnished supplies and personnel and then the rest was handled here.

He found himself puzzled by Sutton's attitude. The man seemed quite content, bore no resentment over being exiled here. They are not monsters, he had said, implying that the men in this operation were reasonable and devoted men working in the public interest. He was convinced that someday his book would be published, according him posthumous vindication. There had been, as well, Latimer remembered, Enid's poems and Dorothy's novel. Had the poems and the novel been published back in prime world, perhaps under pseudonyms, works so excellent that it had been deemed important that they not be lost?

And what about the men who had done the research that had resulted in the discovery of the alternate worlds and had worked out the technique of reaching and occupying them? Not still on prime world, certainly; they would pose too great a danger there. Retired, perhaps, to estates on some of the alternate worlds.

They walked around one of the clumps of trees with which the park was dotted, and from a distance Latimer heard the sound of children happy at their play.

"School is out," said Sutton. "Now it's the children's hour."

"One more thing," said Latimer, "if you don't mind. One more question. On all these other alternate worlds you mention, are there any humans native to those worlds? Is it possible there are other races of men?"

"So far as I know," said Sutton, "man rose only once, on prime world. What I have told you is not the entire story, I imagine. There may be much more to it. I've been too busy to attempt to find out more. All I told you are the things I have picked up in casual conversation. I do not know how many other alternate worlds have been discovered, nor on how many of them stations have been established. I do know that on Auk world there are several stations other than Auk House."

"By stations, you mean the places where they put the undesirables."

"You put it very crudely, Mr. Latimer, but yes, you are quite right. On the matter of humans arising elsewhere, I think it's quite unlikely. It seems to me that it was only by a combination of a number of lucky circumstances that man evolved at all. When you take a close look at the situation, you have to conclude that man had no right to expect to evolve. He is a sort of evolutionary accident."

"And intelligence? Intelligence rose on prime world, and you seem to have evidence that it has risen here as well. Is intelligence something that evolution may be aiming at and will finally achieve, in whatever form on whatever world? How can you be sure it has not risen on Auk world? At Auk House, only a few square miles have been explored. Perhaps not a great deal more around the other stations."

"You ask impossible questions," said Sutton shortly. "There is no way I can answer them."

They had reached a place from which a full view of the headquarters building was possible and now there were many people—men and women walking about or sunning themselves, stretched out on the grass, people sitting on terraces in conversational groups, while children ran gaily, playing childish games.

Sutton, who had been walking ahead of Latimer, stopped so quickly that Latimer, with difficulty, averted bumping into him.

Sutton pointed. "There they are," he said.

Looking in the direction of the pointing finger, Latimer could see nothing unusual. "What? Where?" he asked.

"On top the hill, just beyond the northern gate."

After a moment Latimer saw them, a dozen squatting creatures on top of the hill down which, a few hours ago, he had run for the gate and safety. They were too distant to be seen clearly, but they had a faintly reptilian look and they seemed to be coal-black, but

whether naturally black or black because of their silhouetted position, he could not determine.

"The ones I told you about," said Sutton. "It's nothing unusual. They often sit and watch us. I suspect they
are as curious about us as we are about them."

"The intelligences?" asked Latimer.

"Yes, that is right," said Sutton.

Someone, some distance off, cried in a loud voice—
no words that Latimer could make out, but a cry of
apprehension, a bellow of terror. Then there were other
cries, different people taking up the cry.

A man was running across the park, heading for its
northeast corner, running desperately, arms pumping
back and forth, legs a blur of scissoring speed. He was
so far off that he looked like a toy runner, heading for
the four-foot fence that stood inside the higher fence.
Behind him were other runners, racing in an attempt to
head him off and pull him down.

"My God, it's Breen," gasped Sutton. His face had
turned to gray. He started forward, in a stumbling run.
He opened his mouth to shout, but all he did was gasp.

The running man came to the inner fence and cleared
it with a leap. The nearest of his pursuers was many feet
behind him.

Breen lifted his arms into the air, above his head. He
slammed into the electrified fence. A flash blotted him
out. Flickering tongues of flame ran along the fence—
bright and sparkling, like the flaring of fireworks. Then
the brightness faded and on the fence hung a black blot
that smoked greasily and had a fuzzy, manlike shape.

A hush, like an indrawn breath, came upon the
crowd. Those who had been running stopped running
and, for a moment, held their places. Then some of
them, after that moment, ran again, although some of
them did not, and the voices took up again, although
now there was less shouting.

When he looked, Latimer saw that the hilltop was
empty; the dinosaurs that had been there were gone.
There was no sign of Sutton.

So it was Breen, thought Latimer, who hung there on

the fence. Breen, head of the evaluation team, the one man, Gale had said, who could tell him why he had been lured to Auk House. Breen, the man who pored over psychological evaluations, who was acquainted with the profile of each suspected personage, comparing those profiles against economic charts, social diagnostic indices, and God knows what else, to enable him to make the decision that would allow one man to remain in prime world as he was, another to be canceled out.

And now, thought Latimer, it was Breen who had been canceled out, more effectively than he had canceled any of the others.

Latimer had remained standing where he had been when Sutton and he had first sighted the running Breen, had stood because he could not make up his mind what he should do, uncertain of the relationship that he held or was expected to assume with those other persons who were still milling about, many of them perhaps as uncertain as he of what they should do next.

He began to feel conspicuous because of just standing there, although at the same time he was certain no one noticed him, or if they did notice him, almost immediately dismissed him from their thoughts.

He and Sutton had been on their way to get a drink when it had all happened, and thinking of that, Latimer realized he could use a drink. With this in mind, he headed for the building. Few noticed him, some even brushing against him without notice; others spoke non-committal greetings, some nodded briefly as one nods to someone of whose identity he is not certain.

The lounge was almost empty. Three men sat at a table in one corner, their drinks before them; a woman and a man were huddled in low-voiced conversation on a corner of a davenport; another man was at the self-service bar, pouring himself a drink.

Latimer made his way to the bar and picked up a glass.

The man who was there said to him, "You must be new here; I don't remember seeing you about."

"Just today," said Latimer. "Only a few hours ago."

He found the Scotch and his brand was not among the bottles. He selected his second choice and poured a generous serving over ice. There were several trays of sandwiches and other snack items. He found a plate, put two sandwiches on it.

"What do you make of Breen?" asked the other man.

"I don't know," said Latimer. "I never met the man. Gale mentioned him to me."

"Three," said the other man. "Three in the last four months. There is something wrong."

"All on the fence?"

"No, not on the fence. This is the first on the fence. One jumped, thirteen stories. Christ, what a mess! The other hanged himself."

The man walked off and joined another man who had just come into the lounge. Latimer stood alone, plate and glass in hand. The lounge still was almost empty. No one was paying the slightest attention to him. Suddenly he felt a stranger, unwanted. He had been feeling this all the time, he knew, but in the emptiness of the lounge, the feeling of unwantedness struck with unusual force. He could sit down at a table or in one of a group of chairs or on the end of an unoccupied sofa, wait for someone to join him. He recoiled from the thought. He didn't want to meet these people, talk with them. For the moment, he wanted none of them.

Shrugging, he put another sandwich on the plate, picked up the bottle, and filled his glass to the top. Then he walked out into the hallway and took the elevator to his floor.

In his room, he selected the most comfortable chair and sat down in it, putting the plate of sandwiches on a table. He took a long drink and put down the glass.

"They can all go to hell," he told himself.

He sensed his fragmented self pulling back together, all the scattered fragments falling back into him again, making him whole again, his entire self again. With no effort at all, he wiped out Breen and Sutton, the events of the last hours, until he was simply a man seated comfortably in his room.

So great a power, he thought, so great and secret. Holding one world in thrall, planning to hold others. The planning, the foresight, the audacity. Making certain that when they moved into the other worlds, there would be no silly conservationists yapping at their heels, no environmentalist demanding environmental impact statements, no deluded visionaries crying out in protest against monopolies. Holding steadily in view the easy business ethic that had held sway in that day when arrogant lumber barons had built mansions such as Auk House.

Latimer picked up the glass and had another drink. The glass, he saw, was less than half full. He should have carried off the bottle, he thought; no one would have noticed. He reached for a sandwich and munched it down, picked up a second one. How long had it been since he had eaten? He glanced at his watch and knew, even as he did, that the time it told might not be right for this Cretaceous world. He puzzled over that, trying to figure out if there might be some time variance between one world and another. Perhaps there wasn't— logically there shouldn't be—but there might be factors . . . he peered closely at the watch face, but the figures wavered and the hands would not stay in line. He had another drink.

He woke to darkness, stiff and cramped, wondering where he was. After a moment of confusion, he remembered where he was, all the details of the last two days tumbling in upon him, at first in scattered pieces, then subtly arranging themselves and interlocking into a pattern of reality.

He had fallen asleep in the chair. The moonlight pouring through the window showed the empty glass, the plate with half a sandwich still upon it, standing on the table at his elbow. The place was quiet; there was no noise at all. It must be the middle of the night, he thought, and everyone asleep. Or might it be that there was no one else around, that in some strange way, for some strange reason, the entire headquarters had been evacuated, emptied of all life? Although that, he knew, was unreasonable.

He rose stiffly from the chair and walked to the window. Below him, the landscape was pure silver, blotched by deep shadows. Somewhere just beyond the fence, he caught a sense of movement, but was unable to make out what it was. Some small animal, perhaps, prowling about. There would be mammals here, he was sure, the little skitterers, frightened creatures that were hard-pressed to keep out of the way, never having had the chance to evolve as they had back in prime world when something had happened millions of years before to sweep the world clean of its reptilian overlords, creating a vacuum into which they could expand.

The silver world that lay outside had a feel of magic—the magic of a brand-new world as yet unsullied by the hand and tools of men, a clean place that had no litter in it. If he went out and walked in it, he wondered, would the presence of himself, a human who had no right to be there, subtract something from the magic?

Out in the hall, he took the elevator to the ground floor. Just off the corridor lay the lounge and the outer door opened from the lounge. Walking softly, although he could not explain why he went so softly, for in this sleeping place there was no one to disturb, he went into the lounge.

As he reached the door, he heard voices and, halting in the shadow, glanced rapidly over the room to locate the speakers. There were three of them sitting at a table in the far end of the lounge. Bottles and glasses stood upon the table, but they did not seem to be drinking; they were hunched forward, heads close together, engaged in earnest conversation.

As he watched, one of them reared back in his chair, speaking in anger, his voice rising. "I warned you," he shouted. "I warned Breen and I warned you, Gale. And you laughed at me."

It was Sutton who was speaking. The man was too

distant and the light too dim for Latimer to recognize his features, but the voice he was sure of.

"I did not laugh at you," protested Gale.

"Perhaps not you, but Breen did."

"I don't know about Breen or laughter," said the third man, "but there's been too much going wrong. Not just the three suicides. Other things as well. Miscalculations, erroneous data processing, bad judgments. Things all screwed up. Take the generator failure the other day. Three hours that we were without power, the fence without power. You know what that could mean if several big carnivores . . ."

"Yes, we know," said Gale, "but that was a mere technical malfunction. Those things happen. The one that worries me is this fellow, Latimer. That was a pure and simple foul-up. There was no reason to put him into Auk House. It cost a hell of a lot of money to do so; a very tricky operation. And when he got there, what happens? He escapes. I tell you, gentlemen, there are too many foul-ups. More than can be accounted for in the normal course of operation."

"There is no use trying to cover it up, to make a mystery out of it," said Sutton. "You know and I know what is happening, and the sooner we admit we know and start trying to figure out what to do about it, the better it will be. If there is anything we can do about it. We're up against an intelligence that may be as intelligent as we are, but in a different way. In a way that we can't fight. Mental power against technical power, and in a case like that, I'd bet on mental power. I warned you months ago. Treat these jokers with kid gloves, I told you. Do nothing to upset them. Handle them with deference. Think kindly toward them, because maybe they can tell what you're thinking. I believe they can. And then what happens? A bunch of lunkheads go out for an afternoon of shooting and when they find no other game, use these friends of ours for casual target practice . . ."

"But that was months ago," said the third man.

"They're testing," said Sutton. "Finding out what

they can do. How far they can go. They can stop a generator. They can mess up evaluations. They can force men to kill themselves. God knows what else they can do. Give them a few more weeks. And, by the way, what particular brand of idiocy persuaded prime world to site the base of operations in a world like this?"

"There were many considerations," said Gale. "For one thing, it seemed a safe place. If some opposition should try to move in on us . . ."

"You're insane," shouted Sutton. "There isn't any opposition. How could there be opposition?"

Moving swiftly, Latimer crossed the corner of the lounge, eased his way out of the door. Looking back over his shoulder, he saw the three still sitting at the table. Sutton was shouting, banging his fist on the tabletop.

Gale was shrilling at him, his voice rising over Sutton's shouting: "How the hell could we suspect there was intelligence here? A world of stupid lizards . . ."

Latimer stumbled across the stone-paved terrace and went down the short flight of stone stairs that took him to the lawn. The world still was silver magic, a full moon riding in a cloudless sky. There was a softness in the air, a cleanness in the air.

But he scarcely noticed the magic and the cleanness. One thing thundered in his brain. A mistake! He should not have been sent to Auk House. There had been a miscalculation. Because of the mental machination of a reptilian intelligence on this world where the Cretaceous had not ended, he had been snatched from prime world. Although the fault, he realized, did not lie in this world, but in prime world itself—in the scheme that had been hatched to make prime world and the alternate worlds safe, safe beyond all question, for prime world's business interests.

He walked out across the sward and look up at the northern hilltop. A row of huddled figures sat there, a long row of dumpy reptilian figures solemnly staring down at the invaders who had dared to desecrate their world.

He had wondered, Latimer remembered, how one man alone might manage to put an end to the prime-world project, knowing well enough that no one man could do it, perhaps that no conceivable combination of men could do it.

But now he need wonder no longer. In time to come, sooner or later, an end would come to it. Maybe by that time, most of the personnel here would have been transferred to Auk House or to other stations, fleeing this doomed place. It might be that in years to come, another operations center would be set up on some safer world and the project would go on. But at least some time would be bought for the human race; perhaps the project might be dropped. It already had cost untold billions. How much more would the prime-world managers be willing to put into it? That was the crux of it, he knew, the crux of everything on prime world: Was it worth the cost?

He turned about to face the hilltop squarely and those who squatted there. Solemnly, David Latimer, standing in the magic moonlight, raised an arm in salutation to them.

He knew even as he did it that it was a useless gesture, a gesture for himself rather than for those dumpy figures sitting on the hilltop, who would neither see nor know. But even so, it was important that he do it, important that he, an intelligent human, pay a measure of sincere respect to an intelligence of another species in recognition of his belief that a common code of ethics might be shared.

The figures on the hilltop did not stir. Which, he told himself, was no more than he had expected of them. How should they know, why should they care what he instinctively had tried to communicate to them, not really expecting to communicate, but at least to make some sign, if to no other than himself, of the sense of fellowship that he, in that moment, felt for them?

As he was thinking this, he felt a warmness come upon him, encompassing him, enfolding him, as when he had been a child, in dim memory, he remembered his mother tucking him snugly into bed. Then he was moving, being lifted and impelled, with the high guard fence below him and the face of the great hill sliding underneath him. He felt no fright, for he seemed to be in a dreamlike state inducing a belief, deep-seated, that what was happening was not happening and that, in consequence, no harm could come to him.

He faced the dark and huddled figures, all sitting in a row, and although he still was dream-confused, he could see them clearly. They were nothing much to look at. They were as dumpy and misshapen as they had seemed when he had seen them from a distance. Their bodies were graceless lumps, the details vague even in the bright moonlight, but the faces he never would forget. They had the sharp triangle of the reptilian skull, the cruelty of the sharpness softened by the liquid compassion of the eyes.

Looking at them, he wondered if he was really there, if he was facing them, as he seemed to be, or if he still might be standing on the greensward of the compound, staring up the hill at the huddled shapes, which now seemed to be only a few feet distant from him. He tried to feel the ground beneath his feet, to press his feet against the ground, a conscious effort to orient himself, and, try as he might, he could feel no ground beneath his feet.

They were not awesome creatures and there was nothing horrible about them—just a faint distastefulness. They squatted in their lumpy row and stared at him out of the soft liquid of their eyes. And he felt—in some strange way that he could not recognize, he felt the presence of them. Not as if they were reaching out physically to touch him—fearing that if they did touch him, he would recoil from them—but in another kind of reaching, as if they were pouring into him, as one might pour water in a bottle, an essence of themselves.

Then they spoke to him, not with voice, not with words, with nothing at all that he could recognize— perhaps, he thought wildly, they spoke with that essence of themselves they were pouring into him.

"Now that we have met," they said, "we'll send you back again."

And he was back.

He stood at the end of the brick-paved driveway that led up to the house, and behind him he heard the damp and windy rustle of a primeval forest, with two owls chuckling throatily in the trees behind him. A few windows in the house were lighted. Great oaks grew upon the spreading lawn, and beneath the trees stood graceful stone benches that had the look of never being used.

Auk House, he told himself. They had sent him back to Auk House, not back to the grassy compound that lay inside the fence in that other world where the Cretaceous had not ended.

Inside himself he felt the yeasty churning of the essence that the squatting row of monstrosities had poured into him, and out of it he gained a knowledge and a comfort.

Policemen, he wondered, or referees, perhaps? Creatures that would monitor the efforts of those entrepreneurs who sought a monopoly of all the alternate worlds that had been opened for humans, and perhaps for many other races. They would monitor and correct, making certain that the worlds would not fall prey to the multinational financial concepts of the race that had opened them, but would become the heritage and birthright of those few intelligent peoples that had risen on this great multiplicity of worlds, seeing to it that the worlds would be used in a wiser context than prime world had been used by humans.

Never doubting for a moment that it would or could be done, knowing for a certainty that it would come about, that in the years to come men and other intelligences would live on the paradise worlds that Sutton had told him of—and all the other worlds that lay waiting to be used with an understanding the human race had missed. Always with those strange, dumpy ethical wardens who would sit on many hilltops to keep their vigil.

Could they be trusted? he wondered, and was

ashamed of thinking it. They had looked into his eyes and had poured their essence into him and had returned him here, not back to the Cretaceous compound. They had known where it was best for him to go and they would know all the rest of it.

He started up the driveway, his heels clicking on the bricks. As he came up to the stoop the door came open and the man in livery stood there.

"You're a little late," said the butler. "The others waited for you, but just now sat down to dinner. I'm sure the soup's still warm."

"I'm sorry," said Latimer. "I was unavoidably detained."

"Some of the others thought they should go out looking for you, but Mr. Jonathon dissuaded them. He said you'd be all right. He said you had your wits about you. He said you would be back."

The butler closed the door behind him. "They'll all be very happy to find you're back," he said.

"Thank you," said Latimer.

He walked, trying not to hurry, fighting down the happiness he felt welling up inside himself, toward the doorway from which came the sound of bright laughter and sprightly conversation. ✢

About the Editor

Judy-Lynn del Rey, editor of the *Stellar* series, was the managing editor of *Galaxy* and *IF* science-fiction magazines for eight and a half years. She has been a contributor to the *World Book Encyclopedia* on science fiction. In addition she is currently a Senior Editor at Ballantine Books and the Editor-in-Chief of DEL REY Books, Ballantine's enormously successful SF/Fantasies. Mrs. Del Rey lives in New York City with her husband Lester, who has written memorable science fiction over the last forty years and who is now Fantasy Editor for the Del Rey line.